*The Authors' Press Series
of the Works of
Elinor Glyn*

LOVE ITSELF

British Library Cataloguing-in-Publication Data
A catalogue record for this book is available from the
British Library

Elinor Glyn

Elinor Glyn was born on 17th October 1864 in Saint Helier, Jersey. She was the youngest daughter of a civil engineer, Douglas Southerland, and his wife Elinor Saunders. Elinor's father died when she was only two months old, leaving her mother alone with Elinor and her older sister Lucy Christiana.

After the death of their father, Elinor and her sister were taken to Canada, the place of their mother's parental home. There they were home-schooled by their grandmother, Lucy Anne Saunders, an Anglo-Irish aristocrat, who taught the girls the ways of society and upper-class etiquette. This education proved to be extremely useful for both sisters, Lucy going on to become Lady Duff-Gordon and successful fashion designer "Lucile", and Elinor becoming an authority on style and breeding in Hollywood. In 1871, Glyn's mother remarried and the family returned to Jersey to live at their stepfather's house.

In 1892, Elinor married a wealthy landowner with whom she had two children, Margot and Juliet. The marriage was not a successful one and she began to have a string of affairs with various British aristocrats. One particular relationship, with Lord Alistair Innes Ker, caused a great scandal after the publication of her novel *Three Weeks,* which was allegedly inspired by their liaison.

Elinor Glyn began her writing career in 1900 and was a pioneer of the risqué and romantic fiction genre. She went on to write many popular books such as *Beyond the Rocks* (1906), *Love's Blindness* (1926), and *It* (1927), in which she coined the term 'It', meaning the animal magnetism that some individuals possess.

In 1920 she moved to Hollywood to work in the movie industry as a script-writer. Glyn also helped develop the careers of such stars as Gloria Swanson and Clara Bow.

Elinor Glyn died at the age of 78 in Chelsea, London in 1943.

"And now they are past the last blue headland and in the open sea; and there is nothing round them but the waves and the sky and the wind. But the waves are gentle and the sky is clear, and the breeze is tender and low; for these are the days when Halcyone and Ceyx build their nest and no storms ever ruffle the pleasant summer sea. And who were Halcyone and Ceyx? Halcyone was a fairy maiden, the daughter of the beach and of the wind. And she loved a sailor-boy and married him; and none on earth were so happy as they. But at last Ceyx was wrecked; and before he could swim to the shore, the billows swallowed him up. And Halcyone saw him drowning and leapt into the sea to him; but in vain. Then the Immortals took pity on them both, and changed them into two fairy sea-birds, and now they build a floating nest every year and sail up and down happily for ever upon the pleasant seas of Greece."

THE HEROES, *Kingsley.*

LOVE ITSELF

CHAPTER I

OUTSIDE one of the park gates there was a little house. In the prosperous days of the La Sarthe it had been the land steward's—but when there was no longer any land to steward it had gone with the rest, and for several years had been uninhabited.

One day in early spring Halcyone saw smoke coming out of the chimney. This was too interesting a fact not to be investigated; she resented it, too—because a hole in the park paling had often let her into the garden and there was a particularly fine apple tree there whose fruit she had yearly enjoyed.

She crept nearer, a tall, slender shape, with mouse-colored hair waving down her back, and a scarlet cap pulled jauntily over her brow—the delightful feeling of adventure tingling in her veins. Yes, the gap was there, it had not been mended yet—she would penetrate and see for herself who this intruder could be.

She climbed through and stole along the orchard and up to the house. Signs of mending were around the windows, in the shape of a new board here and there in the shutters; but nothing further. She peeped over the low sill, and there her eyes met those of an old man seated in a shabby armchair, amid piles and piles of books. He had evidently been reading while he smoked a long, clay pipe.

He was a fine old man with a splendid presence, his gray hair was longer than is usual and a silvery beard flowed over his chest.

Halcyone at once likened him to Cheiron in the picture of him in her volume of Kingsley's "Heroes."

They stared at one another and the old man rose and came to the window.

Halcyone did not move.

1

"Who are you, little girl?" he said. "And what do you want?"

"I want to know who you are, and why you have come here?" she answered fearlessly. "I am Halcyone, you know."

The old man smiled.

"That ought to tell me everything," he said gravely, "but unfortunately it does not! Who is Halcyone?"

"I live at La Sarthe Chase with the Aunts La Sarthe," she said proudly, as though La Sarthe Chase had been Windsor Castle—"and I have been accustomed to play in this garden. I don't like your being here much."

"I am sorry for that, because it suits me and I have bought it. But how would it be if I said you might come into the garden and play? Would you forgive me then for being here?"

"I might," said Halcyone. "What are all these books for?"

"They are to read."

"I knew that"—and she frowned, beetling her delicate dark brows, "but why such a lot? You can never read them all."

The old man smiled.

"I have read most of them already," he said. "I have had plenty of time, you see."

"Yes, I dare say you are old," said Halcyone—"and what are they about? I would like to know that. My books so seldom interest me."

He handed her one through the window, but it was written in Greek and she could not read it. She frowned again as she turned over the pages.

"Perhaps there is something nice in that," she said.

"Possibly."

"Well, won't you tell me what?"

"That would take a long time—suppose you come in and have tea with me, then we could talk comfortably."

"That sounds a good plan," she said gravely. "Shall I climb through the window—I can quite easily—or would you like me to go round by the door?"

"The window will serve," said the old man.

And with one bound as light as a young kid, Halcyone was in the room.

There was a second armchair beyond the pile of books, and into that she nestled, crossing her knees and clasping her hands round them.

"Now we can begin," she said.

"Tea or talk?" asked the old man.

"Why, talk, of course; there is no tea—"

"But if you rang that bell some one might come."

Halcyone jumped up again and looked about for the bell. She was not going to ask where it was—she disliked stupid people herself. The old man watched her from under the penthouse of his eyebrows with a curious smile.

The bell was hidden in the carving of the mantelpiece, but she found it at last and gave it a lusty pull.

It seemed instantaneously answered by a strange-looking man,—a dark, extremely thin person with black, dull eyes.

The old man spoke to him in an unknown language and he retired silently.

"Who was that?" asked Halcyone.

"That is my servant—he will bring tea."

"He is not English?"

"No—does that matter?"

"Of course not—but what country does he come from?"

"You must ask him some day."

"I want to see countries," and she stretched out her slender arms, "I want to fly away outside the park and see the world."

"You have time," said the old man.

"When I am big enough I shall run away—I get very tired of only the Aunts La Sarthe. They never understand a word I say."

"What do you say?"

"I want to say all sorts of things, but if it isn't what they have heard a hundred times before, they look shocked and pained."

"You must come and say them to me then, perhaps I might understand, and in any case I should not be shocked or pained."

"They remind me of the Three Gray Sisters, although there are only two of them—one eye and one tooth between them."

"I see—there is something we can talk about at all events," said the old man. "The Three Gray Sisters are friends of yours—are they?"

"Not *friends!*" Halcyone exclaimed emphatically. "I can't bear them, silly old things nodding there, with their ridiculous answers to Perseus, saying old things were better than new—and their day better than his—I should have thrown their eye into the sea if I had been he. Do all old

people do that?—pretend their time was the best?—do you?
I don't mean to."

"You are right. It is a bad habit."

"But are they better, the old things?"

The old man did not answer for a moment or two. He
looked his visitor through and through with his wise gray
eyes—an investigation which might have disconcerted some
people, but Halcyone was unabashed.

"I know what you are doing," she said. "You are seeing
the other side of my head—and I wish I could see the other
side of yours, I can the Aunts' La Sarthe and Priscilla's,
in a minute, but yours is different."

"I am glad of that—you might be disappointed, though, if
you did see what was there."

"I always want to see," she said simply—"see everything;
and sometimes I find the other side not a bit what this is
—even in the birds and trees and the beetles. But you must
have a huge big one."

The old man laughed.

"You and I are going to be good acquaintances," he said.
"Tell me some more of Perseus. What more do you know
of him?"

"I have only read 'The Heroes,'" Halcyone admitted,
"but I know it by heart—and I know it is all true though
my governess says it is fairy-tales and not for girls. I want
to learn Greek, but they can't teach me."

"That is too bad."

"When things are put vaguely I always want to know
then—I want to know why Medusa turned into a gorgon?
What was her sin?"

The old man smiled.

"I see," said Halcyone, "you won't tell me, but some day
I shall know."

"Yes, some day you shall know," he said.

"They seem such great people, those Greeks; they knew
everything—so the preface of my 'Heroes' says, and I want
to learn the things they knew—mathematics and geometry,
rather—and especially logic and metaphysics, because I want
to know the meanings of words and the art of reasoning,
and above everything I want to know about my own
thoughts and soul."

"You strange little girl," said the old man. "Have you a
soul?"

"I don't know, I have something in there," and Halcyone
pointed to her head—"and it talks to me like another voice,

and when I am alone up a tree away from people, and all is beautiful, it seems to make it tight round here,—and go from my head into my side," and she placed her lean brown paw over her heart.

"Yes—you perhaps have a soul," said the old man, and then he added, half to himself—"What a pity."

"Why a pity?" demanded Halcyone.

"Because a woman with a soul suffers, and brings tribulation—but since you have one we may as well teach you how to keep the thing in hand."

At that moment, the dark servant brought tea, and the fine oriental china pleased Halcyone whose perceptions took in the texture of every single thing she came in contact with.

The old man seemed to go into a reverie, he was quite silent while he poured out the tea, forgetting to inquire her tastes as to cream and sugar—he drank his black—and handed Halcyone a cup of the same.

She looked at him, her inquiring eyes full of intelligence and understanding, and she realized at once that these trifles were not in his consideration for the moment. So she helped herself to what she wanted and sat down again in her armchair. She did not even rattle her teaspoon. Priscilla often made noises which irritated her when she was thinking.

The old man came back to a remembrance of her presence at last.

"Little girl," he said—"would you like to come here pretty often and learn Greek, and about the Greeks?"

Halcyone bounded from her chair with joy.

"But of course I would!" she said. "And I am not stupid —not really stupid Mademoiselle says, when I want to learn things."

"No— I dare say you are not stupid," the old man said. "So it is a bargain then; I shall teach you about my friends the Greeks, and you shall teach me about the green trees, and your friends the rabbits and the beetles."

Then those instinctive good manners of Halcyone's came uppermost, inherited, like her slender shape and balanced head, from that long line of La Sarthe ancestors, and she thanked the old man with a quaint, courtly, sweetly pedantic grace. Then she got up to go—

"I like being here—and may I come again to-morrow?" she said afterwards. "I must go now or they will be disagreeable and perhaps make difficulties."

The old man watched her as she curtsied to him and

vaulted through the window again, and on down the path, and through the hole in the paling, without once turning round. Then he muttered to himself:

"A woman thing who refrains from looking back!— Yes, I fear she has a soul."

Then he returned to his pipe and his Aristotle.

CHAPTER II

HALCYONE struck straight across the park until she came to the beech avenue, near the top, which ran south. The place had been nobly planned by that grim old La Sarthe who raised it in the days of the seventh Henry. It stood very high with its terraced garden in the center of four splendid avenues of oak, lime, beech and Spanish chestnut running east, west, north and south. And four gates in different stages of dilapidation gave entrance through a broken wall of stone to a circular drive which connected all the avenues giving access to the house, a battered, irregular erection of gray stone.

To reach the splendid front door you entered from the oak avenue and crossed the pleasance, now only an overgrown meadow where the one cow grazed in the summer.

Then you were obliged to mount three stately flights of stone steps until you reached the first terrace, which was flagged near the house and bordered with stiff flower-beds. Here you might turn and look back due west upon a view of exquisite beauty—an undulating fertile country beneath, and then in the far distance a line of dim blue hills.

But if you chanced to wish to enter your carriage unwetted on a rainy day, you were obliged to deny yourself the pleasure of passing through the entrance hall in state, and to go out at the back by stone passages into the courtyard where the circular avenue came up close to a fortified door, under the arch of which you could drive.

Everything spoke of past grandeur and present decay— only the flower-beds of the highest terrace appeared even partly cultivated; the two lower ones were a wild riot of weeds and straggling rose trees unpruned and untrained, and if you looked up at the windows in the southern wing of the house, you saw that several panes in them were missing and that the holes had been stuffed with rags.

At this time of the year the beech avenue presented an indescribably lovely sight of just opening leaves of tender green. It was a never-failing joy to Halcyone. She walked the few paces which separated her from it and turning, stood leaning against the broken gate now, drinking in every tone

7

of the patches the lower sun made of gold between the green. For her it was full of wood nymphs and elves. It did not contain gods and goddesses like the others. She told herself long stories about them.

The beech avenue was her favorite for the spring, the lime for the summer, the chestnut for the autumn, and the oak for the winter. She knew every tree in all four, as a huntsman knows his hounds. And when, in the great equinoctial storm of the previous year, three giant oaks lay shattered and broken, the sight had caused her deep grief, until she wove a legend about them and turned them into monsters for Perseus to subdue with Medusa's head. One, indeed, whose trunk was gnarled and twisted, became the serpent of the brazen scales who sleepeth not, guarding the Golden Fleece.

"As the tree falls so shall it lie," seemed to be the motto of La Sarthe Chase. For none were removed.

Halcyone stretched out her arms and beckoned to her fairy friends.

"Queen Mab," she called, "come and dance nearer to me —I can see your wings and I want to talk to you to-day!"

And as if in answer to this invitation, the rays of the lowered sun shifted to an opening almost at her feet, and with a cry of joy the child began to dance in the gorgeous light.

"Come follow, follow me, ye fairy elves that be," she sang softly.

And the sprites laughed with gladness, and gilded her mouse hair with gold, and lit up her eyes, and wove scarves about her with gossamer threads, and beneath her feet tall bluebells offered their heads as a carpet.

But Halcyone sprang over them, she would not have crushed the meanest weed.

"Queen Mab!" she said at last, as she sat down in the middle of the sunlight, "I have found an old gentleman— and he is Cheiron, and if one could see it in the right light, he may have a horse's body, and he is going to teach me just what Jason learnt—and then I shall tell it to you."

The rays shifted again to a path beyond, and Halcyone bounded up and went on her way.

Old William was drawing the elder Miss La Sarthe in a dilapidated basket-chair, up and down on the highest terrace. She held a minute faded pink silk parasol over her head— it had an ivory handle which folded up when she no longer needed the parasol as a shade. She wore one-buttoned gloves, of slate-colored kid, and a wrist-band of black velvet clasped with a buckle. An inverted cake-tin of weather-beaten straw, trimmed with rusty velvet, shadowed her old, tired eyes; an Indian shawl was crossed upon her thin bosom.

"Halcyone!" she called querulously. "Where have you been, child? You must have missed your tea."

And Halcyone answered:

"In the orchard."

For of what use to inform Aunt Ginevra about that enchanting visit to Cheiron! Aunt Ginevra who knew not of such beings!

"The orchard's let," grunted old William—"they do say it's sold—"

"I had rather not hear of it, William," said Miss La Sarthe frowning. "It does not concern one what occurs beyond one's gates."

Old William growled gently, and continued his laborious task—one of the wheels squeaked as it turned on the flags.

"Aunt Ginevra, you must have that oiled," said Halcyone, as she screwed up her face. "How can you bear it? You can't see the lovely spring things, with that noise."

"One does not see with one's ears, Halcyone," quavered Miss La Sarthe. "Take me in now, William."

"And she can't even see them with her eyes—poor Aunt Ginevra!" Halcyone said to herself, as she walked respectfully by the chair until it passed the front door on its way to the side. Then she bounded up the steps and through the paneled, desolate hall, taking joy in climbing the dog-gates at the turn of the stairs, which she could easily have opened—and she did not pause until she reached her own room in the battered south wing, and was soon curled up in the broad window sill, her hands clasped round her knees.

For this was a wonderful thing which had come into her life—She had met someone who could see the other side of her head! Henceforth there would be a human voice, not only a fairy's, to converse with her. Indeed, the world was a very fair place!

Here, Priscilla found her when it was growing dark, still with the rapt expression of glad thought on her face. And the elderly woman shook her head. "That child is not canny," she muttered, while aloud she chided her for idleness and untidiness in having thrown her cap on the floor.

But Halcyone flung her arms round Priscilla's neck and laughed in her beard.

"Oh, you dear old goosie! I have been with the Immortals on the blue peaks of Olympus and there we did not wear caps!"

"Them Immortals!" said Priscilla. "Better far you were attending to things you can see. They'll be coming down and carrying you off, some of these fine nights!"

"The Immortals don't care so much about the nights, Priscilla—unless Artemis is abroad—she does—but the others like the sunlight and great white clouds and a still blue sky. I am quite safe—" and Halcyone smiled.

Priscilla began tidying up.

"Ma'm'selle's wrote to the mistresses to say she won't come back, she can't put up with the place any longer."

This sounded too good to be true! Another governess going! Surely they would see it was no use asking any more to come to La Sarthe Chase—Halcyone had never had one who could appreciate its beauties. Governesses to her were poor-spirited creatures afraid of rats, and the dark passages—and one and all resentful of the rag-stuffed panes in the long gallery. Surely with the new-found Cheiron to instruct her about those divine Greeks a fresh governess was unnecessary.

"I shall ask Aunt Ginevra to implore my stepfather not to send any more. We don't want them, do we, Priscilla?"

"That we don't, my lamb!" agreed Priscilla. "But you must learn something more useful than gods and goddesses. Your poor, dear mother in heaven would break her heart if she knew you were going to be brought up ignorant."

Halcyone raised her head haughtily.

"I shan't be ignorant—don't be afraid. I would not remain ignorant even if no other governess ever came near me. I can read by myself, and the dear old gentleman I saw to-day will direct me." And then when she perceived the look of astonishment on Priscilla's face: "Ah! That is a secret; I had not meant to tell you—but I will. The orchard cottage is inhabited and I've seen him, and he is Cheiron, and I am going to learn Greek!"

"Bless my heart!" said Priscilla. "Well, now, it is long past seven o'clock and you must dress to go down to dessert."

And all the time she was putting Halcyone into her too short white frock, and brushing her mane of hair, the child kept up a brisk conversation. Silent for hours at a time, when something suddenly interested her she could be loquacious enough.

One candle had to be lit before her toilet was completed, and then at half past seven she stole down the stairs, full of shadows, and across the hall to the great dining-room, where the Misses La Sarthe dined in state at seven o'clock, off some thin soup and one other dish, so that at half past seven the cloth had been cleared away by old William (in a black evening coat now and rather a high stock), and the shining mahogany table reflected the two candles in the superb old silver candlesticks.

At this stage, as Halcyone entered the room, it was customary for William to place the dish of apples on the table in front of Miss La Sarthe, and the dish of almonds and raisins in front of Miss Roberta. The dessert did not vary much for months—from October to late June it was the same; and only on Sundays was the almond and raisin dish allowed to be partaken of, but an apple was divided into four quarters, after being carefully peeled by Miss La Sarthe, each evening, and Miss Roberta was given two quarters and Halcyone one, while the eldest lady nibbled at the remaining piece herself.

In her day, children had always come down to dessert, and had had to be good and not greedy, or the fate of Miss Augusta Noble of that estimable book, "The Fairchild Family," would certainly fall upon them. Halcyone, from her earliest memory, had come down to dessert every night —except at one or two pleasant moments when the measles or a bad cold had kept her in bed. Half past seven o'clock, summer and winter, had meant for her the quarter of an apple, two or three strawberries or a plum—and almost always the same conversation.

Miss La Sarthe sat at the head of the table, in a green silk dress cut low upon the shoulders and trimmed with a bertha of blonde lace. Miss Roberta—sad falling off from dignity—had her thin bones covered with a habit shirt of tulle, because she was altogether a poorer creature than her sister, and felt the cold badly. Both ladies wore ringlets at the sides of their faces and little caps of ribbon and lace.

Even within Halcyone's memory, the dining-room had lost some of its adornments. The Chippendale chairs had gone, and had been replaced by four stout kitchen ones. The bits of rare china were fewer—but the portrait of the famous Timothy La Sarthe, by Holbein, still frowned from his place of honor above the chimney-piece. All the La Sarthes had been christened Timothy since that time.

The affair of the governess seemed to be troubling Miss Roberta. At intervals she had found comfort in these denizens of the outer world, and free from the stern eye of Sister Ginevra, had been wont to chat with one and another. They never stayed long enough for her to know them well, and now this lady—the fifth within two years—had refused to return. Life seemed very dull.

"Need I have any more governesses, Aunt Ginevra?" Halcyone said. "There is an old gentleman who has bought the orchard house and he says he will teach me Greek—and I already know a number of other tiresome things."

Halcyone had not meant to tell her aunts anything about Cheiron—this new found joy—but she reasoned after she heard of Mademoiselle's non-return that the knowledge that she would have some instructor might have weight with those in charge of her. It was worth risking at all events.

Miss La Sarthe adjusted a gold pince-nez and looked at the little girl.

"How old are you, Halcyone?" she asked.

"I was twelve on the seventh of last October, Aunt Ginevra."

"Twelve—a young gentlewoman's education is not complete at twelve years old, child—although governesses in the house are not very pleasant, I admit"—and Miss La Sarthe sighed.

"Oh, I know it isn't!" said Halcyone, "but you see, I can speak French and German quite decently, and the other things surely I might learn myself in between the old gentleman's teaching."

"But what do you know of this—this stranger?" demanded Miss La Sarthe. "You allude to someone of whom neither your Aunt Roberta nor I have ever heard."

"I met him to-day. I went into the orchard as usual, and found the house was inhabited, and I saw him and he asked me in to tea. He is a very old gentleman with a long white beard, and very, very clever. His room is full of Greek books and we had a long talk, and he was very kind and said he would teach me to read them."

This seemed to Halcyone to be sufficient in the way of credentials for anyone.

"I have heard from Hester," Miss Roberta interposed timidly, "that the orchard house has been bought by an Oxford professor—it sounds most respectable, does it not, sister?"

Miss La Sarthe looked stern:

"More than thirty-five years ago, Roberta, I told you I disapproved of Hester's chattering. I cannot conceive personally, how you can converse with servants as you do. Hester would not have dared to gossip to me!"

Poor Miss Roberta looked crushed. She had often been chided on this point before.

Halycone would like to have reminded her elder aunt that William, who was equally a servant, had announced some such news to her that afternoon; but she remained silent. She must gain her point if she could, and to argue, she knew, was never a road to success.

"I am sure if we could get a really nice English girl," hazarded Miss Roberta, wishing to propitiate, "it might be company for us all, Ginevra—but if Mrs. Anderton insists upon sending another foreign person—"

"And of course she will," interrupted the elder lady; "people of Mrs. Anderton's class always think it is more genteel to have a smattering of foreign languages than to know their own mother tongue. We may get another German—and that I could hardly bear."

"Then do write to my stepfather, please, please," cried Halcyone. "Say I am going to be splendidly taught—lots of interesting things—and oh—I will try so hard by myself to keep up what I already know. I will practice—really, really, Aunt Ginevra—and do my German exercises and dear Aunt Roberta can talk French to me and even teach me the Italian songs that she sings so beautifully to her guitar!"

This last won the day as far as Miss Roberta was concerned. Her faded cheeks flushed pink. The trilling Italian love-songs, learnt some fifty years ago during a two years' residence in Florence, had always been her pride and joy. So she warmly seconded her niece's pleadings, and the momentous decision was come to that James Anderton should be approached upon the subject. If the child learned Greek—from a professor—and could pick up a few of Roberta's songs as an accomplishment, she might do well enough—and a governess in the house, in spite of the money paid by Mr. Anderton to keep her, was a continual gall and worry to them.

Halcyone knew very little about her stepfather. She was aware that he had married her mother when she was a very poor and sorrowful young widow, that she had had two stepsisters and a brother very close together, and then that the pretty mother had died. There was evidently something so sad connected with the whole story that Priscilla never cared much to talk about it. It was always, "your poor sainted mother in heaven," or, "your blessed pretty mother" —and with that instinctive knowledge of the feelings of other people which characterized Halcyone's point of view, she had avoided questioning her old nurse. Her stepfather, James Anderton, was a very wealthy stock broker—she knew that, and also that a year or so after her mother's death he had married again—"a person of his own class," Miss La Sarthe had said, "far more suitable to him than poor Elaine."

Halcyone had only been six years old at her mother's death, but she kept a crisp memory of the horror of it. The crimson, crumpled-looking baby brother, in his long clothes, whose coming somehow seemed responsible for the loss of her tender angel, for a long time was viewed with resentful hatred. It was a terrible, unspeakable grief. She remembered perfectly the helpless sense of loss and loneliness.

Her mother had loved her with passionate devotion. She was conscious even then that Mabel and Ethel, the stepsisters, were as nothing in comparison to herself in her mother's regard. She had a certainty that her mother had loved her own father very much—the young, brilliant, spendthrift, last La Sarthe. And her mother had been of the family, too—a distant cousin. So she herself was La Sarthe to her finger tips—slender and pale and distinguished-looking. She remembered the last scene with her stepfather before her coming to La Sarthe Chase. It was the culmination after a year of misery and unassuaged grieving for her loss. He had come into the nursery where the three little girls were playing—Halcyone and her two stepsisters—and he had made them all stand up in his rough way, and see who could catch the pennies the best that he threw from the door. His brother, "Uncle Ted," was with him. And the two younger children, Mabel of five and Ethel of four, shouted riotously with glee and snatched the coins from one another and greedily quarreled over those which Halcyone caught with her superior skill and handed to them.

She remembered her stepfather's face—it grew heavy and sullen and he walked to the window, where his brother followed him—and she remembered their words and had pondered over them often since.

"It's the damned breeding in the brat that fairly gets me raw, Ted," Mr. Anderton had said. "Why the devil couldn't Elaine have given it to my children, too. I can't stand it— a home must be found for her elsewhere."

And soon after that, Halcyone had come with her own Priscilla to La Sarthe Chase to her great-aunts Ginevra and Roberta, in their tumble-down mansion which her father had not lived to inherit. Under family arrangements, it was the two old ladies' property for their lives.

And now the problem of what James Anderton—or rather the second Mrs. James Anderton—would do was the question of the moment. Would there be a fresh governess or would they all be left in peace without one? Mrs. James Anderton, Miss Roberta had said once, was a person who "did her duty," as people often did "in her class"—"a most worthy woman, if not quite a lady"—and she had striven to do her best by James Anderton's children—even his step-child Halcyone.

Miss La Sarthe promised to write that night before she went to bed—but Halcyone knew it was a long process with her and that an answer could not be expected for at least a week. Therefore there was no good agitating herself too soon about the result. It was one of her principles never to worry over unnecessary things. Life was full of blessed certainties to enjoy without spoiling them by speculating over possible unpleasantnesses.

The old gentleman—Cheiron—and old William and the timid curate who came to dine on Saturday nights once a month were about the only male creatures Halcyone had ever spoken to within her recollection—their rector was a confirmed invalid and lived abroad—but Priscilla had a supreme contempt for them as a sex.

"One and all set on themselves, my lamb," she said; "even your own beautiful father had to be bowed down to and worshiped. We put up with it in him, of course; but I never did see one that didn't think of himself first. It is their selfishness that causes all the sorrow of the world to women. We needn't have lost your angel mother but for Mr. Anderton's selfishness—a kind, hard, rough man—but as selfish as a gentleman."

It seemed a more excusable defect to Priscilla in the upper class, but had no redeeming touch in the status of Mr. Anderton.

Halcyone, however, had a logical mind and reasoned with her nurse:

"If they are *all* selfish, Priscilla, it must be either women's fault for letting them be, or God intended them to be so. A thing can't be *all* unless the big force makes it."

This "big force"—this "God" was a real personality to

Halcyone. She could not bear it when in church she heard the meanest acts of revenge and petty wounded vanity attributed to Him. She argued it was because the curate did not know. Having come from a town, he could not be speaking of the same wonderful God she knew in the woods and fields—the God so loving and tender in the spring-time to the budding flowers, so gorgeous in the summer and autumn and so pure and cold in the winter. With all that to attend to He could not possibly stoop to punish ignorant people and to harbor anger and wrath against them. He was the sunlight and the moonlight and the starlight. He was the voice which talked in the night and made her never lonely.

And all the other things of nature and the universe were gods, also—lesser ones obeying the supreme force and some-how fused with Him in a whole, being part of a scheme which He had invented to complete the felicity of the world He had created—not beings to be prayed to or solicited for favors, but just gentle, glorious, sympathetic, invisible friends. She was very much interested in Christ; He was certainly a part of God, too—but she could not understand about His dying to save the world, since the God she heard of in the church was still forever punishing and torturing human beings, or only extending mercy after His vanity had been flattered by offerings and sacrifices.

"I expect," she said to herself, coming home on Sunday after one of Mr. Miller's lengthy discourses upon God's vengeance, "when I am older and able really to understand what is written in the Bible I shall find it isn't that a bit, and it is either Mr. Miller can't see straight or he has put the stops all in the wrong places and changed the sense. In any case I shall not trouble now—the God who kept me from falling through the hole in the loft yesterday by that ray of sunlight to show the cracked board, is the one I am fond of."

It was the simple and logical view of a case which always appealed to her.

"Halcyone" her parents had called her well—their bond of love—their tangible proof of halcyon days. And always when Halcyone read her "Heroes" she felt it was her beauti-ful father and mother who were the real Halcyone and Ceyx, and she longed to see the blue summer sea and the pleasant isles of Greece that she might find their floating nest and see them sail away happily for ever over those gentle southern waves.

CHAPTER III

Mr. Carlyon—for such was Cheiron's real name—knocked the ashes from his long pipe next day at eleven o'clock in the morning, after his late breakfast and began to arrange his books. His mind was away in a land of classical lore; he had almost forgotten the sprite who had invaded his solitude the previous afternoon, until he heard a tap at the window, and saw her standing there—great, intelligent eyes aflame and rosy lips apart.

"May I come in, please?" her voice said. "I am afraid I am a little early, but I had something so very interesting to tell you, I had to come."

He opened wide the window and let in the May sunshine.

"The first of May and a May Queen," he told her presently, when they were seated in their two chairs. "And now begin this interesting news."

"Aunt Ginevra has promised to write to my stepfather at once, and suggest that no more governesses are sent to me. Won't it be perfectly splendid if he agrees!"

"I really don't know," said Cheiron.

Halcyone's face fell.

"You promised to teach me Greek," she said simply, "and I know from my 'Heroes' that is all that I need necessarily learn from anyone to acquire the other things myself."

This seemed to Mr. Carlyon a very conclusive answer—his bent of mind found it logical.

"Very well," he said. "When shall we begin?"

"Perhaps to-morrow. To-day if you have time I would like to take you for a walk in the park—and show you some of the trees. The beeches are coming out very early this year; they have the most exquisite green just showing, and the chestnuts in some places have quite large leaves. It is damp under foot, though—do you mind that?"

"Not a bit," said Cheiron.

And so they went, creeping through the hole in the paling like two brigands on a marauding expedition.

"There used to be deer when I first came five years ago," Halcyone said. "I remember them quite well, and their sweet little fawns; but the next winter was that horribly cold one, and there was no hay to be put out to them—my

17

Aunts La Sarthe are very poor—and some of them died, and in the summer the Long Man came and talked and talked, and Aunt Roberta had red eyes all the afternoon, as she always does when he comes, and Aunt Ginevra pretended hers were a cold in her head—and the week after a lot of men arrived and drove all the tender, beautiful creatures into corners, and took them away in carts with nets over them—the does—but the bucks had pieces of wood because their horns would have torn the nets."

Her delicate lips quivered a moment, as though at a too painful memory—then she smiled.

"But one mother doe and her fawn got away—and I knew where they were hiding, but I did not tell, of course—and now there are four of them, or perhaps five. But they are very wild and keep in the copses, and fly if they see anyone coming. They don't mind me, of course, but strangers. The mother remembers that awful day, I expect."

"No doubt," said Cheiron; "and who is the 'Long Man' you spoke of as having instigated this outrage?"

"He is the man of business, he was the bailiff once, but is a house agent now in Applewood. And whenever he comes something has to go—we all dread it. Last Michaelmas it was the Chippendale dining-room chairs—"

"I know him then—I bought my cottage from him. I suppose all this is necessary, because he seemed an honest fellow."

"Someone long ago made it necessary—it is not the Aunts' fault—" and then Halcyone stopped abruptly and pointed to the beech avenue which they were approaching now through the bracken, brown and crisp from last year, with only here and there a green shoot showing.

"Queen Mab and the elves live there in May and early June," she said. "They dance every afternoon as the sun sets, and sometimes in the dawn, too, and the early morning. You can see them if you keep quite still."

"Naturally," said Cheiron.

"Do you know, since last winter I have had a great pleasure," and Halcyone's grave, intent eyes looked up into the old gentleman's face. "There was a terrible storm in February—but can you really keep a secret?"—and then, as he nodded his head seriously, she went on. "It blew down a narrow piece of the paneling in the long gallery—it is next to my room, you know—and I heard the noise in the night and lit a candle and went to see. Some of the window panes are broken, so it is very blustery there in storms.

Well, there was a door behind it—a secret door. I was so excited, but I could not keep the candle alight and it was very cold. I saw nothing was broken—only the wind had dislodged the spring. I was able to push it back and pull a little chest against it, and wait till morning. And then what do you think I found?—it led to a staircase in the thickness of the wall, which went down and down until it came to a door right below the cellar—it took me days of dodging Mademoiselle and Priscilla to carry down oil and things to help me to open it—and then it came out in a hollow archway on the second terrace, which has a stone bench in it, and is where old William keeps his tools. It is so cleverly done you could never see it; it looks just as if it was no door, but was only there for ornament. You may fancy I never told anyone! It is my secret—and yours now —and it enabled me to do what I have always longed to do —go out in the night!"

"You go out in the night all alone!" exclaimed Cheiron, almost aghast.

"But of course," said Halcyone. "You cannot think of the joy when there is a moon and stars; and some of the night creatures are such friends—they teach me wonderful things. Only the dreadful difficulty is in avoiding Priscilla —she sleeps in the dressing-room next me. I love her better than anyone else in the world, but she could never understand—she would only worry about the wet feet and clothes being spoilt. I always think it is so fortunate though, don't you, that servants—even a dear like Priscilla—sleep so soundly. Aunt Ginevra says they can't help it, every class has its peculiarity."

Mr. Carlyon was extremely interested—he wanted to hear more of these adventures.

"How do you avoid Priscilla seeing your things in the morning then?" he asked.

"I have got a pair of big gutta-percha boots—they were my father's waders once, and I found them, and have hidden them in one of the chests, and I tuck everything into them —so there are no marks. It is enchanting."

"And do you often have these nocturnal outings, you odd little girl?" Cheiron said, wonderingly.

"Not very. I have to be so careful, you see—and I only choose moonlight or starlight nights, and they are rare—but when the summer comes I hope to enjoy many more of them."

Then Mr. Carlyon's old eyes looked away into distance and seemed to see a slender shape wrapped in a spotted fawn's skin, its head crowned with leaves, joining the throng of those other early worshipers of Dionysus as they beat their weird music among the dark crags of Parnassus— searching for communion with the spiritual beyond in the only way they knew of then to reach it, through a wild ecstasy of emotion. Here was the same impulse, unconscious, instinctive. The probing of nature to discover her secrets. Here was a female thing with a soul unafraid in her pure innocence, alone in the night.

Halcyone did not interrupt his meditations, and presently they came to the broken gate close to the house.

Cheiron paused and leaned on the top bar.

"Is this elves' home?" he asked.

"Yes," she answered gravely. "But so late in the day you cannot see them. You must wait again until the sun is setting; and I expect when it is warm they come in the moonlight, too, but I have not been able to get a fine enough night—as yet. This avenue is the most beautiful of all, because a hundred years ago the La Sarthes had a quarrel with the Wendovers, whose land just touches at the end of it, and they closed the gate, and so the turf has covered the gravel. And look at the tree—you can see the fairy ring where they dance, and I always fancy they sup under the one with the very low branch at the side—but I don't believe I should like 'marrow of mice,' should you?"

"Not at all," said Cheiron.

Then they wandered on. Halcyone led him to each of the favorite points of view, and he became acquainted with the great serpent, and so vivid was her picturing that he almost fancied he saw the Golden Fleece nailed to the tree beyond, and heard Orpheus' exquisite melodies charming the reptile to sleep while Jason stepped over his slumbering coils.

"But I do not have Medea here," she said; "I play her part myself, and I make her different. She was too cunning and had wicked thoughts in her heart, and so the poor Heroes suffered. If she had been good and true and had not killed Absyrtus, things might have had a different ending. I never like to think of Absyrtus in any case—because, do you know, I once hated my baby brother, and would have been glad if anyone had killed him."

Her eyes became black as night with this awful recollection. "It was very long ago, you understand—when I was quite a little girl before I knew the wonderful things the wind and the flowers and the stars tell me."

Cheiron did not ask the cause of this hate; he reserved the

question for a future time, and encouraged her to tell him of her discoveries in wonderland.

Some trees had strange personalities, she said. You could never guess the other side of their heads, until you knew them very well. But all had good in them, and it was wisest never even to see the bad.

"I always find if you are afraid of things they become real and hurt you, but if you are sure they are kind and true they turn gentle and love you. I am hardly ever afraid of anything now—only I do not like a thunderstorm. It seems as if God were really angry then, and were not considering sufficiently just whom He meant to hit."

Justice to her appeared to hold chief place among the virtues.

"Do you stay here all the year round?" asked Cheiron, presently, "or do you sometimes have a trip to the seaside?"

"I have never been away since I first came—I would love to see the sea," and her eyes became dreary. "I can just remember long ago with my mother, we went once—she and I alone—" then she turned to her old companion and looked up in his face.

"Had you a mother? Of course you had, but I mean one that you knew?"

The late Mrs. Carlyon had not meant anything much to her son in her lifetime, and was now a far-off memory of forty years ago, so Cheiron answered truthfully upon the subject, and Halcyone looked grave.

"When we have been friends for a long time I will tell you of my beautiful mother—and I could let you share my memory of her perhaps—but not to-day," she said.

And then she was silent for a while as they walked on. But when they were turning back towards the orchard house she suddenly began to laugh, glancing at the old gentleman with eyes full of merriment.

"It is funny," she said, "I don't even know your name! I would like to call you Cheiron—but you have a real name, of course."

"It is Arnold Carlyon, and I come from Cornwall," the old gentleman said, "but you are welcome to call me Cheiron, if you like."

Halcyone thanked him prettily.

"I wish you had his body—don't you? How we could gallop about, could we not? But I can imagine you have, easily. I always can see things I imagine, and sometimes they become realities then."

"Heaven forbid!" exclaimed Cheiron. "What would my four legs and my hoofs do in the little orchard house, and how should I sit in my armchair?"

Halcyone pealed with merry laughter; her laughs came so rarely and were like golden bells. The comic side of the picture enchanted her.

"Of course it would only do if we lived in a cave, as the real Cheiron did," she admitted. "I was silly, was not I?"

"Yes," said Mr. Carlyon, "but I don't think I mind your being so—it is nice to laugh."

She slipped her thin little hand into his for a moment, and caught hold of one of his fingers.

"I am so glad you understand that," she said. "How good it is to laugh! That is what the birds sing to me, it is no use ever to be sad, because it draws evil and fear to yourself, and even in the winter one must know there is always the beautiful spring soon coming. Don't you think God is full of love for this world?"

"I am sure He is."

"The Aunts' God isn't a very kind person," she went on. "But I expect, since you know about the Greeks, yours and mine are the same."

"Probably," said Cheiron.

Then, being assured on this point, Halcyone felt she could almost entrust him with her greatest secret.

"Do you know," she said, in the gravest voice, "I will tell you something. I have a goddess, too. I found her in the secret staircase. She is broken, even her nose a little, but she is supremely beautiful. It is just her head I have got, and I pretend she is my mother sometimes, really come back to me again. We have long talks. Some day I will show her to you. I have to keep her hidden, because Aunt Ginevra cannot bear rubbish about, and as she is broken she would want to have her thrown away."

"I shall be delighted to make her acquaintance. What do you call her?"

"That is just it," said Halcyone. "When I first found her it seemed to me I must call her Pallas Athené, because of that noble lady in Perseus—but as I looked and looked I knew she was not that; it seems she cannot be anything else but just Love—her eyes are so tender, she has many moods, and they are not often the same—but no matter how she looks you feel all the time just love, love, love—so I have not named her yet. You remember when Orpheus took his lyre and sang after Cheiron had finished his song—it was of

Chaos and the making of the world, and how all things had sprung from Love—who could not live alone in the Abyss. So I know that is she—just Love."

"Aphrodite," said Cheiron.

"It is a pretty name. If that is what it means, I would call her that."

"It will do," said Cheiron.

"Aphrodite—Aphrodite," she repeated it over and over. "It must mean kind and tender, and soft and sweet, and beautiful and glorious, and making you think of noble things, and making you feel perfectly happy and warmed and comforted and blessed. Is it all that?"

"It could be—and more," said Cheiron.

"Then I will name her so."

After this there was a long silence. Mr. Carlyon would not interrupt what was evidently a serious moment to his little friend. He waited, and then presently he turned the channel of her thoughts by asking her if she thought he might call on her Aunts that afternoon.

Halcyone hesitated a second.

"We hardly ever have visitors. Aunt Ginevra has always said one must not receive what one cannot return, and they have no carriage or horses now, so they never see any one. Aunt Roberta would, but Aunt Ginevra does not let her, and she often says in the last ten years they have quite dropped out of everything. I do not know what that means altogether, because I do not know what there was to drop out of. I have scarcely ever been beyond the park, and there do not seem to be any big houses for miles—do there? —except Wendover, but it is shut up; it has been for twenty years."

"Then you think the Misses La Sarthe might not receive me?"

"You could try, of course. You have not a carriage. If you just walked it would make it even. Shall I tell them you are coming? I had better, perhaps."

"Yes, this afternoon."

And if Halcyone had known it, she was receiving an unheard-of compliment! The hermit Carlyon—the old Oxford Professor of Greek, who had come to this out-of-the-way corner because he had been assured by the agent there would be no sort of society around him—now intended to put on a tall hat and frock coat, and make a formal call on two maiden ladies—all for the sake of a child of twelve years, with serious gray eyes—and a soul!

CHAPTER IV

In her heart of hearts Miss Roberta felt fluttered as she walked across the empty hall to the Italian parlor behind her sterner sister, to receive their guest. He would come in the afternoon, Halcyone said. That meant about three o'clock, and it behooved ladies expecting a gentleman to be at ease at some pretty fancy work when he should be announced.

The village was two miles beyond the lime lodge gates, and for the last eight years rheumatism in the knee had made the walk there out of the question for poor Miss Roberta—so even the sight of a man and a stranger was an unusual thing! She had not attempted conversation with anyone but Mr. Miller, the curate, for over eleven years. The isolation in which the inhabitants of La Sarthe Chase lived could not be more complete.

The Italian parlor had its own slightly pathetic *cachet*. The walls and ceiling had been painted by rather a bad artist from Florence at the beginning of the nineteenth century, but the furniture was good of its kind—a strange dark orange lacquer and gilt—and here most of the treasures which had not yet been disposed of for daily bread, were hoarded in cabinets and quaint glass-topped show tables. There were a number of other priceless things about the house, the value of which the Long Man's artistic education was as yet too unfinished to appreciate. And the greatest treasure of all, as we have seen, was probably only understood by Halcyone—but more of that in its place.

At present it concerns us to know that Miss La Sarthe and her sister had reached the Italian parlor, and were seated in their respective chairs—Miss Roberta with a piece of delicate embroidery in her hands, the stitches of which her eyes—without spectacles, to receive company—were too weak adequately to perceive.

Miss La Sarthe did not condescend to any such subterfuges. She sat quite still doing nothing, looking very much as she had looked for the last forty years. Her harp stood on one side of the fireplace, and Miss Roberta's guitar hung by a faded blue ribbon from a nail at the other.

Presently old William announced:

"Mr. Carlyon."

And Cheiron, in his Sunday best, walked into the room.

Halcyone was not present. If children were wanted they were sent for. It was not seemly for them to be idling in the drawing-rooms.

But Miss Roberta felt so pleasantly nervous, that she said timidly, after they had all shaken hands:

"Ginevra, can we not tell William to ask Halcyone to come down, perhaps Mr. Carlyon might like to see her again."

And William, who had not got far from the door, was recalled and sent on the errand.

"What a very beautiful view you have from here," Mr. Carlyon said, by way of a beginning. "It is an ideal spot."

"We are glad you like it," Miss La Sarthe replied, graciously; "as my sister and I live quite retired from the world it suits us. We had much gayety here in our youth, but now we like tranquillity."

"It is, however, delightful to have a neighbor," Miss Roberta exclaimed—and then blushed at her temerity.

The elder lady frowned; Roberta had always been so sadly effusive, she felt. Men ought not to be flattered so.

Mr. Carlyon bowed, and the platitudes were continued, each felt he or she must approach the subject of Halcyone's lessons, but waited for the other to begin.

Halcyone, herself, put an end to all awkwardness after she very gently entered the room. There was no bounding or vaulting in the presence of the aunts.

"Is it not kind of Mr. Carlyon to wish to teach me Greek?" she said, including both her relatives. "I expect he has told you about it though."

The Misses La Sarthe were properly surprised and interested. Most kind they thought it and expressed their appreciation in their separate ways. They both hoped their great-niece would be diligent, and prove a worthy pupil. It was most fortunate for Halcyone, because her stepfather, Mr. James Anderton, might decide at their request not to send another governess, and, "No doubt it will be most useful to her," Miss La Sarthe continued. "In these modern days so much learning seems to be expected of people. When we were young, a little French and Italian were all that was necessary."

Then Mr. Carlyon made friends of them for life, by a happy inspiration.

"I see you are both musicians," he said, pointing to the antiquated musical instruments. "A taste of that sort is a constant pleasure."

"We used to play a good deal at one time," admitted Miss La Sarthe, without a too great show of gratification, "and my sister was quite celebrated for her Italian songs."

"Oh!" gasped Miss Roberta, blushing again.

"I hope I may have the pleasure of hearing you together some day," said the Professor, gallantly.

Both ladies smilingly acquiesced, and they depreciated their powers.

And just before their visitor got up to leave, Miss La Sarthe said with her grand air:

"We hope you find your cottage comfortable. It used to be the land steward's, before we disposed of the property we no longer required. It always used to have a very pretty garden, but no doubt it has rather fallen into decay."

"I shall do my best to repair it," Mr. Carlyon said, "but it will take some time. I and my servant have already begun to clear the weeds away, and a new gardener is coming next week."

"Oh, may I help?" exclaimed Halcyone. "I love gardening, and can dig quite well. I often help William."

"Our old butler does many useful things for us," Miss Roberta explained, with a slightly conscious air.

And then the adieus were said, Halcyone's first lesson having been arranged to begin on the morrow.

When the visitor had gone and the door was shut:

"A very worthy, cultivated gentleman, Roberta," Miss La Sarthe announced to her sister. "We must ask him to dinner the next time Mr. Miller is coming. We must show him some attention for his kindness to our great-niece; he will understand and not allow it to flatter him too much. You remember, Roberta, our Mamma always said unmarried women—of any age—cannot be too careful of *les convenances,* but we might ask him to dinner under the circumstances—don't you think so?"

"Oh, I am sure—yes, sister—but I wish you would not talk so of our age," Miss Roberta said, rather fretfully for her. "You were only seventy-two last November, and I shall not be sixty-nine until March—and if you remember, Aunt Agatha lived to ninety-one, and Aunt Mildred to ninety-four! So we are not so very old as yet."

"The more reason for us to be careful then," retorted the elder lady, and Miss Roberta subsided with a sigh as she took her guitar from the wall and began in her gentle old quavering voice to trill out one of her many love-songs.

The guitar had not been tuned for several days, and had run down into a pitiful flatness; Halcyone could hardly sit still, it hurt her so—but it was only when Miss Roberta had begun a second warble that either she or Miss La Sarthe noticed the jar. Then a helpless look grew in the song-stress's faded eyes.

"Halcyone, dear—I think you might tune the instrument for me," she said. "I almost think the top string is not quite true, and you do it so quickly."

And grateful for the chance, the child soon had it perfectly accorded, and the concert continued.

Meanwhile Mr. Carlyon had got back to the orchard house, and had rung for some of his black tea. He was musing deeply upon events. And at last he sat at his writing-table and wrote a letter to his friend and former pupil, John Derringham, in which he described his arrival at his new home, and his outlook, and made a casual reference to the two maiden ladies in these terms:

"The park and house is still owned by two antediluvian spinsters of the name of La Sarthe—exquisite specimens of Early Victorian gentility. They are very poor and proud and narrow-minded, and they have a great-niece living with them, the most remarkable little female intelligence I have ever come across. My old habit of instruction is not to be allowed to rest, for I am going to teach the creature Greek, as a diversion. She seems to be about twelve years old, and has the makings of a wonderful character. In the summer you had better come down and pay me a visit, if you are not too busy with your potent mistress, your political ambitions."

But John Derringham did not respond to this casual invitation for many a long day. He had other potent interests beside his political ambitions—and in any case, never did anything unless he felt inclined.

Mr. Carlyon did not expect him—he knew him very well.

Thus the days passed and by the end of June, even, Halcyone had learned more than the Greek alphabet; and had listened to many charming stories of that wonderful people. And the night was her friend, and numerous hours were passed in the shadow of his dark wings, as she flitted like some pale ghost about the park and the deserted, dilapidated garden.

CHAPTER V

THE July of that year was very warm with peculiarly still days, and Halcyone and her master, Cheiron, spent most of their time during their hours of study, under the apple tree. They had got to a stage of complete understanding, and seemed to have fitted into each other's lives as though they had always been together.

Mr. Carlyon watched his little pupil from under the shadow of his penthouse brows with the deep speculative interest she had aroused in him from the first. He had theories upon several subjects, which she seemed to be going to show the result of in practice—and in his kindly cynic's heart she was now enshrined in a special niche.

For Halcyone he was "Cheiron," her master, who had the enchanting quality of being able to see the other side of her head. Every idea of her soul seemed to be developing under this touch of sympathy and understanding. Her heterogeneous knowledge culled from the teachings of her many changing governesses, seemed to regulate itself into distinct branches with an upward shoot for each, and Mr. Carlyon watched and encouraged them all.

It was on one glorious Saturday morning when the fairies and nymphs and gods and goddesses were presumably asleep in the sunlight, that she drew up her knees as she sat on the grass by her Professor's chair, and pushing away the Greek grammar, said, with grave eyes fixed upon his face:

"Cheiron, to-day something tells me I can show you Aphrodite. When it is cooler, about five o'clock, will you come with me to the second terrace? There I will leave you and go and fetch her, and as William and Priscilla will be at tea, I can open the secret door, and you shall see where she lives—all in the dark!"

Mr. Carlyon felt duly honored—for they had never referred to this subject since she had first mentioned it. The Professor felt it was one of deep religious solemnity to his little friend, and had waited until she herself should feel he was worthy of her complete confidence.

"She speaks to me more than ever," Halcyone continued. "I took her out in the moonlight on Thursday night, and she seemed to look more lovely than before. It has pleased

28

her that I call her Aphrodite—it was certainly her name."

"It is settled, then," said Cheiron, "at five o'clock I will be upon the terrace."

Halcyone returned to her grammar, and silence obtained between them. Then presently Mr. Carlyon spoke.

"I am going to have a visitor for a week or perhaps more," he announced.

A startled pair of eyes looked up at him.

"That seems odd," Halcyone said. "I hope whoever it is will not be much in our way. I do not think I am glad —are you?"

"Yes, I am glad. It is someone for whom I have a great regard," and Mr. Carlyon knocked the ashes from his long pipe. "It is a young man who used to be at Oxford and to whom also I taught Greek."

"Then he will know a great deal more than I do, being older," returned Halcyone, not at all mollified by this information.

"Yes, he knows rather more than you do as yet," the Professor allowed. "Perhaps you will not like him; he can be quite disagreeable when he wishes—and he may not like you."

Halcyone's dark brows met.

"If he is someone for whom you have a regard he must be of those who count. I shall be angry then, if he dislikes me—is he coming soon?"

"On Monday, by the four o'clock train."

"Our lesson will be over—that is something. You will not want me on Tuesday, I expect?" and a note of regret grew in her voice.

"I thought you might have a holiday for a while, all pupils have holidays in the summer," the Professor returned.

"Very well," was all she said, and then was quiet for a time, thinking the matter over. She wished to hear more of this visitor who was going to interrupt their pleasant intercourse.

"Of what sort is he?" she asked presently. "A hunter like Meleager—or cunning like Theseus—or noble like Perseus, whom I love best of all?"

"He is not very Greek to look at, I am afraid, except perhaps in his length of limb," and the Professor smiled. "He is just a thin, lanky, rather distinguished young Englishman and was considered to be the most brilliant of my pupils, taking a Double First under my auspices and leaving Oxford with flying colors when I retired myself a year or two ago. He has been very lucky since, he is full of ambitions in the political line, and he has a fearless and rather caustic wit."

"I must think of him as Pericles, then, if he is occupied with the state," said Halcyone. "But how has he been lucky since? I would like to know—tell me, please, and I will try not to mind his being here."

"Yes—try—" said Mr. Carlyon. "After he took his degree he studied law and history, you know, as well as the Greek philosophy which you may come to some day—he went to London to the Temple to read for the bar. He never intended to be a practising barrister, but everything is a means to his career. Then his luck came—he has lots of friends and relations in the great world and at one of their country houses he met the Prime Minister, who took a tremendous fancy to him, and the thing going well, the great man finally asked him to be his assistant private secretary, which post he accepted. The chief private secretary last year being made governor of a colony, John has now stepped into his shoes, and presently he will go into Parliament. He is a brilliant fellow and cares for no man—following only his own star. I shall be very glad to see him again."

Halcyone's face fell into a brown study and the Professor watching her mused to himself:

"John Derringham will find her in the way. She is not woman enough yet to attract his eye; he will only perceive she is a rather plain child—and she will certainly see the other side of his head."

As Halcyone walked back to La Sarthe Chase for her early dinner, she mused also:

"I must not feel this dislike towards Cherion's other pupil. After all, Jason could not have the master alone—and if I do feel it then he will be able to harm me, should he dislike me, too—but if I try to like him, then he will be powerless, and when he has gone he will not have left any mark."

Mr. Carlyon felt a perceptible glow of interest as he waited at five o'clock that day upon the dilapidated stone bench in the archway where old William kept his garden tools, and while the subdued light gave him very little chance of studying minutely the walls, the general aspect certainly presented no hint of any door. However, he had not to wait or speculate long, for, with hardly a creak, two stones seemed to turn upon a pivot, and Halcyone came forth from the aperture bending her head.

"After all, I do not think you had better come in with me," she said. "It is low like this for ten yards; it will make your back ache—so I have brought her. If you will hold her, I will run out and see if all is safe; and then we can carry her to the summer house and take off her scarf."

Cherion held out his arms to receive the precious bundle; and he could feel by its weight it was a marble head. It was enveloped in the voluminous folds of the remains of an old blue silk curtain, a relic of other days, when rich stuffs hung before the windows of La Sarthe Chase.

"I took the covering from the Spanish Chest in the long gallery," Halcyone announced. "I had played with it for years, and the color suits her—it must be the same as are her real eyes."

Then she darted out into the sunlight and returned again in a few moments—with shining face. All was safe and the momentous hour had come.

She took her goddess from Mr. Carlyon's arms, and walking with the dignity of a priestess of the Temple, she preceded her master along the tangled path.

A riot of things growing impeded each step. Roses which had degenerated into little better than wild ones, showed late red and pink blooms, honeysuckle and columbines flowered, and foxgloves raised their graceful heads.

At the end there was a broken bower at the corner of the terrace, with a superb view over the park and far beyond to the high blue hills.

This place was cleared, for Halcyone had done the necessary work herself. It was one of her outlooks upon the world and she had even carefully mended the cracked bench with a bit of board and a nail or two. The table, which was of stone, still stood firmly and was quaint and rather Greek in shape—for had not a later Timothy La Sarthe brought it from Paris in the Empire days?

Mr. Carlyon sat down and prepared himself for the solemn moment when the Goddess should be unveiled.

And when the reverent little priestess had removed the folds from the face as it lay upon the table, he started and held his breath, for he instantly realized that indeed this was the work of some glorious old Greek sculptor; none other could have created that perfect head.

And as he looked, the child slipped her hand into his and whispered softly:

"Watch her eyes; she is tender to-day and welcomes us. I was not quite sure how she would receive you."

And lo! it seemed to Mr. Carlyon as though the divine orbs soften into a smile, such was the art of those old Greeks, who marred not the marble with pupil or iris, who stooped to no trick of simulation, but left the perfect modeling to speak for itself.

The eyes of this Aphrodite conveyed volumes of love, with her nobly planned brows and temples and her softly smooth cheeks. The slight break of the nose even did not seem to spoil the perfect beauty of the whole. Her mouth, tender and rather full, seemed to smile a welcome, and the patine, unspoiled by any casts having ever been taken, gleamed as the finest of skin. It was in a wonderful state of preservation and had not darkened to more than a soft cream color.

So there she lay at last! Goddess of Love still for all time. The head was broken off at the base of the slender, rounded throat.

Halcyone perceived that Cherion was appreciating her treasure in a proper spirit and spoke not a word while he examined it minutely, turning it in all lights.

"What consummate genius!" he almost whispered at last. "You have truly a goddess here, child, and you do well to guard her as such. Aphrodite—you have named her well."

"I am glad now that I have shown her to you—at first I was a little afraid—but you understand. And now you can feel how I have my mother always with me. She tells me to hope, and that all mean things are of no importance, and that God intends us all to be as happy as is her beautiful smile."

Then Mr. Carlyon asked again for the story of the Goddess's discovery, and heard all the details of how there was a ray of light in the dark passage, coming from some cleverly contrived crack on the first terrace. Here Halcyone's foot had struck against the marble upon her original voyage of discovery, and by the other objects she encountered she supposed someone long ago, being in flight, had gradually dropped things which were heavy and of least value. There was a breastplate as well, and an iron-bound box which she had never been able to move or open.

"You might help me and we could look into it some day," she said.

Mr. Carlyon took Aphrodite into his hands and raised her head, examining every point with minute care, and now her expression appeared to change and grow sad in the different effect of light.

"I do not want her to be up upon a pillar like Artemis and Hebe, who are still in the hall," Halcyone said. "She could not talk to me then, she would be always the same. I like to hold her this way and that, and then I can see her moods and the blue silk keeps her nice and warm."

"It is a great possession," said Cheiron, "and I understand your joy in it," and he handed the head back to the child with respect.

Halcyone bent and caressed it with her soft little velvet cheek.

"See," she said. "Once I was very foolish and cried about something and the tears made this little mark," and she pointed to two small spots which did not gleam quite so much as the rest of the surface. "Tears always do silly things—I am never so foolish now." And then her young voice became dreamy and her eyes widened with a look as though she saw far beyond.

"Cheiron—all the world is made for gladness if we only do not take the ugly things with us everywhere. There is summer, as it is now, when we rest and play and all the gods come down from Olympus and dance and sing and bask in the light—and then the autumn when the colors are rich and everything prepares for winter and sleeps. But even in the cold and dark we must not be sad, because we know it is only for a time and to give us change, so that we may shout for joy when the spring comes and each year discover in it some new beauty."

Cheiron did not speak for a while, he, too, was musing.

"You are a little Epicurean," he said at last, "and presently we shall read about Epicurus's great principles and his garden where he taught and lived."

CHAPTER VI

JOHN DERRINGHAM had been at the orchard house for three or four days before there was any sign of Halcyone. She had kept away on purpose and was doing her best to repress the sense of resentment the thought of the presence of a stranger caused. Mr. Carlyon had given her some simple books upon the Renaissance which she was devouring with joy. This period seemed to give some echo of the Greek ideas she loved, and as was her habit she was visualizing everything as she read, bringing the people and the places up before her mental eyes, and regulating them into friends or acquaintances. Cheiron did not confine himself to teaching her Greek alone, but directed all her reading, taking a growing delight in her intelligent mind. Thus they had many talks upon history and the natural sciences and poetry and painting. But to hear of the famous statues and learn from pictures to know the styles of the old sculptors seemed to please her best of all.

By the fifth day, a Friday, Mr. Carlyon began to feel a desire to see his little pupil again and sent her a message by his dark, silent servant. Would she not take tea with him that afternoon? So Halcyone came. She was very quiet and subdued and crept through her gap in the hedge without any leaps or bounds.

John Derringham was stretched the whole length of his long, lean limbs under the apple tree—her apple tree! This did not produce a favorable note.

Cheiron watched the meeting with inward amusement.

"This is my little friend Halcyone La Sarthe," he said. "Halcyone, yonder Tityus in these latter days is known by the name of John Derringham—of Derringham in the County of Northampton. Make your bows to one another."

Halcyone inclined her head with dignity, but Mr. Derringham only raised himself a little and said "Good afternoon." He did not care for children, and was busy with his old master discussing other things.

"You will pour out the tea, Halcyone, for us as usual," Cheiron said. "Demetrius will bring it in a minute." And Halcyone sat down demurely upon the basket chair near the table and crossed her hands.

"I tell you I will not take their point of view," John Derringham said, continuing the conversation he had been carrying on before Halcyone arrived. "Everything in England is spoilt by this pandering to the mediocrity. A man may not make a speech but he must choose his words so that uneducated clods can grasp his meaning, he cannot advocate an idea with success unless it can appeal to the lower middle classes. It is this subservience to them which has brought us to where we are. No ideals—no lofty ends—just a means to each one's own hand. I will never pretend we are all equal, I will never appeal to anything but the highest in an audience. So they can throw me out if they will!" And he stretched out his long legs and clasped his hands under his head—so that to Halcyone he seemed seven foot tall.

"Tityus" she thought was a very apt name for him, and she wondered if he would jump if the vulture suddenly gave a gnaw at his liver!

"You are an idealist, John," said Mr. Carlyon. "All this might have been some of use as a principle of propaganda before the franchise was so low, but now the mediocrity is our master—so of what use? If you talked so you would but preach to empty benches."

"I will not do that—I will make them listen. My point is that everyone can rise if he wishes, but until he has done so in fact, there is no use in his pretending in words that he has. I would explain to them the reason of things. I could have agreed with the greatest Athenian democrats because their principle was one of sense. They had slaves to do the lowest offices who had no voice in public affairs, but here we let those who have no more education or comprehension than slaves have the same power as men who have spent their lives in studying the matter. It is all unjust, and no one has the courage to tell them to their faces they are unfitted for the task."

"It will be a grand stalking horse for your first essay in your constituency," Cheiron said with his kindly twinkle of sarcasm. He loved to encourage John Derringham to talk.

But at that moment Demetrius brought the tea and Halcyone gravely began her task.

"Do you take it black like Mr. Carlyon?" she asked of the reclining guest.

He came back to the remembrance of her presence and glancing at her, murmured:

"Oh—ah, no—that is, yes—strong, only with cream and sugar. Thanks awfully."

But Halcyone did not rise to hand it to him, so he was obliged to get up and take it from where she sat. She perceived then that though extremely thin he was lithe and well-shaped. And in spite of her unconquered prejudice, she was obliged to own she liked his steely gray hawk-like eyes and his fine, rather ascetic, clean-shaven face. He did not look at her specially. He may have taken in a small, pale visage and masses of mouse-colored hair and slender legs—but nothing struck him particularly except her feet. As his eyes dropped to the ground he caught sight of them; they were singularly perfect feet. He admired points in man or beast—and when he had returned to his old place stretched out under the apple tree, he still glanced at them now and then; they satisfied his eye.

"What have you been doing in these days, Halcyone?" Mr. Carlyon asked. "I have not seen you since Monday morning. Have you been getting into any mischief?"

Halcyone reluctantly admitted that she had not. There was, she explained, very little chance of any of an agreeable find coming her way at La Sarthe Chase. She had been gardening with William—they had quite tidied the top terrace—and she had been reading French with Aunt Roberta, but the book was great nonsense.

Then she added that she had brought an invitation from the Aunts La Sarthe that Mr. Carlyon's guest should accompany him when he dined with them on the Saturday. It had become the custom for him to partake of this repast on the same occasions that Mr. Miller did—once a month.

John Derringham frowned under his straw hat which he had pulled over his eyes. He had not come into the country to be dragged out to bucolic dinner parties. But upon some points he knew his old master was obdurate and from his firm acceptance of the invitation this appeared to be one of them.

Then Halcyone asked politely if he would have a second cup of tea, but he refused and again addressed Cheiron, ignoring her. Their conversation now ran into philosophical questions, some of them out of her depth, but much of the subject interested her deeply and she listened absorbed.

At last there was a pause and her fresh young voice asked:

"What, then, is the aim of philosophy—is it only words, or does it bring any good?"

And both men looked at her, staggered for a moment, and John Derringham burst into a ringing laugh.

"Upon my word, I don't know," he said. "It was invented so that the Master here and I should pull each other's theories to pieces; that evidently was its aim from the beginning of time. I do not know if it has any other good."

"Everything is so very simple," said Halcyone. "To have to argue about it must be fatiguing."

"You find things simple, do you?" asked John Derringham, now complacently roused to look at her. "What are your rules of life, then, let us hear, oh, Oracle!—we listen with respect!"

Halcyone reddened a little and a gleam grew in her wise eyes. She would have refused to reply, but looking at her revered master, she saw that he was awaiting her answer with an encouraging smile. So she thought a second and then said calmly, measuring her words: "Things are what we make them, they have no power in themselves; they are as inanimate as this wood—" and she touched the table with her fine brown hand. "It is we ourselves who give them activity. So it is our own fault if they are bad—they could just as easily be good. Is not that simple enough?"

"An example, please, Goddess," demanded John Derringham with a cynical smile.

"The dark is an example," she went on quietly. "People fill the dark with their own frightening images and fear it because they themselves have turned it into evil. The dark is as kind as the day."

John Derringham laughed. He was amused as this precocious wisdom and he suddenly remembered that his old master had mentioned some clever child when writing to him first about the place, two months before. This was the creature, then, who was learning Greek. She had picked up these ideas, of course, out of some book and was showing off. Children should be snubbed and kept in their places:

"Then you don't cry when your nurse leaves you at night without a candle. What a good little girl! But perhaps you take a doll to bed," he added mockingly, "or suck your thumb."

Halcyone did not answer, her eyes, benign as a goddess's, looked him through and through—and Cheiron leaned back in his chair and puffed volumes of smoke while he chuckled delightedly:

"Take care, John—you will come off second best, for Halcyone can see the other side of your head."

For some unaccountable reason, John Derringham felt
annoyed; but it was too contemptible to be annoyed by a
child, so he laughed as he answered condescendingly:

"There, I will not tease her. I expect she hates me
already—" and he pushed his hat back from his eyes.

"No," said Halcyone. "One only hates a thing one fears;
hate implies fear. I hated my last but one governess for a
while—because she told lies and was mean and she had the
power to keep me in. But once I reasoned about it, I grew
quite indifferent and she had no effect upon me at all."

"You have not had time to reason about me," returned
John Derringham, "but it is something that you don't hate
me; I ought to feel pleased."

"I do not know that there is occasion for that," Halcyone
remarked, "it is all a level thing which does not matter.
You are Mr. Carlyon's guest and I expect will be staying
some time—"

"So you will have to put up with me!" and John Derringham laughed, furious now with himself for his increasing
irritation.

"I must be going," Halcyone then announced and got up
from her chair—"and I will tell my aunts that they may
expect you to-morrow night," she continued, addressing Mr.
Carlyon.

He rose and prepared to accompany her down the garden.
She bowed to John Derringham with quiet dignity as he still
lay on the ground and walked on by the side of her Professor without further words.

"You don't like my old pupil, Halcyone?" Mr. Carlyon
said when they got to the gap in the hedge. "Tell me, what
do you see at the other side of his head?"

"Himself," was all she answered and she bounded lightly
away laughing, and was soon lost to view in the copse
beyond.

And Cheiron, considerably amused, returned to his pros-
trate guest to find him with a frown upon his face.

"I hope to goodness, Master, you won't bore me with
that brat while I am here," he exclaimed, "chattering aphor-
isms like a parrot. I can't stand children out of their place."

CHAPTER VII

"Since there will be three gentlemen, Ginevra," Miss Roberta said on Saturday morning when they sat together in the Italian parlor after breakfast, "do you not think we had better have Halcyone down to dinner to-night? I know," she added timidly, "it is not in the proper order of things, but we could make an exception."

Miss La Sarthe frowned. Roberta so often was ready to upset regulations. She was difficult to deal with. But this suggestion of hers had some point. They would be two ladies to three of the other sex—and one of their guests appeared to be quite a young man—perhaps it might be more prudent to relax a rule, than to find themselves in an embarrassing position.

"I strongly deplore the fact of children ever being brought from their seclusion except for dessert, but as you say, Roberta, three gentlemen—and one a perfect stranger—might be too much for us. I hardly think our Mamma would have approved of our giving such an unchaperoned party, so for this once Halcyone had better come down. She can have Mr. Miller for her partner, you will be conducted by the Professor—and the new guest will take me in."

Miss Roberta bridled—the Professor was now a hero in her eyes.

"And Sister," she said, "I think we might bring six of the chairs from Sir Timothy's bed- and dressing-room just for to-night, instead of those Windsor ones. It would give the dining-room a better look, do you not think so?"

And to this also Miss La Sarthe agreed. So Miss Roberta joyfully found Halcyone out upon the second terrace and imparted to her the good news. They would arrange flowers in the épergne, she suggested—a few sweet williams and mignonette and a foxglove or two. A pretty posy fixed in sand, such as she remembered there always was in their gala days. Halcyone was enchanted at the prospect.

"Oh, dear Aunt Roberta, do let me do it all," she said. "You sit here on the bench and I will run and fetch the épergne—and we can pick what we think best. Or—don't you think just a big china bowl full of sweet peas would be prettier? The sand might show and, and—the épergne is rather stiff."

But Miss Roberta looked aggrieved. The épergne with its gold and silver fern leaves climbing up a thin stalk of glass to its top dish for fruit had always come out for dinner parties and she liked no innovations. It was indeed as much as Halcyone could do to get all the flowers of the same kind, a nasturtium and a magenta stock had with care to be smuggled away, leaving the sweet peas sole occupants of the sand. But the effect was very festive and the two carried their work into the dining-room well pleased.

The best Sèvres dinner-set was had out, which that traveler Timothy had brought from Paris among other things, and the best cut glass and rat-tailed silver. Old William, assisted by Hester and Priscilla, had been busy polishing most of the day—while the cook and the "young person from the village" were contriving wonders in the vast kitchen. And punctually at seven in broad daylight, the three Misses La Sarthe, the two elder in their finest mauve silk evening dresses, awaited their guests in the Italian parlor.

Miss Roberta's heart had not fluttered like this since a county ball some forty years ago when a certain whiskered captain of a dashing cavalry regiment stationed at Upminster had whispered in her ear.

Priscilla had let down Halcyone's white muslin frock and as the tucks were rather large, it was longer than she intended, so that the child might easily have been taken for a girl of fifteen, and her perfect feet were encased in a pair of old-fashioned bronze slippers with elastics crossed up the legs of her white silk stockings. A fillet of blue silk kept back the soft cloud of her mouse-colored hair.

Mr. Miller was announced first—very nervous, as usual, and saying the wrong things in his flurry. Then up the terrace steps could be seen advancing Mr. Carlyon and his guest. They had walked over from the cottage—and Halcyone, observing from the window, was conscious that against her will she was admiring John Derringham's arrogant, commanding walk.

"He could very well be as Theseus was after he grew proud," she said to herself.

And soon they were announced.

Mr. Carlyon was now on the most friendly terms with both old ladies, and as well as coming to the monthly dinner, sometimes dropped in to tea on Sunday afternoons, but he knew this was a real party and must be treated as such.

How agreeable it felt to be once more in the world, Miss Roberta thought, and her faded pale cheeks flushed a delicate pink.

John Derringham had been sulky as a bear at the idea of coming, but something in the quaintly pathetic refinement of the poor and splendid old house pleased him, and the aroma of untouched early-Victorian prudish grace which the ancient ladies threw around them appealed to his imagination, as any complete bit of art or nature always did. He found himself seated between Miss La Sarthe and Halcyone and quite enjoyed himself. Everything was of the time from the épergne to the way the bread was cut.

Halcyone conversed with Mr. Miller, who always felt he must make nursery jokes with her and ask her the names of her dolls.

"He can't help it," she told Cheiron one day. "If he had any more intelligence God would have put him to work in some busier place.

John Derringham did not address her; he devoted himself to Miss La Sarthe.

He had absolutely no diffidence. He had been spoilt from his cradle, and by the time he had left Eton—Captain of the Oppidans—had ruled all those near him with a rod of iron, imposing his interesting enthusiastic personality upon all companies with unqualified success. Miss La Sarthe fell at once. He said exactly the right things to her and flattered her by his unfeigned interest in all she spoke of. He was studying her as he studied any rare memento of historical value.

"My great-niece reads every morning with Mr. Carlyon," she said presently. "Girls are expected to be so very clever nowadays, we are told. She already knows a little Greek. It would have been considered quite unnecessary in our day."

"And I am sure it is in this," said John Derringham. "Learned women are an awful bore. As a sex they were meant to be feminine, dainty, exquisite creatures as those I see to-night," and he bowed gallantly while Miss La Sarthe thrilled. She thoroughly approved of his appearance.

"So very much of a gentleman, Roberta," she afterwards said. "None of that thick, ill-cut look we are obliged to observe in so many of the younger people we see when we go into Upminster each year."

"And why should he look thick or ill-cut, Sister?" Miss Roberta replied. "Mr. Carlyon told me the Derringhams have been seated at Derringham since fabulous times."

Thus this last of that race was appreciated fully in at least two antiquated female hearts.

But meanwhile the cloth was being removed, and the port wine and old Madeira placed before the elder hostess.

"Our father's cellar was famous for its port," she said, "and we have a few bottles of the '47 left."

But now she felt it was only manners to turn to Mr. Carlyon upon her other hand, so John Derringham was left in silence, no obligation to talk to Halcyone making itself felt. She turned and looked at him, he interested her very much. Mr. Carlyon had quantities of books of photographs of all the famous statues in Europe and especially in Italy and Greece, but she could find any likeness to him in any of her recollection of them. Alas! his face was not at all Greek. His nose was high and aquiline, his forehead high and broad, and there was something noble and dominating in his fearless regard. His hair even did not grow very prettily, though it was thick and dark—and there was not an ounce of superfluous flesh upon his whole person. He never for a moment suggested repose, he gave the impression of vivid, nervous force and action, a young knight going out to fight any impossible dragon with his good sword and shield—unabashed by the smoke from its flaming nostrils, undaunted by any fear of death.

Halcyone watched him, and her prejudice slept.

The silence had lasted quite five minutes when he allowed his natural good manners, which he was quite aware he had kept in abeyance in regard to her, to come uppermost.

"The Professor has been telling me how wonderfully you work with him," he said; "we under him at Oxford were not half so diligent it seems. I wonder what good it will be to you at all."

"If a thing gives pleasure, it is good," she answered gravely. "I wanted to learn Greek because I had a book when I was little which told me about those splendid heroes, and I thought I could read more about them when I am grown up if I knew it—than if I did not."

"There is something in that. What was the book?" he asked.

Her steady eyes looked straight into his as she replied: "It was Kingsley's 'Heroes' and if only I were a boy I would be like Perseus and go and kill the Gorgon and rescue Adromeda from the sea monster. Pallas Athené said some fine things to him—do you remember?—when she asked him the question of which sort of man he would be?"

"No, I don't remember," said John Derringham. "You must tell me now."

Then Halcyone began in a soft dream voice while her eyes widened and darkened with that strange look as though she saw into another and vaster world. "'I am Pallas Athené and I know the thoughts of all men's hearts, and discern their manhood or their baseness. And from the souls of clay I turn away; and they are blest, but not by me. They fatten at ease like sheep in the pasture and eat what they did not sow, like oxen in the stall. They grow and spread like the gourd along the ground, but like the gourd they give no shade to the traveler and when they are ripe death gathers them, and they go down unloved into hell, and their name vanishes out of the land.'"

She paused a second and John Derringham was astonished at himself because he was conscious of experiencing a thrill of deep interest.

"Yes?" he said—and her voice went on:

"'But to the souls of fire I give more fire and to those who are manful I give a might more than man's. These are the heroes, the sons of the Immortals who are blest but not like the souls of clay, for I drive them forth by strange paths, Perseus, that they may fight the Titans and monsters, the enemies of gods and men. Through doubt and need and danger and battle I drive them, and some of them are slain in the flower of youth, no man knows when or where, and some of them win noble names and a fair and green old age—but what will be their latter end, I know not, and none, save Zeus, the father of gods and men—Tell me, now, Perseus, which of these two sorts of men seem to you more blest?'"

It was as if she asked him a personal question and unconsciously he answered:

"I should reply as Perseus did. Tell me his words."

"'Better to die in the flower of youth on the chance of winning a noble name than to live at ease like the sheep and die unloved and unrenowned.'"

He bent nearer to her and answered softly: "They are indeed fine words," and there was no mockery whatever in his eyes as he looked at her—and took in every detail of her pure childish face. "You wonderful, strange little girl— soon I too am going like Perseus to fight the Gorgons, and I shall remember this night and what you have said."

But at that moment Mr. Miller's high, cackling laugh was heard in an explosion of mirth. Mr. Carlyon had made some delightfully obvious joke for his delectation and amidst a smiling company Miss La Sarthe rose with dignity to leave the gentlemen alone with their wine.

CHAPTER VIII

NEXT morning, John Derringham sat at a late breakfast with his whilom master of Greek and discussed things in general over his bacon and tea.

It was three years since he had left Oxford, and life held out many interesting aspects to him. He was standing for the southern division of his county in the following spring when the present member was going to retire, and he was vehement in his views and clear as to the course he meant to take. He was so eloquent in his discourse and so full of that divine spark of enthusiasm, that he was always listened to, no matter how unpalatably Tory the basic principles of his utterances were. He never posed as anything but an aristocrat, and when he whimsically admitted that in the present day to be one was an enormous disadvantage for a man who wished to get on, he endeavored to palliate the misfortune by lucid explanation of what the duties of such a status were, and of the logical advantages which an appreciation of the truths of cause and effect might bring to mankind. Down in his own country he was considered the coming man. He thundered at the people and had facts and figures at his finger tips. His sublime belief in himself never wavered and like any inspired view, right or wrong, it had its strong effect.

Mr. Carlyon thought highly of him, for a number of reasons.

"If women do not make a stumbling-block for you, John, you will go far," he said as he buttered his toast.

"Women!" quoth John Derringham, and he laughed incredulously. "They matter no more to me than the flowers in the garden—enchanting in the summer time, a mere pleasure for sight and touch, but to make or mar a man's life!—not even to be considered as factors in the scheme of things."

"I am glad to hear you say so," said Mr. Carlyon dryly. "And I hope that jade, Fate, won't play you any tricks."

John Derringham smiled.

"I admit that a woman with money may be useful to me by and by," he said, "because, as you know, I am always hard up, and presently when I want to occupy a larger sphere I shall require money for my ends, but for the time being they serve to divert me as a relaxation; that is all."

"You are contracting no ties, dear lad?" asked the Professor with one eyebrow raised, while he shook back his silvery hair. "I had heard vaguely about your attention to Lady Durrend, but I understand she has had many preliminary canters and knows the ropes."

John Derringham smiled. "Vivienne Durrend is a most charming woman," he said. "She has taught me a number of things in the last two years. I am grateful to her. Next season she is bringing a daughter out—and she has a wonderful sense of the fitness of things." Then he sipped his tea and got up and strolled towards the windows.

"Besides," he continued, "I do not admit there are any ties to be contracted. The Greeks understood the place of women; all this nonsense of vows of fidelity and exaltation of sentiment in the home cramps a man's ambitions. It is perfectly natural that he should take a wife if his position calls for it, because the society in which we move has made a figurehead of that kind necessary. But that a woman should expect a man to be faithful to her, be she wife or mistress, is contrary to all nature."

"We have put nature out of the running now for a couple of thousand years," Mr. Carlyon announced sententiously; "We have set up a standard of impossibilities and worship hypocrisy and can no longer see any truth. You have got to reckon with things as they are, not with what nature meant them to be."

"Then you think women are a force now which one must consider?"

"I think they are as deadly as the deep sea—" and Mr. Carlyon's voice was tense. "When they have only bodies they are dangerous enough, but when—as many of the modern ones have—they combine a modicum of mind as well, with all the cunning Satan originally endowed them with— then happy is the man who escapes, even partially whole, from their claws."

"Whew—" whistled John Derringham, "and what if they have souls? Not that I personally admit that such a case exists—what then?"

"When you meet a woman with a soul you will have met your match, John," the Professor said, and opening his *Times*, which Demetrius had brought in with the second post, he closed the conversation.

John Derringham strolled into the garden. The place had been greatly improved since Halcyone's first discovery of its new occupant. The shutters were all a spruce green and the paths weeded and tidy, while the borders were full of bedded-out plants and flowers. A famous gardener from Upminster renowned through all the West had come over and given his personal attention to the matter, and the next year wonderful herbacious borders would spring up on all sides. Mr. Johnson's visits and his council, though at first resented, had at length grown a source of pure delight to Halcyone; she reveled in the blooms of the delicate begonias and salvias and other blossoms which she had never seen before. Mr. Carlyon, although desiring solitude, appreciated a beautiful and cultivated one, and the orchard house was now becoming a very comfortable bachelor's home.

The day was much cooler than it had been of late. There was a fresh breeze though the sun shone. John Derringham wandered down to the apple tree and thence to the gap, and through it and on into the park. His walk was for pleasure, and aimless as to destination, and presently he sat down under a low-spreading oak and looked at the house—La Sarthe Chase. A beautiful view of it could be obtained from there, and it interested him—and from that his thoughts came to Halcyone and her strange, quaint little personality, and he stretched himself out and putting his hands under his head he looked up into the dense foliage of the tree above him—and there his eyes met two grave, quiet ones peering down from a mass of green, and he saw slender brown legs drawn up on a broad branch, and a scrap of blue cotton frock.

"Good morning," Halcyone said quite composedly, "don't make a noise, please, or rustle—the mother doe is just coming out of the copse with her new fawn."

"How on earth did you get up there?" he asked, surprised.

"I swung myself from the lower branch on the other side; it is quite easy—would you like to come up, too? There is plenty of room—and then we could sure the doe would not see you and she might peep out again. I do not wish to frighten her."

John Derringham rose leisurely and went to the further side of the oak, where sure enough there was a drooping branch and he was soon up beside her, dangling his long limbs as he sat in a fork.

"What an enchanting bower you have found," he said. "Away from all the world."

"No, indeed, that cannot be at this time of the year," she answered. "See, there is a squirrel far up in the top and there are birds, and look—down there at the roots there is a rabbit hole with such a family in it. It is only in the winter you can be alone—and not even then, for you know there are the moles even if you cannot see them."

"Creatures are interesting to watch, aren't they?" he said. "I have an old place which I loved when I was a boy. It is let now because I am too poor to live in it, but I used to like to prowl about in the early mornings long ago."

"We are all very poor," said Halcyone simply, "but I am sorry for you that you have to let strangers be in your house —that must be dreadful."

John Derringham smiled, and his face lost the *insouciante* arrogance which irritated his enemies so. His smile, rare enough, was singularly sweet.

"I don't think about it," he said. "It is best not to when anything is disagreeable."

"Cheiron and I often tell one another things like that."

"Cheiron—who is Cheiron?" he asked.

This seemed a superfluous question to Halcyone.

"The Professor, of course. He is just like the picture in my 'Heroes,'" she answered, "and I often pretend we are in the cave on Pelion. I thought you would perhaps be like one of the others since you were his pupil, too, but I cannot find which. You are not Heracles—because you have none of those great muscles—or Æneas or Peleus. Are—are you Jason himself, perhaps—" and her voice sounded glad with discovery. "We do not know, he may not have had a Greek face."

John Derringham laughed. "Jason who led the Argonauts to find the Golden Fleece—it is a good omen. Would you help me to find the Golden Fleece if you could?"

"Yes, I would, if you were good and true—but the end of the story was sad because Jason was not."

"How must I be good and true then? I thought Jason was a straight enough sort of a fellow and that it was Medea who brought all the trouble—Medea, the woman."

Halcyone's grave eyes never left his face. She saw the whimsical twinkle in his but heeded it not.

"He should not have had anything to do with Medea— that is where he was wrong," she said, "but having given her his word, he should have kept it."

"Even though she was a witch?" Mr. Derringham asked.

"It was still his word—don't you see! Her being a witch did not alter his word. He did not give it because she was or was not a witch—but because he himself wanted to at the time, I suppose; therefore, it was binding."

"A man should always keep his word, even to a woman, then?" and John Derringham smiled finely.

"Why not to a woman as well as a man?" Halcyone asked surprised. "You do not see the point at all it seems. It is not to whom it is you give your word—it is to you it matters that you keep it, because to break it degrades yourself."

"You reason well, fair nymph," he said gallantly; he was frankly amused. "What may your age be? A thousand years more or less will not make any difference!"

"You may laugh at me if you like," said Halcyone, and she smiled; his gayety was infectious, "but I am not so very young. I shall be thirteen in October, the seventh of October."

John Derringham appeared to be duly impressed with this antiquity, and went on gravely:

"So you and the Master discuss these knotty points of honor and expediency together, do you, as a recreation from the Greek syntax? I should like to hear you."

"The Professor does not believe in men much," Halcyone said. "He says they are all honorable to one another until they are tempted—and that they are never honorable to a woman when another woman comes upon the scene. But I do not know at all about such things, or what it means. For me there is nothing towards other people; it only is towards yourself. You must be honorable to yourself."

And suddenly it seemed to John Derringham as if all the paltry shams of the world fell together like a pack of cards, and as if he saw truth shining naked for the first time at the bottom of the well of the child's pure eyes.

An extraordinary wave of emotion came over him, finely strung as he was, and susceptible to all grades of feeling. He did not speak for a minute; it was as if he had quaffed some elixir. A flame of noble fire seemed to run in his veins, and his voice was changed and full of homage when at last he addressed her.

"Little Goddess of Truth," he said, "I would like to be with you always that you might never let me forget this point of view. And you believe it would have won for Jason in the end—if he had been true to himself? Tell me—I want greatly to know."

"But how could there be any doubt of that?" she asked surprised. "Good only can bring good, and evil, evil."

At this moment, out from the copse the soft head of a doe appeared, and at the thrilling sight Halcyone slipped her hand into her companion's, and held his tight lest he should move or rustle a leaf.

"See," she whispered right in his ear. "She will cross to the other side by the stream—and oh! there is the fawn! Is he not the dearest baby angel you have ever seen—!"

And the doe, feeling herself safe, trotted by, followed by a minute son in pale drab velvet hardly a month old.

The pair in the tree watched them breathlessly until they had entered the copse again beyond the bend, and then Halcyone said:

"That makes six—and perhaps there are more. Oh! how I hope the Long Man will not see them!"

John Derringham did not let go her hand at once; there was something soft and pleasant in the touch of the cool little fingers.

"I want to hear about everything," he said. "Tell me of the Long Man—and the fawns, and why there are only six. I am having the happiest morning I have had for years."

So Halcyone began. She glossed a good deal over the facts she had told Mr. Carlyon upon the subject because she did not feel she knew this stranger well enough to let him into her aunts' private affairs—so she turned the interest to the deer themselves, and they chatted on about all sorts of animals and their ways, and John Derringham was entranced and felt quiet aggrieved when she said it was getting late and she must go back to the house for her early dinner. He swung himself down from the tree by the high branch with ease and stood ready to catch her, but with a nimbleness he did not expect, she crept round to the lower side and was landed upon the soft turf before he could reach her.

Then he walked back with her to the broken gate, telling her about his own old home the while, and then they paused to say good-by.

Halcyone carried a twig of freshly sprouting oak which she had brought from the tree, having broken it off in her lightning descent.

"Give me one leaf and you keep the other," he said. "And then, whenever I see it, I will try to remember that I must always be good and true."

With grave earnestness she did as he asked, and then opened the gate.

"I want to tell you," she said—and she looked down for a second, and then up into his eyes from beyond the bars. "I did not like the thought of your coming—and at first I did not like you—but now I see something quite different at the other side of your head—Good-by."

And before he could answer, she was off as the young fawn would have been—a flitting shape among the trees. And John Derringham walked slowly back to the orchard house, musing as he went.

But when he got there a telegram from his Chief had arrived, recalling him instantly to London.

And he did not see Halcyone again for several years.

CHAPTER IX

THE seasons came and went with peaceful regularity, unbroken by a jarring note from the outside world. Mr. Anderton, being well assured by the Misses La Sarthe that his stepdaughter was receiving a splendid education, was only too glad to leave her in peace, and Mrs. Anderton felt her duty achieved when at the beginning of each summer and winter she sent a supply of what she considered suitable clothes. It took Priscilla and Hester hours to alter them to Halcyone's slender shape.

Mr. Carlyon was seldom absent from his house during this period, only twice a year, when he spent a fortnight in London in June, and another week in November with his brother, a squire of some note in the Cornish world. Halcyone made green his old age with the exquisite quality of her opening mind. And deep down in her heart there always dwelt the image of John Derringham, and whatever new hero she read about, he unconsciously assumed some of his features or mien. She passed through enthusiasms for all periods, and for quite six months was under the complete spell of the "Morte d'Arthur" and the adventures of the knights contained therein. She read voraciously and systematically, but her first love for all things Greek regained its hold and undoubtedly colored her whole view of life.

Her education was exotic and might have ruined a brain of lesser fiber. But for her it seemed to bring forth all that was clear and fine and polish it with a diamond luster. Twice a week alternately the French and German master from the Applewood Grammar School came to her, and she also learned to read music from the organist at the church, and then played to herself with no technique but much taste.

And of all her masters, Nature and the fearless study of her night moods molded her soul the most.

For the first few months after John Derringham's visit Mr. Carlyon often spoke of him and read aloud bits of his letters, and Halcyone listened with rapt attention, but she never embarked upon the subject herself—and then the Professor had an accident to his knee which kept him a prisoner for months. And somehow the interest of this seemed to dwarf less present things, and as time went on, John Derringham grew to be mentioned only by fits and starts, when his rapidly rising political career called forth cynical grunts of admiration from his old master. There had been a dissolution of Parliament and a short term of office for the other side, and then at the General Election John Derringham's Chief had come in again stronger than ever, and he himself had been made Under-Secretary of State for Foreign Affairs. It was a tremendous rise for one so young. He was at that time not more than twenty-nine years old—but two years before this happened, when Halcyone was about fifteen, he came again to the orchard house for a short Saturday to Monday visit.

From the moment that she knew he was coming a strange stillness seemed to fall upon the child. She had grown long-legged and was at the fledgling stage when even a pretty girl sometimes looks plain, and she, who had as yet no claim to beauty, was at her worst. She was quite aware of it, with her intense soul-worship of all beautiful things. Some unreasoned impulse made her keep away from her master during the first day, but on the Sunday he summoned her, and, as once before, she came and poured out the tea, but it was a cold and windy autumn afternoon, and it was not laid out of doors. John Derringham had been for a walk, and came in while she sat in a shadowy corner behind the table, teapot in hand.

He was greatly changed, she thought, in the three years. He had grown a beard! and looked considerably older, with his thin commanding figure and arrogant head. He was not handsome now, but peculiarly distinguished-looking. He could very well be Pericles, she decided at once. As for him, he had almost forgotten her. Life had been so full of many things; but, seeing a pale, slender, overgrown girl with mouse-colored clouds of hair now confined in a demure pigtail, it came to his mind that this must be the Professor's pupil again. Had she not been called Hebe or Psyche—or Halcyone—some Greek name? And gradually his former recollection of her came back, and of their morning in the tree.

"Why, how do you do," he said politely, and Halcyone bowed without speaking. She felt much as Hans Andersen's Ugly Duckling used to feel, and when John Derringham had said a few ordinary things about her having grown out of all likeness, he turned to the Professor again, and almost forgot her presence.

His talk was most wonderful to listen to, she thought, his language was so polished, and there was a courtesy added to the former vehemence. They spoke of nothing but politics, which she did not understand, and Cheiron chaffed him a good deal in his kindly cynical way. He was still fighting his chimeras, it seemed, and fighting them successfully. As he spoke, Halcyone, behind the teapot, thrilled with a kind of worship. To be strong and young and manful, and to combat modern dragons, appeared to her to be a god-like task.

In the midst of a heated argument she rose to slip away. Her comings and goings were so natural to the Professor that he was unaware that she was leaving the room until John Derringham broke off in the middle of a sentence, to rise and open the door for her.

"Good-by," she said. "Aunt Roberta is not very well to-day, so I must not be late. Good-night, Cheiron"—and she went out and closed the door.

"But it is quite dark!" exclaimed John Derringham. "Is there a servant waiting? She can't go all alone!"

The Professor leaned back in his chair.

"Don't disturb yourself," he said. "Halcyone is accustomed to the twilight. It is a strange night-creature—leave it alone."

John Derringham sat down again.

"She is not nearly so attractive-looking as she used to be. If I remember, she was rather a weirdly pretty child."

"Just a chrysalis now," grunted the professor between puffs of smoke. "But there is more true philosophy and profound knowledge of truth in that little head than either you or I have got in ours, John."

"You always thought the world of her, Master—you, with your ineradicable contempt for women!"

"She is not a woman—yet. She is an intelligence and a brain—and a soul."

"Oh, she has a soul, then!" and John Derringham smiled. "I remember once you said when I should meet a woman with a soul I should meet my match! I do not feel very alarmed."

One of the professor's penthouse brows raised itself about half an inch, but he did not speak.

"In which school have you taught her?" John Derringham asked—"you who are so much of a cynic, Master.

Does she study the ethics of Aristotle with you here in this Lyceum, or do you reconstruct Plato's Academy? She is no sophist, apparently, since you say she can see the truth."

Mr. Carlyon looked into the fire.

"She is almost an Epicurean, John, in all but the disbelief in the immortality of the soul. She has evolved a theory of her own about that. It partakes of Buddhism. After I have discussed metaphysical propositions with her over which she will argue clearly, she will suddenly cut the whole knot with a lightning flash, and you see the naked truth, and words become meaningless, and discussion a jest."

"All this, at fifteen!" John Derringham laughed antagonistically, and then he suddenly remembered her words to himself upon honor in the tree that summer morning three years ago, and he mused.

Perhaps some heaven-taught beings were allowed to come to earth after all, now and then as the centuries rolled on.

"She knows Greek pretty well?" he asked.

"Fairly, for the time she has learnt. She can read me bits of Lucian. She would stumble over the tragedies. I read them to her." Then he continued, as though it were a subject he loved, "She has a concrete view upon every question; her critical faculty is marvelous. She never lays down the law, but if you ask her, you have your answer in a nutshell, the simplest truth, which it always appears to her so strange that you have not seen all the time."

"What is her parentage? Heredity plays so large a part in these things," Mr. Derringham asked.

"The result of a passionate love-match between distant cousins of that fine old race, I believe. Timothy La Sarthe was at Oxford before your day, but not under me—a brilliant, enchanting fellow, drowned while yachting when my little friend was only a few months old."

"And the mother?"

"Married again to pay his debts, to a worthy stock-broker, almost immediately, I believe. She paid the debt with herself and died after having three children for him in a few years."

"So your protégée lives with those cameos of the Victorian era we dined with, and never sees the outside world?"

"Never—from one year's end to another."

"What a fate!" and John Derringham stretched out his arms. "Ye gods, what a fate!"

And again Cheiron smiled, raising his bushy left brow.

Halcyone, meanwhile, was walking with firm certain steps

across the park, where the dusk had fallen. The turbulent Boreas blew in her face, and she stopped and took off her soft cap and unplaited her hair so that it flew out in a cloud as the wind rushed through it. This sensation was a great pleasure to her, and when she came to a rising ground, a kind of knoll where the view of the country was vast and superb, she paused again and took in great deep breaths. She was drawing all the forces of the air into her being and quivered presently with the joy of it.

She could see as only those who are accustomed to the dark can. She was aware of all the outlines of golden bracken at her feet and the head of a buck peeping from the copse near. The sky was a passionate, tempestuous mass of angry clouds scudding over the deep blue, where an evening star could be seen peeping out.

"Bring me your force and strength, that I may grow noble and beautiful, dear wind," she said aloud. "I want to be near him when he comes again," and then she ran and jumped the uneven places, while she hummed a strange song.

And Jeb Hart and Joseph Gubbs, the poachers, saw her, as she passed within a yard of where they lay setting their snares, and Gubbs, who was a good Catholic from Upminster, crossed himself as he muttered in his friend's ear:

"We'll get no swag to-night, Jeb. When she passes, blest if she don't warn the beasts." ,

CHAPTER X

WHEN Halcyone was nearly nineteen and had grown into a rare and radiant maiden, the like of whom it would be difficult to find, an event happened which was of the greatest excitement and importance to the neighborhood. Wendover, which had been shut up for twenty years, was reported to have been taken for a term by a very rich widow—or *divorcée*—from America it was believed, and it was going to be sumptuously done up and would be filled with guests. Mr. Miller took pains to find out every detail from the Long Man at Applewood, and so was full of information at his monthly repast with the old ladies. Mrs. Vincent Cricklander was the new tenant's name. The Long Man had himself taken her over the place when she first came down to look at it, and his report was that she was the most beautiful lady he had ever seen, and with an eye to business that could not be beaten. He held her in vast respect.

Then Mr. Miller coughed; he had now come to the point of his discourse which made him nervous.

For he had learned beyond the possibility of any doubt that Mrs. Cricklander was, alas! not a lonely widow but had been divorced—only a year or two ago. She had divorced her husband—not he her—he hastened to add, and then coughed again and got very red.

"When we were young," Miss La Sarthe remarked severely, "our Mamma would never have allowed us to know any divorced person—and, indeed, our good Queen Victoria would never have received one at her Court. We cannot possibly call, Roberta."

Poor Miss Roberta's face fell. She had been secretly much elated by the thoughts of a neighbor, and to have all her hopes thus nipped in the bud was painful. She had heard (from Hester again, it is to be feared!) that Mrs. Cricklander's maid, who was a cousin of the baker in Applewood, and who had originally instigated her discovery of Wendover, had said that her lady knew all the greatest people in England—lords and duchesses by the dozen, and even an archbishop! Surely that was respectable enough.

But Miss La Sarthe, while again deploring the source of her sister's information, was firm. Ideas might have changed, but *they* had not. Since the last time they had curtsied to the beloved late Queen, in about 1879, she believed new rules had been made, but the La Sarthe had nothing to do with such things!

Halcyone caught Miss Roberta's piteous, subdued eyes, and smiled a tender, kind smile. With years her understanding of her ancient aunts had grown. They were no longer rather contemptible, narrow-minded elders in her eyes, but filled her with a pitiful and gentle respect. Their courage under adversity, their firm self-control, and the force which made them live up to their idea of the fitness of things, appealed to her strongly. She had John Derringham's quality of detached consideration, and appreciated her old relatives as exquisite relics of the past, as well as her own kith and kin.

"In America, divorce is not considered the heinous crime it was once in England," Mr. Carlyon said. "Perhaps this lady may have been greatly sinned again and deserves all our pity and regard."

But Miss La Sarthe remained obdurate. The point was not as to who was in the right, she explained, but that certain conventions, laid down by one whose memory was revered, had been outraged, and she could never permit her sister or Halcyone to have any intercourse with the tenant of Wendover Park!

The preparations for the new arrival went on apace all the autumn and winter. Armies of workpeople were reported to be in possession, and whole train-loads of splendid French furniture were known to have arrived at Applewood to augment the antique and time-worn pieces which were Wendover's own.

Miss La Sarthe sent for the Long Man. Things had been rather better of late, and no more precious belongings had been forced to be parted with. An investment which had been valueless for years now began to produce some interest which was a great comfort, for Miss La Sarthe was now seventy-nine and Miss Roberta seventy-six.

The orders that the agent received were precise. The gate between Wendover and La Sarthe Chase which had been closed for over a hundred years was to be boarded up, and their side of the haw-haw which for nearly a mile divided the two parks was to be deepened and cleared out, and the spikes mended in any places where the ground might have seemed to have fallen in sufficiently, or the irons to have become broken enough to make the passage easy.

This would be unnecessary, Mr. Martin (the Long Man) told her. The haw-haw was still as perfect as ever and a wonder of concealed traps for the unwary, but the gate should be seen to at once.

Thus La Sarthe Chase was armed fully against Wendover, when, about Easter, Mrs. Cricklander decided she would come down and bring a few friends. It was with a sudden violent beating of the heart that Halcyone learned casually from Mr. Carlyon that John Derringham would be of their number.

The aunts took in the *Morning Post*, but until she was eighteen they had rigorously forbidden Halcyone's perusal of it. Newspapers, except one or two periodicals, were not fit for young ladies' reading until they were grown up, they felt. However, their niece, having now come to years of discretion, sometimes had the pleasure of reading John Derringham's speeches and thrilled with joy over his felicitous daring and caustic wit. The Government could not last much longer, but he at least, as far as he could, would keep it full of vigor until the end. She knew, therefore, that the last sitting before the Easter recess had been a storm of words sharp as sword-thrusts—it was before the days of the language of Billingsgate and the behavior of roughs. There were quite a number of gentlemen still in the House of Commons, who often behaved as such.

Those wonderful forces which Halcyone culled from all nature, and especially the night, gave her a serenity over the most moving events, and when the sudden beating of her heart was over, she waited calmly for the moment when she should see John Derringham again.

Mr. Carlyon took in the *Graphic* as well as his *Quarterly Review* and the *Nineteenth Century*, and it was her only medium for guessing even what the outside world looked like, but from it she was quite aware that a beard was a most unusual thing for a young modern man of the world, and that John Derringham for that reason must always be distinguished from his fellows. Carpenters and hedgers and ditchers wore them, and nondescript young fellows she remembered seeing when she went into Upminster with her aunts; but these excursions had been discontinued now for the past five years, so the villagers of Sarthe-under-Crum and the denizens of the rather larger Applewood were the only human beings she ever saw.

The party at Wendover were to arrive on the Thursday before Good Friday—Priscilla had told her that—and it was just possible that some of them might be in church.

The aunts now drove a low basket shay which had been their pride in the sixties, but which for countless years, until the investment began to pay, they had been unable to keep a pair of ponies for. Now, however, the shay was unearthed from the moldy coachhouse and for the past year two very old and quiet specimens of Shetland had been found for them by Mr. Martin and they were able to drive to church every Sunday in state, William sitting up behind, holding the reins between his mistresses, while Miss La Sarthe flourished a small whip whose delicate handle was studded with minute turquoises. From it dangled a ring which she could slip on her finger over her one-buttoned slate-colored glove, and so feel certain of not dropping this treasure. Halcyone always walked.

On Good Friday there was not a sight of the Wendover party in Church, and Halcyone went back by the orchard house to look in at Cheiron, who had had a cold in the last few days.

Stretched in the armchair she found John Derringham.

The brisk walk in the fresh spring air had brought some faint color to her pale cheeks, her soft hair was wound about her head with becoming simplicity, and she wore an ordinary suit which could not disguise her beautiful slender limbs, so long and thin, a veritable Artemis in her chase perfection of balance and proportion.

Halcyone could pass in any crowd and perhaps no one would ever notice her and her mouse-like coloring, but once your eye was arrested, then, like looking at some rare bit of delicate enamel, you began to perceive undreamed-of graces which soothed the sight until you were filled with the consciousness of an exquisite beauty as intangible as her other charm—distinction. An infinite serenity was in her atmosphere, a promise of all pure and tender things in her great soft eyes. The mystery and freshness of the night seemed always to hang about her. Her ways were noiseless—the most creaking door appeared to forget its irritating habit when under her touch. Thus is was that John Derringham, smoking a cigar, never even glanced up until a voice of extreme cultivation and softness said gently:

"Good morning. And how are you?"

Then he bounded from his chair, startled a little, and held out his hand.

"My old friend, Miss Halcyone, the Priestess of Truth!" he exclaimed, "as I am alive!"

She smiled serenely while they shook hands, and sat down demurely by the Professor's side.

"I thought you would have been translated to Olympus long ago," the visitor said. "Have you honored this ordinary earth and our friend Cheiron's cave, ever since?"

"Ever since!"

"There can be nothing left for you to learn. Master, it is you and I whom she could teach," he laughed.

"How do you know all this," asked Halcyone quietly, while her eyes smiled at his raillery. "Do I look such an old-fashioned blue-stocking, then?"

"You look perfectly sweet," and John Derringham's expressive eyes confirmed what he said.

"Enough, enough, John. Halcyone is quite unaccustomed to gallants from the world like you," the Professor growled. "If you pay her compliments she won't believe you can really make a speech."

So Mr. Derringham laughed and continued his interrupted conversation. He seemed in good humor with all the world. He was going to stay at Wendover for the whole of Easter week. Mrs. Cricklander had an amusing party of luminaries of both sides—she was the most perfect hostess and had a remarkable talent for collecting the right people.

"She is quite the best-read woman I have ever met, Master," John Derringham said. "You must let me bring her over here one day to see you—you would delight in her wit and beauty. She does not leave you a dull moment."

"Yes, bring her," the Professor returned between the puffs at his long pipe. "I have never met any of these new hot-house roses grafted upon briar roots. I should like to study how the system has worked."

"Quite admirably, as you will see. I do not know any Englishwomen who are to compare to such Americans in brilliancy and fascination."

Over Halcyone, in spite of her serenity, there crept a feeling of cold. She did not then analyze why, and, as was her habit when anything began to distress her, she looked out of the window, whether it were night or day. She always did this, and when her eyes saw Nature in any of her moods, calm returned to her.

"She will simply revel in La Sarthe Chase when she sees it," Mr. Derringham went on, now addressing Halcyone. "She is a past-mistress in knowledge of the dates of things.

You are going to have the most delicious neighbor, Miss Halcyone, and in learning, a foeman worthy of your steel."

Cheiron was heard to chuckle wickedly, and when his former Oxford pupil asked him with mild humor the reason of his inappropriate mirth, he answered dryly:

"She is never likely to see the inside of the park even. Queen Victoria did not receive divorced persons, and the Misses La Sarthe, in consequence, cannot either. You will have to bring her here by the road, John!"

Halcyone winced a little. She disliked this conversation; it was not as *fine* as she liked to think were the methods of both the men who were carrying it on.

John Derringham reddened up to his temples, where there were a few streaks of gray in his dark hair which added to the distinction of his finely cut, rather ascetic face. The short, well-trimmed beard was very becoming, Halcyone thought, and gave him a look of great masculinity and strength. His hawk's eyes were shadowed, as though he sat up very late at night; which indeed he did. For John Derringham, at this period of his life, burnt the candle at both ends and in the middle, too, if it could add to the pleasure or benefit of his calculated career, mapped out for himself by himself.

A sensation almost of wrath rose in his breast at his old master's words. These ignorant country people, to dare to criticise his glittering golden pheasant, whom he was very nearly making up his mind to take for a wife! This aspect of the case, that even these unimportant old ladies could question the position of his choice, galled him. He had spent up to the last penny of his diminished income in his years of man's estate, and Derringham was mortgaged to its furthest acre—and a gentleman must live—and with his brilliant political future expanding before him, lack of means must not be allowed to stand in his way. He would give this woman in gratified ambition as much or more than she would give him in wealth, so it would be an equal bargain and benefit them both. And, above all, he was more than half in love with her, and could get quite a large share of pleasure out of the affair as well. He had been too busy to trouble much over women as a sex since he had left the University—except in the way he had once described to his old master, regarding them as flowers in a garden—mere pleasures for sight and touch, and experiencing ephemeral passions which left no mark. But women either feared or adored him; and this woman, the desired of a host of his friends, had singled him out for her especial favors. It had amused him the whole of the last season; he had defied her efforts to chain him to her chariot wheels, and in the winter she had gone to Egypt, and had only just returned. But the charm was growing, and he felt he would allow himself to be caught in her net.

"Mrs. Cricklander would be very much amused could she hear this verdict of the country," he said with a certain tone in his voice which did not escape Halcyone. "In London we do not occupy ourselves with such unimportant things—but I dare say she will get over it. And now I really must be going back. May I walk with you through the park, Miss Halcyone, if you are going, too? I am sure there must be an opening somewhere, as the two places touch."

"Yes, there is just one," Halcyone said. "The haw-haw runs the whole way, and it is impossible to pass, except in the one spot, and I believe no one knows of it but myself. There are a few bricks loose, and I used to take them out and put them back when I wanted to get into Wendover—long ago."

"Then it will be an adventure; come," he said, and Halcyone rose.

"Only if you will not give away my secret. Promise you will not tell anyone else," she bargained.

"Oh! I promise," and John Derringham jumped up—his movements were always quick and decided and full of nervous force. "I will bring my hostess to see you on Monday or Tuesday, Master," he announced, as he said good-by. "And prepare yourself to fall at her feet like all the rest of us—Merlin and Vivien, you knew. It will be a just punishment for your scathing remarks."

When they were outside in the garden Halcyone spoke not a word. The beds were a glory of spring bulbs, and every bud on the trees was bursting with its promise of coming leaf. Glad, chirruping bird-notes called to one another, and a couple of partridges ran across the lawn.

John Derringham took in the lines of Halcyone's graceful person as she walked ahead. She had that same dignity of movement from the hips which the Niké of Samothrace seems to be advancing with as you come up the steps of the Louvre.

How tall she had grown! She must be at least five feet nine or ten. But why would she not speak?

He overawed her here in the daylight, and she felt silent and oppressed.

"Whereabouts is our tree that we sat in when I was young and you were old?" he asked, after they had got through the gap in the hedge. A little gate had been put in the last years to keep out the increasing herd of deer.

"It is over there by the copse," she said shyly. "The lower branch fell last winter, and it makes a delightful seat. One is not obliged to climb into the tree now. See: Demetrius helped me to drag it close, and we nailed on these two arms," and she pointed to a giant oak not far from them, which John Derringham pretended to recognize.

He tried his best to get her to talk to him, but some cloud of timid aloofnes on her part seemed to hang between them, and very soon below the copse they came to the one vulnerable part in all the haw-haw's length. She showed him how to take the bricks out and where to place his feet, and pointed out how secluded from any eye the place was. Then, as he climbed down and then up again, and looked across at her from Wendover lands, she said a sedate good-by, and turning, went on among the thickly growing saplings of the copse and, never looking back, was soon out of sight.

John Derringham watched her disappear with a strange feeling of ruffled disquietude in his heart.

CHAPTER XI

Iᴛ was so warm and charming an April day that Mrs. Cricklander and some of her friends were out of doors before luncheon, walking up and down the broad terrace walk that flanked Wendover's side.

It was a Georgian house, spacious and comfortable, but not especially beautiful. Mrs. Cricklander was a woman of enormous ability—she had a perfect talent for discovering just the right people to work for her pleasure and benefit, while being without a single inspiration herself. If she engaged a professional adviser to furnish her house, and decorate it, you could be sure he was of the best and that his services had been measured and balanced beforehand, and that he had been generously paid whatever he had obtained by bargaining for it, and that the agreement was signed and every penny of the cost entered in a little book. It was so with everything that touched her life. She had a definite idea of what she wanted, although she did not always want the same thing for long; but while she did, she went about getting it in a sensible, practical way, secured it, paid for it,—and then often threw it away.

She had felt she wanted Vincent Cricklander because he belonged to one of the old families in New York and played polo well, and, being a great heiress though of no pretensions to birth, she wished to have an undisputed entry into the inner circle of her own country. He fulfilled her requirements for quite three years, and then she felt she was "through" with America, and wanted fresh fields for her efforts. Paris was too easy, Berlin doubtful, Vienna and Petersburg impossible to conquer, but London would hold out everything that she could wish for. Only, it must be the very best of London, not the part of its society that any-one can struggle and push and pay to get into, but the real thing. She was "quite finished" with Vincent Cricklander, too, at this period; to see him play polo no longer gave her any thrill. So one morning at their lunch, on a rare occasion when they chanced to be alone, she told him so, and asked him practically how much he would take to let her divorce him.

But Vincent Cricklander was a gentleman, and, what is more, an American gentleman, which means of a chivalry towards women unknown in other countries.

"I do not want any of your money, Cis," he said. "I will be quite glad to go, if it will make you happier. We'll phone T. V. Ryan this afternoon and let him think out a scheme so that it can be done without a scandal of any sort. My mother has old-fashioned ideas, and I would hate to pain the poor dear lady."

It took nearly two years, but the divorce was completed at last, and Cecilia Cricklander found herself perfectly free and with all the keen scent of the hunter for the chase dilating her fine nostrils as she stood upon the deck of the great ocean liner bound for Liverpool.

She was a very beautiful woman, and refined in every point, with exquisite feet and hands, pure, brilliant, fair coloring and a superb figure, and even a fairly sweet voice. Her education had been a good deal neglected because she was too spoilt by a doting father to profit by the instruction he provided for her. She felt this keenly directly she began to go out into the world, and immediately commenced to remedy the defect. For her, from the very beginning, life appeared in the light of a game. Fate was an adversary from whom she meant to win all the stakes, and it behooved a clever woman not to overlook a single card that might be of use to her in her play. She was quite aware of her own limitations, and her own forces and advantages. She knew she was beautiful and charming; she knew she was kind and generous and extremely "cute," as her old father said. She knew that literature and art did not interest her one atom in themselves, that most music bored her, and that she had a rather imperfect memory; but during her brief visits to England, when she was making up her mind that this country would be the field for her next exertions, she had decided that to be beautiful and charming was not just enough; there were numbers of other Americans who were both, and they were all one as successful and sought after as the other. She must be something beyond this—a real Queen. To beauty and wealth and charm she must add culture as well. She must be able to talk to the prime minister upon his pet foibles, she must be able to quote erudite passages from all the cleverest books of the day to the brilliant politicians and diplomats and men of polished brain who made up the society over which she wished to rule. And how was this to be done? She thought it all out, and during her two years of living quietly to obtain her divorce without a breath of scandal, she had hit upon and put into practice an admirable plan.

She searched for and found a poor, very plain and highly cultivated English gentlewoman, one who had been governess in a foreign Royal family and was now trying to support an aged mother by giving private lessons. Arabella Clinker was this treasure's name—Miss Arabella Clinker, aged forty-two, and as ugly as it is possible for a thoroughly nice woman to be.

Mrs. Cricklander made no mysteries about what she required Miss Clinker's companionship for. She explained minutely that should any special dinner-party or *rencontre* with any great person be in view, Miss Clinker must do a sort of preparatory cramming for her, as boys are prepared for examinations.

"You must make it your business, when I give you the names of the people I am to meet, to post me up in what they are likely to talk about. You must read all the papers in the morning with the political speeches in them, and then give me a quick *résumé* if it should be any diplomat or great artist or one of those delightful Englishmen who knows everything, then you must suggest some suitable authors to speak of that they will like, and I have quite enough sense myself to turn the conversation off any that I should not know about. In this way you will soon learn what I require of you, and I shall learn a great deal and gradually can launch out into much more difficult things."

Arabella Clinker had a sense of humor, and she adored her mother and wished to give her a comfortable old age. Mrs. Cricklander's terms for this unique position were according to her accustomed liberality.

"I like to give splendid prices for things, and then I expect them to be splendidly done," she said.

Miss Clinker had promised to do her best, and their partnership had lasted for nearly three years with the most satisfactory results to both of them. Their only difficulty was Mrs. Cricklander's defective memory. She *could not* learn anything by heart, and if she were at all tired had to keep herself tremendously in hand to make no mistakes. But the three years of constant trying had enabled her to talk upon most subjects in a shibboleth of the world which imposed upon everyone. Her real talent which called for the greatset admiration was the way in which she manipulated what she knew, and skimmed a fresh subject.

She would do so with such admirable skill and wording as to give the impression that she was acquainted with its profoundest depths; and then when she was safely over the chasm the first moment she was free she would rush to Arabella for the salient points, doggedly repeat them over and over, and on the next occasion come out with them to the same person, convincing him more than ever of her thorough knowledge of the subject. But her memory was her misfortune, for if Miss Clinker instructed her, for instance, in all the different peculiarities of the styles of Keats and Shelley, a week after she would have forgotten which was which—because both bored her to distraction—and she would have to be reminded again. One awful moment came when, rhapsodizing upon the sensibility of Keats' character, she said to Sir Tedbury Delvine, the finest litterateur of his time, that there must have come moments during Keats' latter years when he must have felt as his own "Prometheus Unbound!" But, seeing her mistake immediately by her listener's blank face, she regained her ground with a skill and a flow of words which made Sir Tedbury Delvine doubt whether his own ears had heard aright.

"Arabella," Mrs. Cricklander said when next morning she lay smoking in her old-rose silk bed, while she went through her usual lessons for the day, "you must give me just a point each about those wretched old two, so that I will remember them again. I must have a sort of keynote. Shelley's would do with that horrible statue of him drowned, at Oxford, that would connect his chain—but what for Keats?"

So at last Miss Clinker invented a plan, almost Pythagorean in its way, and it proved very helpful to her patroness.

When she went on light, amusing excursions to Egypt and such places, she allowed Arabella to remain with her mother, and these were months of pure happiness to Miss Clinker.

It had not taken Mrs. Cricklander long to conquer London with her money, and her looks, and her triumphant belief in herself. At the end of two years, when John Derringham was first presented to her, she had almost reached the summit of her ambitions. To become his wife she had decided would place her there. For was he not certain to climb to the top of the tree, as well as being the most brilliant and most sought after young man in all England. Of love—the love that recks not of place or gain but just gives its being to the loved one—to such emotion she was happily a complete stranger. John Derringham attracted her greatly, and until now had successfully evaded all her snares and had remained beyond the thrall of her will. To have got him to come for this whole week of Easter was a triumph and exulted her accordingly. She particularly affected politicians, and her house in Grosvenor Square was a meeting-place for both parties, provided the members of each were of the most distinguished type. And there were not more than two or three people out of all her acquaintances, besides Arabella, who smiled a little over her brilliant culture.

By all this it can be seen that Mrs. Cricklander was a wonderful character—tenacious, indomitable, full of nerve and deserving of the greatest respect in consequence.

The only thing the least vulgar about her was her soul —if she had one—and it is not the business of society to look into such things. Scrutiny of the sort is left for creatures like the Professor, Cheiron, who have nothing else to do—but his impressions upon this subject must come in their proper place.

Meanwhile, John Derringham had joined the party on the terrace, and was joyously acclaimed, and then minutely questioned as to the cause of his lengthy absence. He had not been to church—that was certain. He had not been out of the park, because the lodges were not in the direction from which he had been seen advancing. Where had he been, then? All alone? He would not give any account of himself, as was his way, and presently his hostess drew him on ahead and down the terrace steps. She wanted to point out to him some improvements which she contemplated. The garden must be the most beautiful in the country— and he knew so much about gardens, he could tell her exactly which style would suit the house best.

John Derringham was in a bad temper. That unaccountable sense of a discordant note with himself still stayed with him. He unconsciously, during his walk, had dwelt upon the Professor's information as to the view of the old ladies of The Chase, and then Halcyone's silence and stiffness. He felt excluded from the place which he recollected he had held in the child's regard. His memory had jumped the brief glimpse of her during her fledgling period, and had gone back with distinct vividness to the summer morning in the tree, almost seven years ago.

He answered with a carelessness which was not altogether

pleasing to Cecilia Cricklander. She saw instantly that her favorite guest was ruffled by something. Although never fine, she was quick at observing all the moods of her pawns, and had brought the faculty of watching for signs from castles, knights and kings to a science. John Derringham must be humored and cajoled by a proof of her great under-standing of him—he must be left in silence for a minute, and then she would pause and look over the balustrade, so that he might see her handsome profile and take in the exquisite simplicity of her perfect dress. She knew these things pleased him. She would look a little sad, too, and far away.

It had its effect.

"What are you dreaming about, fair châtelaine?" he asked after a while. "Your charming mouth has its corners drooped."

"I was wondering—" and then she stopped.

"Yes?" asked John Derringham. "You were wonder-ing what?"

"I was wondering if one could ever get you to really take an interest in anything but your politics, and your England's advancement? How good it would be if one could interest you for a moment in anything else."

He leaned upon the balustrade beside her.

"You are talking nonsense," he said. "You know very well that you interest me every time I see you—and it is growing upon me. That was not the only thing revolving in your clever mind."

"Yes, indeed," and she looked down.

"Well, then, I am interested in your garden. What do you think of doing? Tell me."

She explained an elaborate plan, and quoted the names of famous gardeners and their styles, with her accustomed erudition. For had not Arabella got them up for her only that morning, as she smoked her seventh cigarette in bed? She inclined to French things, and she thought that this particular part—a mere rough bit in the park—could very well be laid out as a *Petit Trianon*. She could procure copies of the plans of Mique, and even have a *Temple d'Amour*.

"I love to create," she said. "The place would not have amused me if everything had been complete, and if you will help me I shall be so grateful."

"Of course I will," he said. "The *Temple d'Amour* would look quite well up upon that rising ground, and you could have a small winding lake dug to complete the illusion. Nothing is impossible, and I suppose you can get permission from the old Wendover who lives in Rome to do what you wish?"

"I should like to have been able to take the park of the next place, La Sarthe Chase, too—that impassable haw-haw and the boarded-up gate irritate me. The boards have been put since I came to look over everything last autumn. I did instruct the agent, Martin, in Applewood to offer a large price for it, but he assured me it would be quite useless; it belongs, it appears, to the most ridiculous old ladies, who are almost starving, but would rather die than be sensible."

Suddenly John Derringham was conscious that his sympathies had shifted to the Misses La Sarthe, and he could not imagine why.

"You told me, I think," she went on, "that you knew this neighborhood. Do you happen to be aware of any bait I could hold out to them?"

"No, I do not," he said. "That sort of pride is foolish, if you like; but there it is—part of an inheritance of the spirit which in the past has made England great. They are wonderful old ladies. I dined with them once long ago."

"I must really go over and see them one day. Perhaps I could persuade them to my view."

The flicker of a smile came into the eyes of John Derringham, and she noticed it at once. It angered her, and deepened the pretty pink in her fresh cheeks.

"You think they would not be pleased to see me?" she flashed.

"They are ridiculously old-fashioned," he said . "Not your type at all."

"But I love curiosities," she returned, smiling now. "I am not absolutely set upon any type. All human beings are a delightful study. If you know them, you must bring them to see me then some day."

But at this John Derringham laughed outright.

"If you could picture them, you would laugh, too," he said. "There is someone, though, whom I do want you to know, who lives close here—my old Oxford professor of Greek, Arnold Carlyon. He is a study who will repay you. The most whimsical cynic, as well as one of the greatest scholars I have ever come across in my life. I promised him to-day I would persuade you to let me take you to see him."

"How enchanting," she replied with enthusiasm. "And we must make him come here. When shall we go? To-morrow?"

"No, I said Monday or Tuesday—with your permission," and he bent over her with caressing homage.

"Of course—when you will. That, then, is where you were this morning. But how did you get back through the park?" she asked. "There is no opening at that side whatever. It is all blocked by the wicked La Sarthe Chase."

"I came round the edge," he said, and felt annoyed—he hated lying—"and then turned upwards. I wanted to see the boundaries."

"I hate boundaries," she laughed. "I always want to overstep them."

"There is the chance of being caught in snares."

"Which adds to the excitement," and she allowed her radiant eyes to seek his with a challenge.

He was not slow to take it up.

"Enchantress," he whispered softly, "it is you whose charm lays snares for men. You have no fear of falling into them yourself."

She rippled a low laugh of satisfaction. And, having tamed her lion, she now suggested it was time to go in to luncheon.

CHAPTER XII

ARABELLA CLINKER took Sunday afternoons generally to write a long letter to her mother, and Good Friday seemed almost a Sunday, so she went up to her room from force of habit. But first she looked up some facts in the countless books of reference she kept always by her. Mrs. Cricklander had skated over some very thin ice at luncheon upon a classical subject, when talking to the distinguished Mr. Derringham, and she must be warned and primed up before dinner. Arabella had herself averted a catastrophe and dexterously turned the conversation in the nick of time. Mrs. Cricklander had a peculiarly unclassical brain, and found learning statistics about ancient philosophies and the names of mythological personages the most difficult of all. Fortunately in these days, even among the most polished, this special branch of cultivation was rather old-fashioned, Miss Clinker reflected, but still, as Mr. Derringham seemed determined to wander along this line (Arabella had unconsciously appropriated some apt Americanisms during her three years of bondage), she must be loyal and not allow her employer to commit any blunders. So she got her facts crystalized, or "tabloided," as Mrs. Cricklander would mentally have characterized the process, and then she began her letter to her parent. Mrs. Clinker, an Irishwoman and the widow of a learned Dean, understood a number of things, and was clear-headed and humorous, for all her seventy years, and these passages in her daughter's letter amused her.

We are entertaining a number of distinguished visitors, and among them Mr. John Derringham, the Under Secretary of State for Foreign Affairs. He is a most interesting personality, as perfectly sure of what he wants in life as is M. E. (M. E. stood for "My Employer—" names were invidious). They would be a perfect match, each as selfish as the other, I should say. He is really very cultivated, and believes her to be so, too. She has not made a single mistake as yet, but frightened me at luncheon a little. I must try and get her to keep him off classical subjects. She intends to marry him —and then she will not require me, I suppose; or rather, I do not think he would permit her to keep me. If it came to a measure of wills, he would win, I think—at first, at least— but she could wear away a stone in the end, as you know. The arranging of this place is still amusing her, so she may decide to spend a good deal of time here. She closed her mouth with that firm snap this morning that I have described to you often, and said that it was going to be her delight to make them put themselves out and come so far away from London for her. "Them," for the moment, are Mr. Derringham and Mr. Hanbury-Green, almost a Socialist person, who is on the other side—very brilliantly clever but with a Cockney accent in one or two words. M. E. does not notice this, of course. Mr. H. G. is in love with her—Mr. D. is not, but she is determined that he shall be. I do not know if he intends to marry her. He is making up his mind, I think, therefore I must be doubly careful not to allow her to commit any mistakes, because if she did it would certainly estrange him, and as to keep her free is so much to our advantage, I feel I must be extra careful in doing my duty.

Arabella was a person of scrupulous honor.

She then proceeded to describe the party, and concluded with,

There is one American girl I like very much—perfectly natural and bubbling with spirits, saying aloud everything she thinks, really well educated and taking so much outdoor exercise that she has not yet begun to have the nervous attacks that are such a distressing feature of so many of her countrywomen. I am told it is their climate. M. E. says it is because the men out there have always let them have their own way. I should think so much smoking has something to do with it.

John Derringham meanwhile had gone with his hostess and some of the rest of the party, Mr. Hanbury-Green among them, to inspect the small golf links Mrs. Cricklander was having constructed in the park. Her country-house must be complete with suitable amusements. She had taken all the Wendover shooting, too, and what she could get of Lord Graceworth's beyond. "You cannot drag people into the wilds and then bore them to death," she said. What she most enjoyed was to scintillate to a company of two or three, and fascinate them all into a desire for a *tête-à-tête*, and then, when with difficulty one had secured this privilege, to be elusive and tantalize him to death. To passion she was a complete stranger, and won all her games because with her great beauty she was as cold as ice.

She was not feeling perfectly content this Good Friday afternoon. Something had happened since the evening before which had altered John Derringham's point of view towards her. She felt it distinctly with her senses, trained like an animal's, to scent the most subtle things in connection with herself. It was impossible to seize; she could not analyze it, but there it was; certainly there seemed to be some change. He was brilliant, and had been even *empressé* before lunch, but it was not spontaneous, and she was not perfectly sure that it was not assumed. It was his cleverness which attracted her. She could not see the other side of his head—not that she would have understood what that meant, if she had heard the phrase.

But her habit was not to sit down under an adverse circumstance, but to probe its source and eradicate it, or, at least, counteract it. Thus, while she chatted eloquently to Sir Tedbury Delvine, her keen brain was weighing things. John Derringham had certainly had a look of aroused passion in his eyes when he had pressed her hand in a lingered good night; he had even said some words of a more advanced insinuation as to his intentions towards her than he had ever done before. They were never exact—always some fugitive hint to which afterwards she would try to fix some meaning as she reviewed their meetings. She had not seen him at breakfast because she never came down in the morning until eleven or twelve, and he had already gone out, she heard, when she did descend.

It followed then that either he had received some disturbing letter by the post—only one on Good Friday—or something had occurred during his visit to his old master. It would be her business to find out which of these two things it was. Could the Professor be married, and might there be some woman in the family? Or was it nothing to do with the Professor or with a letter, or was there a more present reason? Had Cora Lutworth attracted him with her youth and high spirits? They were walking ahead now, and she could hear his laugh and see how they were enjoying themselves.

She had been a perfect fool to ask Cora. She did not fear a single Englishwoman, the powers of most of whom in her heart she despised—but Cora was of her own race, and well equipped to rival her in a question of marriage. Cora was only twenty-one, and she herself was thirty—and there was the divorce which, although she had found it no bar to her entrance into the most exclusive English society,

still might perhaps rankle unconsciously in the mind of a
man mounting the political ladder, and determined to secure the highest honors.

She felt she hated Cora, and would have destroyed her
with a look if she had been able.

Miss Lutworth, meanwhile, brimful of the joy of life and
insouciance, was amusing herself vastly. And John Derringham was experiencing that sense of relaxation and
irresponsible pleasure he got sometimes when he was over-
worked from going to an excruciatingly funny Paris farce.
Miss Lutworth did not appeal to his brain at all, although
she was quite capable of doing so; she just made him feel
gay and frolicsome with her deliciously *rusé* view of the
world and life in general. He forgot his ruffled temper of
the morning, and by the time they had returned for tea,
was his brilliant self again, and quite ready to sit in a low
chair at his hostess's side, while she leaned back among the
cushions of her sofa, in her own sitting-room, whither she
had enticed him during that nondescript hour before dinner,
when each person could do what he pleased.

"Is not Cora sweet?" she said, smoothing the brocade beneath her hand. Her sitting-room had been arranged by
the artist who had done the house, as a perfect bower of
Italian Sixteenth Century art. Mr. Jephson, the artist,
had assured her that this period would make a perfect background for her fresh and rather voluptuous coloring; it had
not become so *banal* as any of the French Louis'. And so
Arabella had been instructed to drum into her head the
names of the geniuses of that time, and their works, and she
could now babble sweetly all about Giorgione, Paolo Veronese and Titian's later works without making a single mistake. And while the pictures bored her unspeakably, she
took a deep pleasure in her own cleverness about them, and
delighted in tracing the influence Paolo Veronese must have
had upon Boucher, a hint from Arabella which she had
announced as an inspiration of her own.

She had tea-gowns made to suit this period, and adopted
the stately movements which were evidently the attribute
of that time.

John Derringham thought her superb. If he had been
really in love with her, he might have seen through her—
and not cared—just as if she had not attracted him at all,
he would certainly have taken her measure and enjoyed
laying pitfalls for her. But as it was, his will was always
trying to augment his inclination. He was too busy to ana-

lyze the real meaning of any woman, and until the Professor's words about the divorce and the Misses La Sarthe's view of the affair, it had never even struck him that there could be one single aspect of Mrs. Cricklander's case which he might have to blink at. He had told himself he had better marry a rich woman, since his old maternal uncle, Joseph Scroope, had just taken unto himself a young wife and might any day have an heir. And this was his only other possible source of fortune.

Mrs. Cricklander seemed the most advantageous bargain looming upon the horizon. She was of proved entertaining capabilities. She had passed her examination in the power of being a perfect hostess. She had undoubted and expanding social talents. Women did not dislike her; she was very vivid, very handsome, very rich. What more could a man who in his innermost being had a supreme contempt for women, and a supreme belief in himself, desire?

He had even balanced the advantages of marrying a rich American girl, one like Miss Lutworth, for example. But such beings were unproven, and might develop nerves and fads, which were of no consequence in the delightful creatures with whom he passed occasional leisure hours of recreation, but which in a wife would be a singular disadvantage. Since he must marry—and soon—before the present Parliament broke up and his Government went out, and there came some years of fighting from the Opposition benches, when especially brilliant entertaining might be of advantage to him—he knew he had better make up his mind speedily, and take this ripe and luscious peach, which appeared more than willing to drop into his mouth.

So, this late afternoon, aided by the scents and colors and propinquity, he did his very best to make gradual love to her, and for some unaccountable hideously annoying reason felt every moment more aloof. It almost seemed at last as if he were guarding something fine and free that was being assailed. His dual self was fighting within his soul.

Mrs. Cricklander was experiencing all the exciting emotions which presumably the knights of old enjoyed when engaged in a tournament. She was not even disturbed when the dressing-gown rang and she not yet won. It was only a postponement of one of the most entrancing games she had ever played in her successful life. And Mr. Hanbury-Green was going to sit upon her left hand at dinner and would afford new flint for her steel. He was a recent acquisition, and of undoubted coming value. His views were in reality nearer her heart politically than those of John Derringham. Deep down in her being was a strong class hatred—undreamed of, and which would have been vigorously denied. She remembered the burning rage and the vows of vengeance which had convulsed her as a girl, because the refined and gently bred women of her own New York's inner circle would have none of her, and how it had been her glory to trample upon as many of them as she could, when Vincent Cricklander had placed her as head of his fine mansion in Fifty-ninth Street, having moved from the old family home in Washington Square. And there, underneath, was the feeling still for those of any country who, instinct told her, had inherited from evolution something which none of her money, and none of her talent, and none of her indomitable will, could buy. But of course Mr. Hanbury-Green was not to be considered, except as a foil for her wit—a pawn in the game for the securing of John Derringham.

Thus it was that she was able to walk in her stately way with trailing velvets down the broad stairs of her newly acquired home with a sense of exaltation and complacency which was unimpaired.

John Derringham, on the contrary, was rather abrupt with his valet and spoilt two white ties, and swore at himself because his old Eton hand had lost its cunning. But finally he too went down the shallow steps, and, joining his hostess at the door, sailed in with her to the George I saloon, his fine eyes shining and his bearing more arrogant than before.

CHAPTER XIII

AFTER dinner there was a brisk passage of arms between the two men of opposite party in the group by the fire, and Mrs. Cricklander incited them to further exertions. It had arisen because Mr. Derringham had launched forth the abominable and preposterous theory that the only thing the Radicals would bring England to would be the necessity of returning to barbarism and importing slaves—then their schemes applied to the present inhabitants of the country might all work. The denizens in the casual wards, having a vote and a competence provided by the State, would have time to become of the leisured classes and apply themselves to culture, and so every free citizen being equal, a company of philosophers and an aristocracy of intellect would arise and all would be well!

Mrs. Cricklander glanced stealthily at his whimsical face, to be sure whether he were joking or no—and decided he probably was. But Mr. Hanbury-Green, so irritated by the delightful hostess's evident *penchant* for his rival, allowed his ill-humor to obscure his usually keen judgment, and took the matter up in serious earnest.

"Your side would not import, but reduce us all—we who are the defenders of the people—to being slaves," he said with some asperity. "Your class has had its innings long enough, it would be the best thing in the world for you to have to come down to doing your own housework."

"I should make a capital cook," said John Derringham, with smiling eyes, "but I should certainly refuse to cook for anyone but myself; and you, Mr. Green, who may be an indifferent artist in that respect, would have perhaps a bad dinner."

"I never understand," interrupted Mrs. Cricklander—"when everything is socialistic, shall we not be able to live in these nice houses?"

"Of course not," said Mr. Hanbury-Green gravely. "You will have to share with less fortunate people." And then he drew himself up ready for battle, and began.

"Why, because a man or woman is born in the gutter,

79

should not he or she be given by the State the same chance as though born in a palace? We are all exactly the same human beings, only until now luck and circumstances have been different for us."

"I am all for everyone having the same chance," agreed John Derringham, allowing the smile to stay in his eyes, "although I do not admit we are all the same human beings, any more than the Derby winner is the same horse as the plow horse or the cob. They can all draw some kind of vehicle, but they cannot all win races—they have to excel, each in his different line. Give everyone a chance, by all means, and then make him come up for examination, and if found fit passed on for higher things, and if unfit, passed *out!* It is your tendency to pamper the unfit which I deplore. You have only one idea on your Radical Socialist side of the House, to pull down those who are in any inherited or agreeable authority—not because they are doing their work badly, but because you would prefer their place! The war-cry of boons for the people covers a multitude of objects, and is the most attractive cry for the masses to hear all over the world. The real boon for the people would be to give them more practical sound education and ruthlessly to clear out the unfit." Then his face lost its whimsical expression and became interested.

"Let us imagine a Utopian state of republic. Let every male citizen who has reached twenty-five years, say, pass his examination in the right to live freely, regardless of class, and if he cannot do so, let him go into the ranks of the slaves, because, turn it how you will, we must have some beings to do the lowest offices in life. Who would willingly clean the drains, fill the dust-carts—and, indeed, do the hundred and one things that are simply disgusting, but which must be done?"

Mr. Hanbury-Green had not a sufficiently strong answer ready, so remained loftily silent, while John Derringham went on:

"We obscure every issue nowadays by a sickly sentiment and this craze for words to prove black is white in order to please the mediocrity. If we could only look facts in the face we should see that the idea of equality of all men is perfectly ridiculous. No ancient republic ever worked, even the most purely democratic, like the Athenian, of the fifth and fourth centuries B. C., without an unconsidered and unrepresented population of slaves. You know your Aristotle, Mr. Green," he went on blandly, "and you will remember his admirable remark about some men being born masters and others born to obey, and that, if only Nature had made the difference in their mental capacities as apparent to the eye as is the difference in their bodies, everyone would recognize this at once."

His voice grew intense; the subject interested him.

"You may say," he went on, "that Aristotle, Plato and Socrates accepted the fact of slavery without protest because it was an institution from time immemorial, and so the idea did not appear to them so repugnant. But do you mean to tell me that such consummate geniuses, such unbiased, glorious brains would have glossed over any idea, or under-considered any point in their schemes for the advancement of men? They accepted slavery because they saw that it was the only possible way to make a republic work, where all citizens might aspire to be equal."

"You would advocate slavery, then? Oh! Mr. Derringham, how dreadful of you!" exclaimed Mrs. Cricklander, half playfully.

"Not in the least," he returned, still allowing some feeling to stay in his voice. "I should only have it recognized that there must be some class in my ideal republic who will do the duties of the slaves of old. I would have it so arranged that they should occupy this class only when they had shown they were unfit for anything higher, and I would also arrange it that the moment they appeared capable of rising out of it there should be no bar to their doing so. It is the cry of our all being equal because we have two arms and two legs and a head in common, not counting any mental endowment, which is utter trash and hypocrisy. But when these agitators are shouting for the people's rights and inciting poor ignorant wretches to revolt, they never suggest that the lowest of them is not perfectly suited to the highest position! Those occupying any station above the lowest have got there merely by superior luck and favoritism, not merit—that is what they preach."

Mr. Hanbury-Green was just going to answer with a biting attack when Miss Cora Lutworth's rather high voice was heard interrupting from a tall old chair in which she had perched herself.

"Why, Mr. Derringham, we all want to be something very grand," she laughed merrily. "I hate common people and love English dukes and duchesses—don't you, Cis?" and she looked at Mrs. Cricklander, who was standing in a position of much stately grace by the lofty mantelpiece.

"You sweet girl!" exclaimed Lord Freynault, who was next to her. "I cannot get any nearer to those favored folk than my uncle's being a duke, but won't you let me in for some of your friendly feelings on that account?"

"I certainly will," she answered archly, "because I like the way you look. I like how your hair is brushed, and how your clothes are cut, and your being nice and clean and outdoor—and long and thin—" and then she whispered—"ever so much better than Mr. Hanbury-Green's thick appearance. He may be as clever as clever, but he is common and climbing up, and I like best the people who are there!"

John Derringham now addressed himself exclusively to his hostess.

"I agree with the point of view of the old Greeks—they were so full of common sense. Balance and harmony in everything was their aim. A beautiful body, for instance, should be the correlative of a beautiful soul. Therefore in general their athletics were not pursued, as are ours, for mere pleasure and sport, and because we like to feel fit. They did not systematically exercise just to wrest from some rival the prize in the games, either. Their care of the body had a far higher and nobler end: to bring it into harmony as a dwelling-place for a noble soul."

"How divine!" said Mrs. Cricklander.

John Derringham went on:

"You remember Plato upon the subject—his reluctance to admit that a physical defect must sometimes be overlooked. But nowadays everything is distorted by ridiculous humanitarian nonsense. With our wonderful inventions, our increasing knowledge of sanitation and science, and the possibilities and limitations of the human body, what glorious people we should become if we could choke this double-headed hydra of rotten sentiment and exalt common sense!"

But now Mrs. Cricklander saw that a storm was gathering upon Mr. Hanbury-Green's brow and, admirable hostess that she was, she decided to smooth the troubled waters, so she went across the room to the piano, and began to play a seductive valse, while John Derringham followed her and leaned upon the lid, and tried to feel as devoted as he looked.

"Why cannot we go to-morrow and see your old master?" she asked, as her white fingers, with their one or two superb rings, glided over the keys. "I feel an unaccountable desire to become acquainted with him. I should love to see what the person was like who molded you when you were a boy."

"Mr. Carlyon is a wonderful-looking old man," John

Derringham returned. "Someone—who knows him very well—described him long ago as 'Cheiron.' You will see how apt it is when you meet."

Mrs. Cricklander crashed some chords. She had never heard of this Cheiron. She felt vaguely that Arabella had told her of some classical or mythological personage of some such sounding name, a boatman of sorts—but she dare not risk a statement, so she went on with the point she wished to gain, which was to investigate at once Mr. Carlyon's surroundings and discover, if possible, whether there was any influence there that would be inimical to herself.

"I dare say we can go to-morrow," John Derringham said. "You and I might walk over—and perhaps Miss Lutworth and Freynault. We can't go a large party, the house is so small."

"Why cannot you and I go alone, then?" she asked.

"Oh, I think he would like to see Miss Cora. She is such a charming girl," and John Derringham looked over to where she sat, still dangling a pair of blue satin feet from the high chair. And inwardly Mrs. Cricklander burned.

Cora was a second cousin of her divorced husband, and belonged by birth to that inner cream of New York society which she hated in her heart. Never, never again would she be so foolish as to chance crossing swords with one of her own nation. But aloud she acquiesced blandly and arranged that they should start at eleven o'clock.

"Perhaps we could persuade him to return to lunch with us?" she hazarded. "And that would be so nice."

"You must do what you can with him," John Derringham said. "I have prepared him to find you beautiful—as you are."

"You say lovely things about me behind my back, then?" she laughed. "Now he will be disappointed!"

"Yes, I admit it was a *bêtise*—but, being my real thoughts, they slipped out when I was there to-day. You will have to be extra charming to substantiate them."

Before Mrs. Cricklander went to bed, she called Arabella Clinker into her room.

"Arabella," she said, "who was Cheiron?" But she pronounced the "ei" as an "a," so Miss Clinker replied without any hesitation:

"He was a boatman who carried the souls of the dead over the River Styx, and to whom they were obliged to pay an obolus—son of Erebus and Nox. He is represented as an old man with a hideous face and long white beard and piercing eyes."

"Is there anything else I ought to know about him?" her employer asked, and Arabella thought for a moment.

"There is the story of Hercules not showing the golden bow. Er—it is a little complicated and has to do with the superstitions of the ancients—er—something Egyptian, I think, for a moment—I will look it up to-morrow. I can't say offhand."

"Thanks, Arabella. Good night."

And it was not until after the party of four had started next morning that Miss Clinker suddenly thought, with a start: "She may have been alluding to quite the other Cheiron—the Centaur—and in that case I have given her some wrong lights!"

CHAPTER XIV

CORA was being more than exasperating, Mrs. Cricklander thought, as they went through the park. Not content with Lord Freynault, who was plainly devoted to her, she kept every now and then looking back at John Derringham with some lively sally, and although he was being particularly agreeable to herself, he responded to Miss Lutworth's piquant attacks with a too ready zeal.

Mrs. Cricklander grew more and more certain that her hold over him had lessened in these last two days, and every force in her indomitable personality stiffened with determination to win him at all costs.

The Professor received them graciously. He was seated in his library, which now was a most comfortable room surrounded with bookcases in which lived all his rare editions of loved books. Nothing could be more fascinating than Mrs. Cricklander's manner to him—a mixture of deference and friendly familiarity, as though he would appreciate the fact of a tacit understanding between them that she too had a right in John Derringham's friends. She had been so reassured by finding that Mr. Carlyon was unmarried and lived alone, that a glow of real warmth towards the Professor emanated from her, while the conviction grew that it was nothing but the influence of Cora Lutworth which had even momentarily cooled her whilom ardent friend.

Mr. Carlyon's imperturbable countenance gave no hint of what he thought of her, although John Derringham watched him furtively and anxiously. He listened to their conversation when he could, and it jarred upon him twice when the lady of his choice altogether missed the point of Cheiron's subtle remarks. She whom he had always considered so understanding.

Of Halcyone there was no sign and no mention, and for some reason which he could not explain John Derringham felt glad.

It seemed an eternity before Mrs. Cricklander got up to go, having been unable to persuade Mr. Carlyon to return with them to luncheon. He had a slight cold, he said, and meant to remain in his warm library.

"Mr. Derringham says you are called Cheiron," Mrs. Cricklander announced laughingly. "How ridiculous to find in you any likeness to that old ferryman of the piercing eye. I see see no resemblance but in the beard."

"So John relegates me to the post of ferryman to the dead already, does he?" Mr. Carlyon responded. "I had *hoped* he still allowed me my horse's hoofs and my cave—I have been deceiving myself all these years, evidently."

A blank look grew in Mrs. Cricklander's eye. What had caves and horse's hoofs to do with the case? She had better turn the conversation at once, or she might be out of her depth, she felt; and this she did with her usual skill, but not before the Professor's left eyebrow had run up into his forehead, and his wise old eyes beneath had met and then instantly averted themselves from those of John Derringham.

All the way back to the house Mrs. Cricklander had the satisfaction of listening to a much more advanced admiration of herself than she had hoped to obtain so soon, and arrived in the best of restored humors—for John Derringham had clenched his teeth as he left the orchard house, and had told himself that he would not be influenced or put off by any of these trifling things, and that it was some vixenish turn of Fate to have allowed these currents of disillusion about a woman who was so eminently suitable to reach him through the medium of his old friend.

A strange thing happened to Halcyone that morning. She had made up her mind to keep away from her usual visit to Cheiron on the Monday and Tuesday when John Derringham had announced he might bring over his hostess to see the Professor. She did not wish to cause complications with her aunts by making Mrs. Cricklander's acquaintance, and underneath she had some strange reluctance herself. Her unerring instincts warned her that this woman might in some way trouble her life, but she thought Saturday would be perfectly safe and was preparing to start, when some vague longing came over to see her goddess. She had felt less serene since the day before, and John Derringham and his words and looks absorbed her thoughts. The home of Aphrodite was now in a chest in the long gallery, of which she kept the key, and as this old room was always empty—none of the servants, not even Priscilla, caring about visiting it—haunted, it was, they said—she had plenty of time to spend what hours she liked with her treasure without having to do so by stealth, as in the beginning. For any place indoors she loved the long gallery better than any other place. The broken window panes had been mended when the turn for the better came for the whole house, and now she herself kept it all dusted and tidy and used it as a sitting-room and work-room as well; and, above all, it was the temple of the goddess wherein was her shrine.

This day when Aphrodite was uncovered from her blue silk wrappings, her whole expression seemed to be one of appeal; however Halcyone would hold her, in high or low light, the eyes appeared to be asking her something.

"What is it, sweet mother and friend?" she said. "Do you not want me to leave you to-day? If so, indeed I will not. What are you telling me with those beautiful, sad eyes? That something is coming into my existence that you promised me always, and that it will cause me sorrow, and I must pause?"—and she shivered slightly and laid her cheek against the marble cheek. "I am not afraid, and I want whatever it must be, since it is life." Then she put the head back, and started upon her walk. But first one thing and then another delayed her, until last of all she sat down under the oak near the gap in the hedge and asked *herself* if all these things could be chance. And here she took to dreaming and watching the young rabbits come out of their holes, and to wondering what Fate held in store for her in the immediate future. What was going to be her life? That nothing but good could happen she always knew, because since the very beginning God—the same personal kindly force that she had always worshiped, unaltered by her deep learning, unweakened by any theological dissertations—was there manifesting the whole year round His wonderful love for the world.

And so she sat until the clock of the church at Sarthe-under-Crum struck one, and she started up, realizing that she was too late now to go on to Cheiron's and would only just have time to return for lunch with her aunts. She must go instead in the afternoon. So she walked briskly to the house, with a strange feeling of relief and joy, which she was quite unable to account for in any explicable way.

Nothing delayed her on her second attempt to reach the orchard house, and she found Cheiron placidly smoking while he read a volume of "Lucian." She was quite aware what that meant. When the Professor was in an amused and cynical humor he always read "Lucian," and although he knew every word by heart, it still caused him complete satisfaction, plainly to be discerned by the upward raising of the left penthouse brow.

Halcyone sat down and smiled sympathetically while she tried to detect which volume it was, that she might have some clew as to the cause of her Professor's mood. But he carefully closed the book, so that she could not see—it was the "Judgment of Paris" in the dialogue of the gods—and she was unable to have her curiosity gratified.

"Something has entertained you, Cheiron?" she said.

"I have had the visit of two goddesses," he answered, chuckling. "Our friend John Derringham brought them. He wanted to show them off and get my opinion, I think."

"And did you give him one?" she asked. "I suppose not!"

"He went away with his teeth shut—" and Mr. Carlyon's smile deepened as he stroked his white beard.

Halcyone laughed. She seldom asked questions herself. If the Professor wished to tell her anything about the ladies he would do so—she was dying to hear! Presently a set of disjointed sentences flowed from her master's lips between his puffs of smoke.

"Girl—worth something—showy—honest—sure of herself —clever—pretty—on her own roots—not a graft."

"Girl"—who was the girl? Halcyone wondered. But Cheiron continued his laconic utterances.

"Woman—beautiful—determined—thick—roots of the commonest—grafting of the best—octopean, tenacious—dangerous—my poor devil of a John!"

"And did you give the apple to either, Cheiron?" Halcyone asked with a gleam of fine humor in her wise eyes. "Or, one of the trio being absent, did you feel yourself excused?"

Mr. Carlyon glanced at her sharply, and then broke into a smile.

"Young woman, I do not think I have ever allowed you to read the Judgment of Paris," he said. "Wherefore your question is ill-timed and irrelevant."

Then they laughed together. How well they knew one another!—not only over things Greek. And presently they began their reading. They were in the middle of Symonds' "Renaissance," and so forgot the outer world.

But after Halcyone had gone in the dusk through the park, the Professor sat in the firelight for a while, and did not ring for lights. He was musing deeply, and his thoughts ran something in this line:

"John must dree his weird. Nothing anyone could say

has ever influenced him. If he marries this woman she will eat his soul; having only a sham one of her own, she will devour his. She'll do very well to adorn the London house and feed his friends. He'll find her out in less than a year —it will kill his inspirations. Well, Zeus and all the gods cannot help a man in his folly. But my business is to see that he does not ensnare the heart of my little girl. If he had waited he could have found her—the one woman with a soul."

. . . .

Miss Roberta had, unfortunately, a bad attack of rheumatism on Easter Sunday, augmented by a cold, and Halcyone stayed at home to rub her poor knee with hot oil, so she did not see the Wendover party, several of whom came to church. Miss La Sarthe occupied the family pew alone, and was the source of much amusement and delight to the smart inhabitants of the outer world.

"Isn't she just too sweet, Cis?" whispered Miss Lutworth into Mrs. Cricklander's ear. "Can't we get Mr. Derringham to take us over there this afternoon?"

But when the subject was broached later at luncheon by his hostess, John Derringham threw cold water upon the idea. He had stayed behind for a few minutes to renew his acquaintance with the ancient lady, and had given her his arm down the short church path, and placed her with extreme deference in the Shetland pony shay, to the absolute enchantment of Miss Lutworth, who, with Lord Freynault, stood upon the mound of an old forgotten grave, the better to see. It was in the earlier days of motor-cars, and Mrs. Cricklander's fine open Charron created the greatest excitement as it waited by the lych-gate. The two Shetlands cocked their ears and showed various signs of nervous interest, and William had all he could do to hold the minute creatures. But Miss La Sarthe behaved with unimpaired dignity, never once glancing in the direction of the great green monster. She got in, assisted by the respectful churchwarden, and allowed John Derringham to wrap the rug round her knees, and then carefully adjusted the ring of her turquoise-studded whip handle.

"Good day, Goddard," she said with benign condescension to the churchwarden. "And see that Betsy Hodges' child with the whooping-cough gets some of Hester's syrup and is not brought to church again next Sunday." And she nodded a gracious dismissal. Then, turning to John Derringham, she gave him two fingers, while she said with some show of haughty friendliness: "My sister and I will be very pleased to see you if you are staying in this neighborhood, Mr. Derringham, and care to take tea with us one day."

"I shall be more than delighted," he replied, as he bowed with homage and stood aside, because William's face betrayed his anxiety over the fidgety ponies.

Miss La Sarthe turned her head with its pork-pie hat and floating veil, and said with superb tranquillity, "You may drive on now, William." And they rolled off between a lane of respectful, curtseying rustics.

Mrs. Cricklander and Lady Maulevrier had already entered the motor and were surveying the scene with amused interest, while Miss Lutworth and Lord Freynault, chaperoned by Arabella Clinker, were preparing to walk. It was not more than a mile across the park, and it was a glorious day. John Derringham joined them.

"I think I will come with you, too," he said. "You take my place, Sir Tedbury. It is only fair you should drive one way."

And so it was arranged, not altogether to the satisfaction of the hostess, who would have preferred to have walked also. However, there was nothing to be done, and so they were whizzed off, while with the tail of her eye Cecilia Cricklander perceived that Lord Freynault had been displaced from Cora's side and was now stalking behind the other pair, beside Arabella Clinker.

"What an extraordinary sight that was," she said to Sir Tedbury Delvine as they went along. "I thought no villagers curtsied any more now in England. That very funny-looking old lady might have been a royalty!"

"It is because she has never had a doubt but what she is— or something higher—complete owner of all these souls," he returned, "that they have not yet begun to doubt it either. They and their forebears have bobbed to the La Sarthe for hundreds of years, and they will go on doing it if this holder of the name lives to be ninety-nine. They would never do so to any new-comer, though, I expect."

"But I am told they have not a penny left, and have sold every acre of the land except the park. Is it not wonderful, Kitty?" Mrs. Cricklander went on, turning to Lady Maulevrier. "I am dying to know them. I hope they will call."

But Sir Tedbury had already chanced to have talked the matter over with John Derringham, because he himself was most anxious to see La Sarthe Chase, which was of deep historical interest, and had incidentally been made aware by the gentleman of the old ladies' views, so he hastily turned the conversation, rather awkwardly, to other things.   And a wonder grew in Mrs. Cricklander's mind.

That anyone should not be enchanted to recieve her beautiful and sought-after self could not enter her brain, but there was evidently some bar between the acquaintance of herself and her nearest neighbors, and Arabella should be sent to find out of what it consisted.

CHAPTER XV

"Do let us go around by the boundary," Miss Lutworth said when they got through the Wendover gates. "I long to see even the park of that exquisite old lady; it must look quite different to anybody else's, and I feel I want an adventure!"

So they struck in towards the haw-haw—the four walking almost abreast.

When they came to beyond the copse, after it touched the Professor's garden, they paused and took in the view. It was unspeakably beautiful from there, rolling away towards the splendid old house, which could only be just distinguished through the giant trees, not yet in leaf. And suddenly, hardly twenty yards from them across the gulf, coming from the gap in Mr. Carlyon's hedge, they saw a tall and very slender mouse-colored figure, as Halcyone emerged on her homeward way—she had run down to see Cheiron when her duties with Miss Roberta were over, and was now going back to lunch.

"Good morning!" called John Derringham, and the four advanced to the very edge of their side, and Halcyone turned and also bordered hers, while she bowed serenely.

"Isn't it a day of the gods!" he continued. "And may I from across this Stygian lake (there was a little water collected in the haw-haw here from the recent rains) introduce Miss Lutworth to you—and Miss Clinker and Lord Freynault? Miss Halcyone La Sarthe."

Everyone bowed, and Halcyone smiled her sweet, grave smile.

"We would love to jump over—or you come to us," Cora Lutworth said with her frank, friendly charm. "Isn't there any way?"

"I am afraid not," responded Halcyone. "You are across in another world—we live in the shades, this side."

"Remember something about a fellow named Orpheus getting over to fetch his girl"—"gail" Lord Freynault pronounced it—"since old John will use Eton cribs in describing the horrid chasm. Can't we sop old Cerberus and somehow manage to swim, if there is no ferryman about?"

"You would certainly be drowned," said Halcyone. "In this place the lake is quite ten inches deep!"

Cora Lutworth was taking in every bit of her with her clever, kindly eyes.

"What a sweet, distinguished violet-under-the-mossy bank pet of a girl!" she was saying to herself. "No wonder Mr. Derringham goes to see his Professor! How mad Cis would be! I shan't tell her." And aloud she said:

"You cannot imagine how I am longing to get a nearer peep of your beautiful old house. Do we get a chance further on?"

"No," said Halcyone. "I am so sorry. You branch further off once you have passed the closed gate. It was very stupid—the La Sarthe quarreled with the Wendovers a hundred years ago, and it was all closed up then, and these wicked spikes put."

"It is too tantalizing. But won't you walk with us to where we have to part?" Miss Lutworth said, while John Derringham had a sudden longing to turn back and carefully remove certain bits of iron and brick he wot of, and ask this nymph of the woods to take him on to their tree, and tell him more stories about Jason and Medea in that exquisitely refined voice of hers, as she had done once before, long ago. But even though he might not have this joy, he got rather a fine pleasure out of the fact of sharing the secret of the crossing with her, and he had the satisfaction of meeting her soft eyes in one lightning comprehending glance.

They chatted on about the view and the beauties of the neighborhood, and they all laughed often at some sally of Cora's—no one could resist her joyous, bubbling good-fellowship. She had all the sparkle of her clever nation, and the truest, kindest heart. Halcyone had never spoken to another young girl in her life, and felt like a yearling horse—a desire to whinny to a fellow colt and race up and down with him beside the dividing fence of their paddocks. A new light of youth and sweetness came into her pale face.

"I do wish I might ask you to come round by the road," she said, "and see it near, but, as Mr. Derringham knows, my aunts are very old, and one is almost an invalid now, so we never have any visitors at all."

"Of course, we quite understand," said Cora, quickly, touched at once by this simple speech. "But we should so love you to come over to us."

"Alas!" said Halcyone, "it is indeed the Styx."

And here they arrived at the boarded-up gate, where further view was impossible, and from which onwards the lands ceased to join.

"Good-by!" they called to one another, even Arabella Clinker joining in the chorus, while Cora Lutworth ran back to say:

"Some day we'll meet—outside the Styx. Let us get Mr. Derringham to manage it!"

And Halcyone cried a glad "Oh, yes!"

"What a darling! What a perfect darling!" Miss Lutworth said enthusiastically, taking Arabella's arm as they struck rapidly inward and up a knoll. "Did you ever see anything look so like a lady in that impossible old dress? Tell us about her, Mr. Derringham. Does she live with those prehistoric ladies all alone in that haunted house? Could anything be so mysterious and romantic? Please tell us all you know."

"Yes, she does, I believe," John Derringham said. "My old master tells me she never sees or speaks to anyone from one year's end to another. I have only met her very rarely myself."

"Does it not seem too awful?" returned Cora, aghast, thinking of her own merry, enjoyable life, with every whim gratified. "To be so young and attractive and actually buried alive! Don't you think she is a dream, Arabella?"

"I was greatly impressed with her distinction and charm," Miss Clinker said. "I wish we could do something for her to make things brighter."

"Let us ask Ci—" and then Miss Lutworth paused, returning to her first thought—she knew her hostess well. No, it could not bring any pleasure into the life of this slender, lithe English lady with the wonderful Greek name, to be made acquainted with Cecilia Cricklander, who would tear her to pieces without compunction the moment she understood in what direction John Derringham's eyes would probably be cast. He saw Cora's hesitation and understood, and was grateful.

"I believe this girl is trumps. I don't think she will even mention our meeting," he said to himself.

Now for a few steps Miss Lutworth drew Arabella Clinker on ahead.

"Arabella, you dear," she whispered, "I don't want to say a word against Cis—who, of course, is all right—but I have a feeling we won't tell her we've met this dryad of a Halcyone La Sarthe. Have you got that instinct, too?"

"Quite strongly," said Arabella, who never wasted words. "I was going to mention to you the same idea myself."

"Then that is understood!" and she laughed her happy laugh. "I'll see that Freynie doesn't peach!"

Thus it was that four demure and healthful-looking beings joined the party on the terrace of Wendover, and described their pleasant walk, without one word spoken of their *rencontre* with the youngest Miss La Sarthe. And once or twice Cora Lutworth's mischievous eyes met those of John Derringham, and they both laughed.

CHAPTER XVI

JOHN DERRINGHAM made a point of slipping away on the Easter Tuesday afternoon; he determined to drink tea with the Misses La Sarthe. He went to his room with important letters to write, and then sneaked down again like a truant schoolboy, and when he got safely out of sight, struck obliquely across the park to the one vulnerable spot in the haw-haw, and after fumbling a good deal, from his side, managed to get the spikes out and climb down, and repeat the operation upon the other side. There was no water here, it was on rather higher ground, and he was soon striding up the beech avenue towards the house.

"It would be an extremely awkward place to get over in the dark," he thought, and then he was conscious that Halcyone was far in the distance in front of him, almost entering the house.

So she would be in, then—that was good.

He had never permitted his mind to dwell upon her for an instant, after the Sunday walk. He made himself tell himself that she was a charming child whom he felt great pity for, on account of her lonely life. That he himself took a special interest in her he would not have admitted for a second to his innermost thought. He had now definitely made up his mind to propose to Cecilia Cricklander, and was only awaiting a suitable occasion to put this intention into effect.

Numbers of moments had come—and passed—but he was always able to find good and sufficient fault with them. And once or twice, when Fate itself seemed to arrange things for him, he had a sudden sensation as of a swimmer fighting with the tide, and he had battled to the shore again, and was still free!

But it must come, of course, and before he left for London at the end of the week. Private news had reached him that the Government must soon go out, and he felt this thing must be an accomplished fact before then, for the hand he meant to play.

But meanwhile it was only Tuesday, and he was nearing the battered and nail-bestudded front door of La Sarthe

96

Chase. William said the ladies were at home, and he was shown into the Italian parlor forthwith.

It had not changed in the slightest degree in the seven years since he had seen it first, nor had the two ancient spinsters themselves. They were most graciously glad to receive him, and gave him tea out of the thinnest china cups, and at last Miss Roberta said:

"Our great-niece Halcyone will be coming down in a moment, Mr. Derringham. She has grown up into a very tall girl. You will hardly recognize her, I expect."

And at that instant Halcyone opened the door and said a quiet word of welcome. And if her heart beat rather faster than usual under her simple serge bodice, nothing of any emotion showed in her tranquit face.

She took her tea and sat down in a chair rather in the shadows and aloof.

Miss La Sarthe monopolized the conversation. She had no intention of relinquishing the pleasure of this rare guest, so while Miss Roberta got in a few sentences, Halcyone hardly spoke a word, and if she had really been a coquette, calculating her actions, she could not have piqued John Derringham more.

She looked so very sylph-like as she sat there, bending her graceful head. Her eyes were all in shadow and seemed to gleam as things of mystery from under her dark brows, while the pure lines of her temples and the plaiting of her soft thick hair made him think of some virgin goddess.

But she never spoke.

At last John Derringham began to grow exasperated, and plunged into temptation, which he did not admit that he ought to have avoided.

"I am so very much interested in this wonderful old house," he said, addressing Miss La Sarthe. "That row of bay windows is in a long gallery, I suppose? Would it be a great impertinence if I asked to see it?"

"We shall be pleased for you to do so," the old lady returned, without much warmth. "It is very cold and draughty, my sister and I have not entered it for many years, but Halcyone, I believe, goes there sometimes; she will show it to you if you wish."

Halcyone rose, ready at once to obey her aunts, and led the way towards the door.

"We had better go up the great staircase and along through Sir Timothy's rooms. The staircase which leads directly to it from the hall is not quite safe," she said.

"Except for me," she addded, when they were outside the door. "Then, I know exactly where to put my feet!"

"I would follow you blindly," said John Derringham, "but we will go which way you will. Only, you are such a strange, silent little old friend now—I am afraid of you!"

Halcyone was rather ahead, leading the way, and she turned and paused while he came up close beside her.

Her eyes were quite startled.

"You afraid of me!" she said.

"Yes—you seem so nymph-like and elusive. I do not know if I am really looking at an ordinary earth-maiden, or whether you will melt away."

"I am quite real," and she smiled, "but now you must notice these two rooms a little that we shall pass through. They are very ghostly I think; they were the Sir Timothy's who went to fetch James I from Scotland. I am glad they are not mine, but the long gallery I love; it is my sitting-room—my very own—and in it I keep something which matters to me more than anything else in the world." Then she went on, with a divine shyness which thrilled her companion: "And—I do not know why—but I think I will show it to you."

"Yes, please do that," he responded eagerly, "and do not let us stop to look at the ghostly apartments—where you sit interests me far more."

So they went rapidly through Sir Timothy's rooms, with the great state bed where had slept his royal master, so the tale ran, and on down some uneven steps, and through a small door, and there found themselves in the long, narrow room, with its bays along the southern side, and one splendid mullioned casement at the end with coats-of-arms emblazoned upon each division. And through this, which looked west, there poured the lowered afternoon sun with a broad shaft of glorious light.

The place was almost empty, but for a chest or two and a table near this window with writing material and books. And upon a rough set of shelves close at hand many more volumes reposed.

"So it is here you live and work, you wise, lonely, little Pallas Athené," he said.

"You must not call me that—I am not at all like her," Halcyone answered softly. "She was very clever and very noble—but a little hard, I think. Wait until I have shown you my own goddess. I would rather have her soul than any other of the Olympian gods."

John Derringham took a step nearer to her.

"Do you remember the night at dinner here when you told me Pallas Athené's words to Perseus?" he said. "I have thought of them often, and they have helped me sometimes, I think."

"I am so glad," said Halcyone simply, while she moved towards her treasure chest.

He watched her with satisfied eyes—every action of hers was full of grace, and the interest he felt in her personally obscured any for the moment in what she was going to show him, but at last he became aware that she had unlocked a cupboard drawer, and was taking from it a bundle of blue silk.

His curiosity was aroused, and he went over as near as he could.

"Come!" whispered Halcyone, and walked to the high window-sill of the middle section, and then put down her burden upon the old faded velvet seat.

"See, I will take off her veil gradually," she said, "and you must tell me of what she makes you think."

John Derringham was growing interested by now, but had no idea in the world of the marvel he was going to see. He started more perceptibly than even Mr. Carlyon had done seven years before, when he had realized the superlative beauty of the Greek head.

Halcyone uncovered it reverently, and then took a step back and waited silently for him to speak.

He looked long into the marvelous face, and then he said as though he were dreaming:

"Aphrodite herself!"

"Ah, I felt you would know and recognize her at once— Yes, that is her name. Oh, I am glad!" and Halcyone clapped her hands. "She is my mother, and so, you see, I am never alone here, for she speaks always to me of love."

John Derringham looked at her sharply as she said this, and in her eyes he saw two wells of purity, each with an evening star melted into its depths.

And he suddenly was conscious of something which his whole life had missed—for he knew he did not know what real love meant, not even that which his mother might have given him, if she had lived.

He did not speak for a moment; he gazed into Halcyone's face. It seemed as if a curtain had lifted for one instant and given him a momentary glimpse into some heaven, and then dropped again, leaving a haunting memory of sweetness, the more beautiful because indistinct.

"Love—" he said, still dreamily. "Surely there is yet another and a deeper kind of love."

Halcyone raised her head, while a strange look grew in her wide eyes, almost of fear. It was as though he had put into words some unspoken, unadmitted thought.

"Yes," she said very softly, "I feel there is—but that is not all peace; that must be gloriously terrible, because it would mean life."

He looked at her fully now; there was not an atom of coquetry or challenge; her face was pale and exquisite in its simple intentness. He turned to the goddess again, and almost chaunted:

"Oh! Aphrodite of the divine lips and soulful eyes, what mystery do you hold for us mortals? What do you promise us? What do you make us pay? Is the good worth the anguish? Is the fulfillment a cup worth draining—without counting the cost?"

"What does she answer you?" whispered Halcyone. "Does she say that to live and fulfill destiny as the beautiful years does is the only good? It is wiser not to question and weigh the worth, for even though we would not drink, perhaps we cannot escape—since there is Fate."

John Derringham pulled himself together with an effort. He felt he was drifting into wonderland, where the paths were too tenderly sweet and flowered for him to dare to linger, for there he might find and quaff of the poison cup. So he said in a voice which he strove to bring back to earth:

"Where did you get the beautiful thing? She is of untold value, of course you know?"

Halcyone took the marble into her hands lovingly.

"She came to me out of the night," she said. "Some day I might tell you how—but not to-day. I must put her back again. No one knows but Cheiron and me—and now—you —that she is in existence, and no one else must ever know."

He did not speak; he watched her while she wrapped the head in its folds of silk.

"Aphrodite never had so true a priestess, nor one so pure," he thought, and a strange feeling of sadness came over him, and he thanked her rather abruptly for showing him her treasure, and they went silently back through Sir Timothy's room, and down the stair; and in the Italian parlor he said good-by at once, and left.

The wind had got up and blew freshly in his face. There would be a gale before morning. It suited his mood. He struck across the park, but instead of making for the haw-haw, he turned into Cheiron's little gate. He wanted understanding company, he wanted to talk cynical philosophy, and he wanted the stimulus of his old master's biting wit.

But when he got there, he found Cheiron very taciturn—contributing little more than a growl now and then, while he smoked his long pipe and played with his beard. So at last he got up to go.

"I have made up my mind to marry Mrs. Cricklander, Master," he said.

"I suppose so," the Professor replied dryly. "A man always has to convince himself he is doing a fine thing when he gives himself up to be hanged."

CHAPTER XVII

John Derringham reached Wendover—by the road and the lodge gates—in an impossible temper. He had left the orchard house coming as near to a quarrel with his old master as such a thing could be. He absolutely refused to let himself dwell upon the anger he had felt; and if Fate had given him a distinct and pointed chance to ask the fair Cecilia for her lily hand, when he knocked at her sitting-room door before dinner, he would no doubt have left the next day—summoned again to London by his Chief—an engaged man. But this turn of events was not in the calculations of Destiny for the moment, and he found no less a person than Mr. Hanbury-Green already ensconced by his hostess's side. They were both smoking and looked very comfortable and at ease.

"I just came in to tell you I shall be obliged to tear myself away to-morrow," John Derringham said, "and cannot have the pleasure of staying to the end of the week in this delightful place."

Mrs. Cricklander got up from her reclining position among the cushions. This was a blow. She wished now she had not encouraged Mr. Hanbury-Green to come and sit with her; it might be a lost opportunity which it would be difficult to recapture again. But she had felt so very much annoyed at Mr. Derringham's capriciousness, displayed the whole of the Monday, and then at at his absenting himself to-day, having gone to see the Professor, of course—since he was out of the house at tea-time when she had sent to his room to enquire—that she had determined to see what a little jealousy would do for him. But if he were off on the morrow this might not be a safe moment to try it.

Mr. Hanbury-Green, however, had not the slightest intention of giving up his place, in spite of several well-directed hints, and sat on like one belonging to the spot.

So they all had to go off to dress without any longed-for word having been spoken. And Mrs. Cricklander was far too circumspect a hostess to attempt to arrange a *tête-à-tête* after dinner under the eye of an important social leader like Lady Maulevrier, whom she had only just succeeded in enticing to stay in her country house. So, with the usual semi-political chaff, the evening passed, and good-nights and good-bys were said, and early next day John Derringham left for London.

He would write—he decided—and all the way up in the train he buried himself in the engrossing letters and papers he had received from his Chief by the morning's post.

And for the next six weeks he was in such a turmoil of hard work and deep and serious questions about a foreign State that he very seldom had time to go into society, and when at last he was a little more free, Mrs. Cricklander, he found, had not returned from Paris, whither she always went several times a year for her clothes.

But they had written to one another once or twice.

He had promised in the last letter that he would go down to Wendover again for Whitsuntide, and this time he firmly determined nothing should keep him from his obvious and delectable fate.

Mrs. Cricklander had no haunting fears now. She could discover no reason for John Derringham's change towards her. Arabella had been mute and had put it down to the stress of his life. This tension with the foreign State, it leaked out, had been known to the Ministers for a week before it had been made public—that, of course, was the cause of his preoccupation, and she would simply order some especially irresistible garments in Paris, and bide her time.

He wrote the most charming letters, though they were hardly long enough to be called anything but notes; but there was always the insinuation in them that she was the one person in the world who understood him, and they were expressed with his usual cultivated taste.

It was sheer force of will that kept John Derringham from ever thinking of Halcyone. He resolutely crushed the thought of her every time it presented itself, and systematically turned to his work and plunged into it, if even a mental vision of her came into his mind's eye.

He felt quite calm and safe when, two days before he was expected at Wendover, the idea came to him to propose himself to the Professor, so as not to have to go and see him and endure his cynical reflections *after* he should be engaged to his hostess.

Mr. Carlyon had wired back, "Come if you like," and on this evening in early June John Derringham arrived at the orchard house.

Cheiron made no allusion to the matter that had caused them to part with some breezy words upon his old pupil's side. Mrs. Cricklander or Wendover might not have existed; their talk was upon philosophy and politics, and contained not the shadow of a woman—even Halcyone was not mentioned at all.

Whitsuntide fell late that year, at the end of the first week in June, and the spring having been exceptionally mild, the foliage was all in full beauty of the freshest green.

It was astonishingly hot, and every divine scent of the night came to John Derringham as he went out into the garden before going to bed. A young setting half-moon still hung in the sky, and there were stars. One of those nights, when all the mystery of life seems to be revealing itself in the one word—Love. The nightingale throbbed out its note in the copse amidst a perfect stillness, and the ground was soft without a drop of dew.

John Derringham, hatless, and with his hands plunged in the pockets of his dinner coat, wandered down the garden towards the apple tree, picking an early red rosebud as he passed a bush—its scent intoxicated him a little. Then he went to the gate, and, opening it, he strolled into the park. Here was a vaster and more perfect view. It was all clothed in the unknown of the half dark, and yet he could distinguish the outline of the giant trees. He went on as if in some delicious dream, which yet had some heart-break in it, and at last he came to the tree where he and Halcyone had sat those seven years ago, when she had told him of what consisted the true point of honor in a man. He remembered it all vividly, her very words and the cloud of her soft hair which had blown a little over his face. He sat down upon the fallen log that had been made into a rude bench; and there he gazed in front of him, unconscious now of any coherent thought.

Suddenly he was startled by a laugh so near him and so soft that he believed himself to be dreaming, but he looked round and quickly rose to his feet, and there at the other side of the tree he saw standing the ethereal figure of a girl, while her filmy gray garments seemed to melt into the night.

"Halcyone!" he gasped. "And from where?"

"Ah!" she said as she came towards him. "You have invaded my kingdom. Mortal, what right have you to the things of the night? They belong to me—who know them and love them."

"Then have compassion upon me, sweet dryad!" he pleaded, "who am but a pilgrim who cannot see his way. Let me shelter under your protection and be guided aright."

She laughed again—a ripple of silver that he had not guessed her voice possessed. Her whole bearing was changed from the reserved, demure and rather timid creature whom he knew. She was a sprite now, or a nymph, or even a goddess, for her brow was imperious and her mien one of assured command.

"This is my kingdom," she said, "and if you obey me, I will show you things of which you have never dreamed—" and then she came towards the tree and sat upon the high forked branch of the broken bough while she pointed with shadowy finger to the part which was a bench. "Sit there, Man of Day," she ordered, "for you cannot see beyond your hand. You cannot know how the living things are creeping about, unafraid now of your cruel power. You cannot discern the difference in the colors of the fresh young bracken and the undergrowth; you cannot perceive the birds asleep in the tree."

"No, indeed, Lady of Night," he said, "I admit I am but a mole, but you will let me perceive them with your eyes, will you not?"

She slipped from her perch suddenly, before he could put out a protesting hand to stop her, and glided out of his view into the dark of the copse, and from there he heard the intoxicating silver laughter which maddened his every sense.

"Halcyone! Witch!" he called. "Come back to me—I am afraid, all alone!"

So she came, appearing like a materializing wraith from the shadow, and with an undulating movement of incredible grace she was again seated upon her perch, the fallen forked branch of the tree.

John Derringham was experiencing the strongest emotion he had ever felt in his life.

A maddening desire to seize the elusive joy—to come nearer—to assure himself that she was real and not a spirit of night sent to torture and elude him—overcame all other thought. The startling change from her deportment of the day—the very way she glided about was as the movement of some other being.

And as those old worshippers of Dionysus had grown intoxicated with the night and the desire of communion with the beyond, so he—John Derringham—cool, calculating English statesman—felt himself being drawn into a current of emotion and enthrallment whose end could only be an ecstasy of which he did not yet dare to dream.

It was all so abnormal—to see her here, a shadow, a tantalizing soft shadow with a new personality—it was no wonder he rubbed his eyes and asked himself if he were awake.

"Come with me," she whispered, bending nearer to him, "and I will show you how the wild roses grow at night."

"I will follow you to Hades," he said, "but I warn you I cannot see a yard beyond my nose. You must lead me with your hand, if so ethereal a spirit possesses a hand."

Again the silver laugh, and he saw her not, but presently she appeared from behind the tree. She had let down her misty, mouse-colored hair, and it floated around her like a cloud.

Then she slipped a cool, soft set of fingers into his, and led him onward, with sure and certain steps, while he blundered, not knowing where to put his feet, and all the time she turned every few seconds and looked at him, and he could just distinguish the soft mystery of her eyes, while now and then, as she walked, a tendril of her floating hair flew out and caressed his face, as once before, long ago.

"There are fairy things all about us," she said. "Countless pink campions and buttercups, with an elf in each. They will feel your giant feet, but they will know you are a mortal and cannot help your ways, because, you poor, blind bat, you cannot see!"

"And you?" he asked. "Who gave you these eyes?"

"My mother," she answered softly, "the Goddess of the Night."

And then she drew him on rapidly and stealthily, and he saw at last, in the open space where the stars and the sinking moon gave more light, that they were approaching the broken gate, and were near the terraced garden, which now was better kept.

When they got to this barrier to their path, Halcyone paused and leaned upon it.

"Mortal," she said, "you are wandering in a maze. You have come thus far because I have led you, but you should have fallen if you had walked so fast alone. Now look, and I will show you the lily-of-the-valley cups—there are only a few there under the shelter of the gray stone arch. Come."

And she opened the gate, letting go of his hand as she glided beyond.

"I cannot and will not hazard a step if you leave me," he

called, and she came back and gave him again her soft fingers to hold. So at last they reached the summer house at the end of the second terrace, where the archway was where old William kept his tools.

There were very few flowers out, but a mass of wild roses, and still some May tulips bloomed, while from the meadow beneath them came that indescribable freshness which young clover gives.

John Derringham knew now that he was dreaming—or drunk with some nectar which was not of earth. And still she led him on, and then pointed to the old bench which he could just see.

"We shall sit here," she said, "and Aphrodite shall tell us your future—for see, she, too, loves the night and comes here with me."

And to his intense astonishment, as he peered on to the table, he saw a misty mass of folds of silk, and there lay the goddess's head, that Halcyone had shown to him that day in the long gallery more than a month ago.

He was so petrified with surprise at the whole thing that he had ceased to reason. Everything came now as a matter of course, like the preposterous sequence of events in a dream. The Aphrodite lay, as a woman caressed, half buried in her silken folds, but Halcyone lifted her up and propped her against a stone vase which was near, letting the silk fall so that the broken neck did not show, and it seemed as if a living woman's face gazed down upon them.

John Derringham's eyes were growing more accustomed to the darkness, or Halcyone really had some magic power, for it seemed to him that he could see the divine features quite clearly.

"She is saying," the soft voice of his companion whispered in his ear, "that all the things you will grasp with your hands are but dreams—and the things that you now believe to be dreams are all real."

"And are you a dream, you sweet?" asked John Derringham. "Or are you tangible, and must I drink the poison cup, after all?"

"I would give you no noxious wine," she answered. "If you were strong and wise and true, only the fire which I have stolen from heaven could come to you."

"Long ago," he said, "you gave me an oak-leaf, dryad, and I have kept it still. What now will you grant to me?"

"Nothing, since you fear—" and she drew back.

"I do not fear," he answered wildly. "Halcyone—sweetheart! I want you—here—next my heart. Give me—yourself!"

Then he stretched out his arms and drew her to him, all soft and loving and unresisting, and he pressed his lips to her pure and tender lips. And it seemed as if the heavens opened, and the Night poured down all that was divine of bliss.

But before he could be sure that indeed he held her safely in his arms, she started forward, releasing herself. Then, clasping Aphrodite and her silken folds, with a bound she was far beyond him, and had disappeared in the shadow of the archway, on whose curve the last rays of moonlight played, so that he saw it outlined and clear.

He strode forward to follow her, but to his amazement, when he reached the place, she seemed to vanish absolutely in front of his eyes, and although he lit a match and searched everywhere, not the slightest trace of her could he find, and there was no opening or possible corner into which she could have disappeared.

Absolutely dumbfounded, he groped his way back to the bench, and sitting down buried his head in his hands. Surely it was all a dream, then, and he had been drunk—with the Professor's Falernian wine—and had wandered here and slept. But, God of all the nights, what an exquisite dream!

CHAPTER XVIII

THE half-moon set, and the night became much darker before John Derringham rose from his seat by the bench. A stupor had fallen upon him. He had ceased to reason. Then he got up and made his way back to the orchard house, under the myriads of pale stars, which shone with diminished brilliancy from the luminous summer night sky.

Here he seemed to grow material again and to realize that he was indeed awake. But what had happened to him? Whether he had been dreaming or no, a spell had fallen upon him—he had drunk of the poison cup. And Halcyone filled his mind. He thrilled and thrilled again as he remembered the exquisite joy of their tender embrace—even though it had been no real thing, but a dream, it was still the divinest good his life had yet known.

But what could it lead to if it were real? Nothing but sorrow and parting and regret. For his career still mattered to him, he knew, now that he was in his sane senses again, more than anything else in the world. And he could not burden himself with a poor, uninfluential girl as a wife, even though the joy of it took them both to heaven.

The emotion he was experiencing was one quite new to him, and he almost resented it, because it was upsetting some of his beliefs.

The next day, at breakfast, the Professor remarked that he looked pale.

"You rather overwork, John," he said. "To lie about the garden here and not have to follow the caprices of fashionable ladies at Wendover, would do you a power of good."

There was no sight of Halcyone all the day. She was living in a paradise, but hers contained no doubts or uncertainties. She knew that indeed she had lived and breathed the night before, and found complete happiness in John Derringham's arms.

That, then, was what Aphrodite had always been telling her. She knew now the meaning of the love in her eyes. This glorious and divine thing had been given to her, too—out of the night.

It was fully perceived at last, not only half glanced at

almost with fear. Love had come to her, and whatever might reck of sorrow, it meant her whole life and soul.

And this precious gift of the pure thing from God she had given in her turn to John Derringham as his lips had pressed her lips.

She spent the whole day in the garden, sitting in the summer house surveying the world. The blue hills in the far distance were surely the peaks of Olympus and she had been permitted to know what existence meant there.

Not a doubt of him entered her heart, or a fear. He certainly loved her as she loved him; they had been created for each other since the beginning of time. And it was only a question of arrangement when she should go away with him and never part any more.

Marriage, as a ceremony in church, meant nothing to her. Some such thing, of course, must take place, because of the stupid conventions of the world, but the sacrament, the real mating, was to be together—alone.

In her innocent and noble soul John Derringham now reigned as king. He had never had a rival, and never would have while breath stayed in her fair body.

By the evening of that day he had reasoned himself into believing that the whole thing was a dream—or, if not a dream, he had better consider it as such; but at the same time, as the dusk grew, a wild longing swelled in his heart for its recurrence, and when the night came he could not any longer control himself, and as he had done before he wandered to the tree.

The moon, one day beyond its first quarter, was growing brighter, and a strange and mysterious shimmer was over everything as though the heat of the day were rising to give welcome and fuse itself into the night.

He was alone with the bird who throbbed from the copse, and as he sat in the sublime stillness he fancied he saw some does peep forth. They were there, of course, with their new-born fawns.

But where was she, the nymph of the night?

His heart ached, the longing grew intense until at was a mighty force. He felt he could stride across the luminous park which separated them, and scale the wall to the casement window of the long gallery, to clasp her once more in his arms. And, as it is with all those beings who have scorned and denied his power, Love was punishing him now by a complete annihilation of his will. At last he buried his face in his hands; it was almost agony that he felt.

When he uncovered his eyes again he saw, far in the distance, a filmy shadow. It seemed to be now real, and now a wraith, as it flitted from tree to tree, but at last he knew it was real—it was she—Halcyone! He started to his feet, and there stood waiting for her.

She came with the gliding movement he now knew belonged in her dual personality to the night.

Her hair was all unbound, and her garment was white.

All reason, all resolution left him. He held out his arms. "My love!" he cried. "I have waited for you—ah, so long!"

And Halcyone allowed herself to be clasped next his heart, and then drawn to the bench, where they sat down, blissfully content.

They had such a number of things to tell one another about love. He who had always scoffed at its existence was now eloquent in his explanation of the mystery. And Halcyone, who had never had any doubts, put her beautiful thoughts into words. Love meant everything—it was just he, John Derringham. She was no more herself, but had come to dwell in him.

She was tender and absolutely pure in her broad loyalty, concealing nothing of her fondness, letting him see that if she were Mistress of the Night, he was Master of her Soul.

And the complete subservience of herself, the sublime transparency without subterfuge of her surrender, appealed to everything of chivalry which his nature held.

"Since the beginning," she whispered, in that soft, sweet voice of hers which seemed to him to be of the angels, "ever since the beginning, John, when I was a little ignorant girl, it has always been you. You were Jason and Theseus and Perseus. You were Sir Bors and Sir Percival and Sir Lancelot. And I knew it just waiting—Fate."

"My sweet, my sweet," he murmured, kissing her hair.

"And the time you came, when I was so ugly," she went on, "and so over-grown—I was sad then, because I knew you would not like me. But the winds and the night were good to me. I have grown, you see, so that I am now more as you would wish, but everything has been for you from that first day in the tree—our tree."

That between two lovers the thing could be a game never entered her brain. The thought that it might be wiser to watch moods and play on this one or that, and conceal her feelings and draw him on with mystery, could meet with no faintest understanding in her fond heart.

She just loved him, and belonged to him, and that was the whole meaning of heaven and earth. Any trick of calculation would have been a thousand miles beneath her feet. And while he was there with her, clasping her slender willowy form to his heart, John Derringham felt exalted. The importance of his career dwindled, the imperative necessity of possessing Halcyone for his very own augmented, until at last he whispered in her ear as her little head lay there upon his breast:

"Darling child, you must marry me at once—immediately—next week. We will go through whatever is necessary at the registry-office, and then you must come away with me and be my very own."

"Of course," was all she said.

"It is absolutely impossible that we could let anyone know about it at present—even Cheiron—" he went on, a little hurriedly. "The circumstances are such that I cannot publicly own you as my wife, although it would be my glory so to do. I should have to give up my whole career, because I have no money to keep a splendid home, which would be your due. But I dare say these things do not matter to you any more than they do to me. Is it so, sweet, darling child?"

"How could they matter?" Halcyone whispered from the shelter of his clasped arms. "Of what good would they be to me? I want to be with you when you have time; I want to caress you when you are tired, and comfort you, and inspire you, and love you, and bring you peace. How could the world—which I do not know—matter to me? Are you not foolish to ask me such questions, John!"

"Very foolish, my divine one," he said, and forgot what more he would have spoken in the delirium of a worshiping kiss.

But presently he brought himself back to facts again.

"Darling," he said, "I will find out exactly how everything can be managed, and then you will meet me here, under this tree, and we will go away together and be married, and for a week at least I will make the time to stay with you, as your lover, and you shall be absolutely and truly my sweetest wife."

"Yes," said Halcyone, perfectly content.

"And after that," he went on, "I will arrange that you stay somewhere near me, so that every moment that I am free I can come back to the loving glory of your arms."

"I cannot think of any other heaven," the tender creature

murmured. And then she nestled closer, and her voice became dreamy.

"This is what God means in everything," she whispered. "In the Springtime, which is waiting for the Summer—in all the flowers and all the trees. This is the secret the night has taught me from the very beginning, when I first was able to spend the hours in her arms."

Then this mystery of her knowledge of the night he had to probe; and she told him, in old world, romantic language, how she had discovered the stairs and Aphrodite, and even of the iron-bound box which she had never been able to move.

"It contains same papers of that Sir Timothy, I expect," she said. "We know by the date of the breastplate that it was when Cromwell sent his Ironsides to search La Sarthe that he must have escaped through the door and got to the coast; but he was drowned crossing to France, so no one guessed or ever knew how he had got away—and I expect the secret of the passage died with him, and I was the first one to find it."

"Then what do you make of the goddess's head?" asked John Derrinbham. "Was that his, too?"

"Yes, I suppose so," she answered. "He was a great, grand seigneur—we know of that—and had traveled much in Italy when a young man, and stayed at Florence especially. He married a relative of the Medici belonging to some female branch, and he is even said to have been to Greece; but in the court of the Grand Duke of Tuscany he would certainly have learned to appreciate the divine beauty of Aphrodite. He must have brought her from there as well as the Hebe and Artemis, which are not nearly so good. They stand in the hall—but they say nothing to me."

"It would be interesting to know what the papers are about," John Derringham went on. "We must look at them together some day when you are my wife."

"Yes," said Halcyone, and thrilled at the thought.

"So it was through the solid masonry you disappeared last night? No wonder, sprite, that I believed I was dreaming! Why did you fly from me? Why?"

"It was too great, too glorious to take all at once," she said, and with a sudden shyness she buried her face in his coat.

"My darling sweet one," he murmured, drawing her to him, passion flaming once more. "I could have cried madly"— and he quoted in Greek:

"Wilt thou fly me and deny me?
By thine own joy I vow,
By the grape upon the bough,
Thou shalt seek me in the midnight, thou shalt love me
even now."

Mr. Carlyon had not restricted Halcyone's reading: she
knew it was from the "Bacchæ" of Euripides, and answered:

"Ah, yes, and, you see, I have sought you in the midnight, and I am here, and I love you—even now!"

After that for a while they both seemed to fall into a
dream of bliss. They spoke not, they just sat close together, his arms encircling her, her head upon his his breast;
and thus they watched the first precursors of dawn streak
the sky and, looking up, found the stars had faded.

Halcyone started to her feet.

"Ah! I must go, dear lover," she said, "though it will
only be for some few hours."

But John Derringham held her two hands, detaining her.

"I will make all arrangements in these next few days,"
he said. "I am going to Wendover for Whitsuntide. I
will get away from there, though, and come across the park
and meet you, darling, here at our tree, and we will settle
exactly what to do and when to go."

Then, after a last fond, sweet embrace, he let her leave
him, and watched her as she glided away among the giant
trees, until she was out of sight, a wild glory in his heart.

For Love, when he wins after stress, leaves no room but
for gladness in his worshiper's soul.

CHAPTER XIX

IT was John Derringham who was taciturn next morning, not the Professor!

The light of day has a most sobering effect, and while still exalted in a measure by all the strong forces of love, he was enabled to review worldly events with a clearer eye, and could realize very well that he was going to take a step which would not have a forwarding impetus upon his career, even if it proved to be not one of retrogression.

He must give up the thought of using a rich wife as an advancement; but then, on the other hand, he would gain a companion whose divine sweetness would be an ennobling inspiration.

How he could ever have deceived himself in regard to his feelings he wondered now, for he saw quite plainly that he had been drifting into loving her from the first moment he had seen her that Good Friday morning, the foundations having been laid years before, on the day in the tree.

He felt rather uncomfortable about his old master, who he knew would not approve of any secret union with Halcyone. Not that Cheiron would reck much of conventionalities, or care in the least if it were a marriage at a registry-office or not, but he would certainly resent any aspect of the case which would seem to put a slight upon his much-loved protégée or place her in a false position.

He would tell him nothing about it until it was an accomplished fact and Halcyone was his wife—then they would let him into the secret.

All the details of what she would have to say to her aunts in her letter of farewell on leaving them would have to be thought out, too, so that no pursuit or inopportune prying into the truth would be the consequence.

Of any possibility of her stepfather's ultimate interference he did not think, not knowing that she had even any further connection with him. To satisfy in some way the ancient aunts was all that appeared a necessity. And that was difficult enough. He had certainly undertaken no easy task, but he did not regret his decision. The first and only strong passion he had ever known was mastering him.

But there was yet one more unpleasant aspect to face—that was the situation regarding Mrs. Cricklander. He had assuredly not committed himself or even acted very unfairly to her. She had been playing a game as he had been. He did not flatter himself that she really loved him —now that he knew what love meant—and her ambition could be gratified elsewhere; but there remained the fact that he was engaged to stay with her for Whitsuntide, and whether to do so, and plainly show her that he had meant nothing and only intended to be a friend, or whether to throw the visit over, and go to London, returning just to fetch Halcyone about Wednesday, he could not quite decide.

Which would be the best thing to do? It worried him —but not for long, because indecision was not, as a rule, one of his characteristics, and he soon made up his mind to the former course.

He would go to Wendover on Saturday, as was arranged, take pains to disabuse his hostess's mind of any illusion upon the subject of his intentions, and, having run over to Bristol this afternoon to give notice to the registrar and procure the license, he would leave with the other guests on the Tuesday, after lunch, having sent his servant up to London in the morning to be out of the way.

Then he would sleep that night in Upminster, getting his servant to leave what luggage he required there—it was the junction for the main line to London, and so that would be easy. A motor could be hired, and in it, on the Wednesday, he would come to the oak avenue gate, as that was far at the other side of the park upon the western road; there he would arrange that Halcyone should be waiting for him with some small box, and they would go over to Bristol, be married, and then go on to a romantic spot he knew in Wales, and there spend a week of bliss!

By the time he got thus far in his meditations he felt intoxicated again, and Mr. Carlyon, who was watching him as he sat there in his chair reading the *Times* opposite him, wondered what made him suddenly clasp his hand and draw in his breath and smile in that idiotic way while he gazed into space!

Then there would be the afterwards. Of course, that would be blissful, too. Oh! if he could only claim her before all the world how glorious it would be—but for the present that was hopeless, and at all events her life with him would not be more retired than the one of monotony which she led at La Sarthe Chase, and would have his tenderest love to brighten it. He would take a tiny house for her somewhere—one of those very old-fashioned ones shut in with a garden still left in Chelsea, near the Embankment—and there he would spend every moment of his spare time, and try to make up to her for her isolation. Well arranged, the world need not know of this—Halcyone would never be *exigeante*—or if it did develop a suspicion, ministers before his day had been known to have *chèries amies*.

But as this thought came he jumped from his chair. It was, when faced in a concrete fashion, hideously unpalatable as touching his pure, fair star.

"You are rather restless to-day, John," the Professor said, as his old pupil went hastily towards the open window and looked out.

"Yes," said John Derringham. "It is going to rain, and I must go to Bristol this afternoon. I have to see a man on business."

Cheiron's left penthouse went up into his forehead.

"Matters complicating?" was all he said.

"Yes, the very devil," responded John Derringham.

"Beginning to feel the noose already, poor lad?"

"Er—no, not exactly," and he turned round. "But I don't quite know what I ought to do about her—Mrs. Cricklander."

"A question of honor?"

"I suppose so."

The Professor grunted, and then chuckled.

"A man's honor towards a woman lasts as long as his love. When that goes, it goes with it—to the other woman."

"You cynic!" said John Derringham.

"It is the truth, my son. A man's point of view of such things shifts with his inclinations, and if other people are not likely to know, he does not experience any qualms in thinking of the woman's feelings—it is only of what the world will think of *him* if it finds him out. Complete cowards, all of us!"

John Derringham frowned. He hated to know this was true.

"Well, I am not going to marry Mrs. Cricklander, Master," he announced after a while.

"I am very glad to hear it," Cheiron said heartily. "I never like to see a fine ship going upon the rocks. All your vitality would have been drawn out of you by those octopus arms."

"I do not agree with you in the least about any of those points," John Derringham said stiffly. "I have the highest respect for Mrs. Cricklander—but I can't do it."

"Well, you can thank whichever of your stars has brought you to this conclusion," growled the Professor.

"I suppose I'll pull through somehow financially," the restless visitor went on, pacing the floor—"anyway, for a few years; there may be something more to be squeezed out of Derringham. I must see."

"Well, if you are not marrying that need not distress you," Cheiron consoled him with. "Those things only matter if a man has a son."

John Derringham stopped abruptly in his walk and looked at his old master.

His words gave him a strange twinge, but he crushed it down, and went on again:

"It is a curse, this want of money," he said. "It makes a man do base things that his soul revolts against." And then, in his restless moving, he absently picked up a volume of Aristotle, and his eye caught this sentence: "The courageous man therefore faces danger and performs acts of courage for the sake of what is noble."

And what did an honorable man do? But this question he would not go further into.

"You were out very late last night, John," Mr. Carlyon said presently. "I left this window open for you on purpose. The garden does one good sometimes. You were not lonely, I hope?"

"No," said John Derringham; but he would not look at his old master, for he knew very well he should see a whimsical sparkle in his eye.

Mr. Carlyon, of course, must be aware of Halcyone's night wandering proclivities. And if there had been nothing to conceal John Derringham would have liked to have sat down now and rhapsodized all about his darling to his old friend, who adored her, too, and knew and appreciated all her points. He felt bitterly that Fate had not been as kind to him as she might have been. However, there was nothing for it, so he turned the conversation and tried to make himself grow as interested in a question of foreign policy as he would have been able to be, say, a year ago. And then he went out for a walk.

And Cheiron sat musing in his chair, as was his habit.

"The magnet of her soul is drawing his," he said to himself. "Well, now that this has begun to work, we must leave things to Fate."

But he did not guess how passion on the one side and complete love and trust upon the other were precipitously forcing Fate's hand.

The possibility of John Derringham's sending a message to Halcyone was very slender. The post was out of the question—she probably never got any letters, and the arrival of one in a man's handwriting would no doubt be the cause of endless comment in the household. The foolishness had been not to make a definite appointment with her when they had parted before dawn. But they had been too overcome with love to think of anything practical in those last moments, and now the only thing would be for him to go again to-night to the tree, and hope that she would meet him there. But the sky was clouding over, and rain looked quite ready to fall. As a last resource he could send Demetrius—his own valet he would not have trusted a yard.

The rain kept off for his journey to Bistol, and his business was got through with rapidity. And if the registrar did connect the name of John Derringham, barrister-at-law, of the Temple, London, with John Derringham, the Under-Secretary of State for Foreign Affairs, he was a man of discretion and said nothing about it.

It was quite late when Mr. Carlyon's guest returned to his roof—cross-country trains were so tiresome—and it had just begun to pour with rain, so there was no use expecting that Halcyone would be there by the tree. And bed, with a rather feverish sensation of disappointment, seemed John Derringham's portion.

Halcyone had passed a day of happy tranquillity. She was of that godlike calm which frets not, believing always that only good could come to her, and that, as she heard nothing from her lover, it was because—which was indeed the truth—he was arranging for their future. If it had been fine she had meant to go to the tree, but as it rained she went quietly to her room, and let her Priscilla brush her hair for an hour, while she stared in the old dark glass, seeing not her own pale and exquisite face, but all sorts of pictures of future happiness. That she must not tell her old nurse, for the moment, of her good fortune was her one crumpled rose-leaf, but she had arranged that when she went she would post a letter at once to her, and Priscilla would, of course, join her in London, or wherever it was John Derringham would decide that she should live. The thought of leaving her aunts did not so much trouble her. The ancient ladies had never made her their companion or encouraged her to have a single interest in common with them. She was even doubtful if they would really miss her, so little had they ever taken her into their lives. For them she was still the child to be kept in her place, however much she had tried to grow a little nearer. Then her thoughts turned back to ways and means.

She so often spent the whole day with Cheiron that her absence would not be marked upon until bedtime. But then she suddenly remembered, with a feeling of consternation, that the Professor intended to leave on the Tuesday in Whitsun week for his annual fortnight in London. If the household knew of this, it might complicate matters, and was a pity. However, there was no use speculating about any of these things, since she did not yet know on which day she was to start—to start for Paradise—as the wife of her Beloved!

Next morning it was fine again, and she decided she would go towards their tree, and if John were not there, she would even go on to the orchard house, because she realized fully the difficulty he would find in sending her a message.

But he was there waiting for her, in the bright sunlight, and she thought him the perfection of what a man should look in his well-cut gray flannels.

John Derringham knew how to dress himself, and had even in his oldest clothes that nameless, indescribable distinction which seems often to be the birthright of Englishmen of his class.

The daylight made her timid again; she was no more the imperious goddess of the night. It was a shy and tender little maiden who nestled into the protecting strong arms of her lover.

He told her all his plans: how he had given notice for the license, and that it would be forthcoming. And he explained that he had chosen Bristol rather than Upminster because in this latter place everyone would know the name of La Sarthe—even the registrar's clerk and whoever else they would secure as a witness—but in Bristol it might pass unnoticed.

They discussed what should be done about Cheiron and the old ladies, and decided that when to apprise the former of their marriage must be left to John's discretion; and as Halcyone would not be missed until the evening, they would simply send two telegrams from Bristol in the late afternoon, one to Miss La Sarthe and one to Priscilla, the former briefly to announce that Halcyone was quite safe and was writing, and the latter asking her old nurse not to let the old ladies feel worried, and promising a letter to her, also.

"Then," John Derringham said, "you will be my wife by that time, sweetheart, and you will tell your aunts the truth, ask them to keep our secret, and say that you will return to them often, so that they shall not be lonely. We will write it between us, darling, and I do not think they will give us away."

"Never," returned Halcyone, while she looked rather wistfully towards the house. "They are too proud."

He dropped her hand for an instant; the unconscious inference of this speech made him wince. She understood, then, that she was going to do something which her old kinswomen would think was a hurt to their pride, and so would be silent over it in consequence. And yet she did not hesitate. She must indeed love him very much.

A tremendous wave of emotion surged through him, and he looked at her with reverence and worship. And for one second his own part of utter selfishness flashed into his understanding, so that he asked, with almost an axious note in his deep, assured voice:

"You are not afraid, sweetheart, to come away—for all the rest of your life—alone with me?"

And often in the after days of anguish there would come back to him the memory of her eyes, to tear his heart with agony in the night-watches—her pure, true eyes, with all her fresh, untarnished soul looking out of them into his as they glistened with love and faith.

"Afraid?" she said. "How should I be afraid—since you are my lord and I am your love? Do we not belong to one another?"

"Oh, my dear," he said, as he folded her to his heart in wild, worshiping passion, "God keep you always safe, here in my arms."

And if she had known it, for the first time in his life there were tears in John Derringham's proud eyes. For he knew now he had found her—the one woman with a soul.

Then they parted, when every smallest detail was settled, for she had promised to help Miss Roberta with a new design for her embroidery, and he had promised to join Mrs. Cricklander's party for an early lunch. They intended to make an excursion to see the ruins of Graseworth Tower in the afternoon.

"And indeed we can bear the separation now, my darling," he said, "because we shall both know that we must go through only four more days before we are together—for always!"

But even so it seemed as if they could not tear themselves apart, and when he did let her go he strode after her again and pleaded for one more kiss.

"There!" she whispered, smiling while her eyes half filled with mist. "This tree is forever sacred to us. John, it is listening now when I tell you once more that I love you."

And then she fled.

CHAPTER XX

WHEN once John Derringham had definitely made up his mind to any course in life, he continued in it with decision and skill, and carried off the situation with a high-handed assurance. Thus he felt no qualms of awkwardness in meeting Mrs. Cricklander and treating her with an enchanting ease and friendliness which was completely disconcerting. She had no *casus belli;* she could not find fault with his manner or his words, and yet she was left with the blank conviction that her hopes in regard to him were over. She despised men in her heart because, as a rule, she was able to calculate with certainty every move in her games with them. Feeling no slightest passion, her very mediocre intellect proved often more than a match for the cleverest. But her supreme belief in herself now received a heavy blow. She was never so near to loving John Derringham as during this Whitsuntide when she felt she had lost him. Cora Lutworth once said of her:

"Cis is one of the happiest women in the world, because when she looks in the glass in the morning she never sees anything but herself, and is perfectly content. Most of us find shadows peeping over our shoulders of what we would like to be."

Arabella found her employer extremely trying during the Saturday and Sunday, and was almost in tears when she wrote to her mother.

"Mr. Derringham has plainly determined not to be ensnared yet. If this did not render M. E. so difficult to please, the situation would be very instructive to watch. And I am not even now certain whether he will escape eventually, because her whole pride in herself is roused and she will stick at nothing. I have a shrewd suspicion as to what has caused the change in his feelings and intentions towards M. E., but I have not imparted my ideas to her, since doing so might do no good, and would in some way certainly injure an innocent person. As yet I believe she is unaware of this person's existence. We have done everything we can for Mr. Derringham with the most erudite conversation. I have

123

been up half of the night ascertaining facts upon all sorts of classical subjects, as that seems to be more than ever the bent of his mind in these last two visits. (I am given to understand from other sources that the person of whom I made mention above is a highly-trained Greek scholar and of exceptional refinement and cultivation, so that may be the reason.) The strain of preparing M. E. for these talks and then my anxiety when, at meals or after them, I hear her upon the brink of some fatal mistake, has caused me to have most unpleasant headaches, and really, if it were not so modern and silly a phrase, I should say the thing was getting on my nerves. However, all the interesting guests are leaving on Tuesday afternoon. Mr. Derringham, I understand from what he said to me, intends to go over to his old master, Professor Carlyon's, and catch a later train from there, but M. E. does not know this, and I have not felt it my duty to inform her of it, because it might involve some awkwardness connected with the person about whom I have already given you a hint. I must close now, as I have some facts to look up concerning the worship of Dionysus which M. E. is going to bring in to-night. It was only yesterday I told her who he was, and I had the greatest difficulty to get her to understand he was Bacchus as well, as she had learned of him when younger under that name as the God of Drunkards, and did not consider him a very nice person to mention. But Mr. Derringham held forth upon the rude Tracian Dionysus last night and the fundamental spirituality of his original cult, and so she felt it might seem rather *bourgeois* to be shocked, and has committed to memory as well as she can some facts to-day.''

It will be seen from Miss Clinker's frank letter to her parent that Mrs. Cricklander was leaving no stone unturned to gain her object, and such praiseworthy toil deserves the highest commendation.

John Derringham, meanwhile, having successfully smoothed matters to his own satisfaction, felt at liberty to dream in his spare moments of his love. He already began to wonder how he had ever felt any emotion towards the fair Cecilia—she was perfectly charming, but left him as cold as ice!

And so at last the good-bys were said, and he got into the motor with some of the other guests, ostensibly for the station, but in reality to get out at the Lodge gates upon the pretense of going to see the Professor. He intended, instead of this, to cross the haw-haw and reconnoiter upon the hope of meeting his beloved, because there was no necessity for him to spend a dull afternoon in Upminster when perhaps some more agreeable hours could be snatched under the tree. He had attended to every point, he believed, even having written a letter to Cheiron which he had taken the precaution to give to his servant to post from London on the following morning, so that there would be no Bristol mark as a clew to their whereabouts. In this he merely stated that when his old master would receive it Halcyone would be his wife, and that for a time they had decided to keep the marriage secret, and he hoped his old master would understand and sympathize.

The only qualm of any sort he experienced during these three days was when he was composing this letter, so he finished it quickly and did not even read it over. And now, as he strode across the Wendover park, it was safe in his servant's pocket and would be despatched duly next day. He was unaware of the fact that Mr. Carlyon had left for London by a morning train.

As he came within view of the haw-haw, he saw in the far distance Halcyone just flitting towards the beech avenue gate, and in his intense haste to catch up with her before she should get too near the house, he removed the bricks very carelessly, not even remarking that one, and the most important, was disposed of in such a manner that the spike left beneath would not bear his weight.

He had got thus far, his eyes fixed upon the slender white figure rapidly disappearing from his view, when with a tremendous crash his foothold gave way and he fell with a fearful force into the ditch beneath, his head striking one of the fallen bricks. And after that, all things were blank and his soul wandered into shadowland and tasted of the pains of death.

.   .   .   .

From the first break of day on that Tuesday when Helcyone awoke she was conscious that some sorrow was near her. Every sense of hers, every instinct, so highly trained by her years of communion with Nature seemed always to warn her of coming events.

She was restless—a state of being quite at variance with her usual calm. The air was sultry and, though no rain fell, ominous clouds gathered and faint thunder pealed afar off.

"What is it? What is it, God?" she asked of the sky. But no answer came, and at least she went out into the park and towards the tree. She had made all her simple preparations—everything that she must take had been put into a small bag and was safely waiting in the secret passage, ready for her to fetch on the morrow.

Cheiron, she knew, had gone to London. Had they not said good-by on the evening before? And his last words had made her smile happily at the time.

"Things are changing, Halcyone," he had said, with the whimsical raising of his left penthouse brow. "Perhaps you will not want to learn Greek much longer with your crabbed old Cheiron in his cave."

And she had flung her arms round his neck and buried her face in his silver beard, and assured him she would always want to learn—all her life. But now she felt a twinge of sadness—she would indeed miss him, her dear old master, and he, too, would be lonely without her. Then she fought with herself. Feelings of depression were never permitted to stay for a moment, and she looked away into the trees for comfort—but only a deathly stillness and a sullen roll of distant thunder answered, and left her uncomforted.

And then some force stronger than her will seemed to drive her back to the house, and to the long gallery, and just at the very moment when she had passed beyond her lover's sight it was as if something chased her, so that she ran the last few yards, and paused not until she stood in front of Aphrodite's shrine.

It would be difficult to carry the marble head with the other few things she proposed to take, but none the less was the necessity imperative. She could not be married without the presence of her beloved mother to bless her.

As she lifted her goddess out, with her silken wrappings, the first flash of the nearing storm lit up the dark room with lurid flame.

Halcyone shivered. It was the one aspect of Nature with which she was out of harmony. When thunder rolled and lightning quivered, her vitality seemed to desert her and she experienced what in her came nearest to fear.

"Ah! someone has angered God greatly," she whispered aloud; and then she carried the head to the secret door, knowing full well she would be unwatched in her entry there —on such a day, with thunder pealing, not a servant would have ventured into the long gallery.

Another and louder rumble reached her with muffled sound, as she made her way in the dark underground, and as she came to the place where there was the contrived gleam of light and outer air, the lightning turned the narrow space into a green dusk.

Halcyone was trembling all over, and when she had put her precious bundle safely into the bag with the rest of her simple preparations, she laid it on the iron-bound box which had never been stirred, all ready for her to lift up and take with her in the morning. Then she ran back, cold and pale, and hastily sought Priscilla in her own room, and talked long to her of old days, glad indeed to hear a human voice, until presently the rain began to pour in torrents and the storm cried itself out.

But with each crash before this came her heart gave a bound, as if in pain. And a wild longing grew in her for the morrow and safety in her lover's arms.

And he—alas! that hapless lover!—was lying there in the haw-haw, with broken ankle and damaged head, half recovering consciousness in the pouring rain, but unable to stir or climb from his low bed, or even to cry aloud enough to make any one hear him. And so at last the night came, and the pure moonlight, and when her usual evening duties were over with her aunts, Halcyone was free to go to bed.

She opened her window wide, but she did not seek to wander in the wet park. John would not be there, and she must rest, so as to be fair for him when to-morrow they should start on life's sweet journey—together.

But her heart was not quiet. All her prayers and pure thoughts seemed to bring no peace, and even when, after a while, she fell into a sleep, it was still troubled.

And thus the day dawned that was to have seen her wedding!

She told herself that the dull, sullen oppression she awoke with was the result of the storm in the night, and with firm determination she banished all she could of heaviness, and got through her usual avocations until the moment came for her to start for the oak avenue gate. She timed her arrival to be exactly at ten o'clock so that she need not wait, as this of the three outlets was the one where there might be a less remote chance of a passer-by. They had had to choose it because it was on the road to Bristol.

The sun was shining gorgeously again when she emerged from the secret door, carrying her heavy bundle, and except in the renewed freshness of all the green there seemed no trace of the storm. Yes—as she got near the gate she saw that one huge tree beyond that old friend who had played the part of the holder of the Golden Fleece was stricken and cleft through by the lightning. It had fallen in helpless fashion, blackened and yawning, his proud head in the dust.

This grieved her deeply, and she paused to pass a tender hand over the gaping wound. Then she went on to the gate, and there waited—waited first in calm belief, then in expectancy, and at last in a numb agony.

The sun seemed to scorch her, the light hurt her eyes, every sound made her tremble and start forward, and at last she cried aloud:

"O God, why do I feel so troubled? I who have always had peace in my heart!"

But no bird even answered her. There was a warm stillness, and just there, under these trees, there were no rabbits which could have comforted her with their living forms scuttling to and fro.

She tried to reason calmly. Motors were uncertain things—this one might have broken down, and that had delayed her lover. She must not stir, in case he should come and think his lateness had frightened her and that she had gone back to the house. Whatever befell, she must be brave and true.

But at last, when the afternoon shadows were lengthening the agony became intense. Only the baker had passed with his cart, and a farm wagon or two, during the whole day. Gradually the conviction grew that it could not only be an accident to the motor—if so, John would have procured some other vehicle, or, indeed, he could have come to her on foot by now. Something had befallen him. There must have occurred some accident to himself; and in spite of all her calm fortitude, anguish clutched her soul.

She knew not what to do or which way to go. At last, as the sun began to sink, faint and weary, she decided the orchard house would be the best place. There, if there was any news of an accident, Sarah Porrit, the Professor's one female servant, would have heard it.

She started straight across the park, carrying her heavy bag, and crossed the beech avenue, and so on to the trysting tree. A cold feeling like some extra disquietude seemed to overcome her as she neared the haw-haw and the copse. It was as if she feared and yet longed to get there. But she resisted the temptation, and went straight on to the little gate and so up the garden to the house.

Mrs. Porrit received her with her usual kindly greeting. All was calm and peaceful, and while Halcyone controlled

herself to talk in an ordinary voice, the postman's knock
was heard. He passed the Professor's door on the road to
Applewood and left the evening mail, when there chanced
to be any.

Mrs. Porrit received the letters—three of them—and then
she adjusted her spectacles, but took them off again.

"After all, since you are here, miss, perhaps as you write
better than I you will be so good as to redirect them on to
the master. You know his address, as usual." And she
named an old-fashioned hotel in Jermyn Street.

Halcyone took them in her cold, trembling fingers, and
then nearly dropped them on the floor, for the top envelope
was addressed in the handwriting of her beloved! She knew
it well. Had she not, during the past years, often seen such
missives, from which the Professor had read her scraps of
news?

She carried it to the light and scrutinized the postmark.
It was "London," and posted that very morning early!

For a moment all was black, and she found herself grasp-
ing the back of Cheiron's big chair to prevent herself from
falling.

John had been in London at the moment when she was
waiting by the tree! What mystery was here?

At first the feeling was one of passionate relief. There
had been no accident, then; he had been obliged to go—there
would be some explanation forthcoming. Perhaps he had
even written to her, too—and she gave a bound forward, as
though to run back to La Sarthe Chase. But then she
recollected the evening postman did not come to the house,
and they got no letters as Cheiron did, who was on the road.
Hers could not be there until the morning—she must wait
patiently and see.

With consummate self-control she made her voice sound
natural as she said, "Oh, I am so late, Mrs. Porrit. I must
go," and, bidding the woman a gracious good evening, walked
rapidly to the house. A telegram might have come for her,
and she had been out all day. What if her aunts had
opened it!

This thought made her quicken her pace so that at last
she arrived at the terrace breathless with running; and having deposited her bag in safety, she came out again from
the secret passage and got hastily to the house.

But there was no sign of a telegram in the hall, and she
mounted to find Priscilla in her room, which she discovered

to be in great disorder, her few clothes lying about on every available place.

"Oh, my lamb, where have you been?" the elderly woman exclaimed. "At four o'clock who should come in a fly from the Applewood station but your stepfather's wife! She was staying at Upminster, and says she thought she would come over and see you—and now it's settled that we go back with her to London to-morrow. Think of it, my lamb! You and me to see the world!" Then she cried in fear: "My precious, what is it?"

For Halcyone, overwrought and overcome, had staggered to a chair and, falling into it, had buried her face in her hands.

CHAPTER XXI

Mrs. James Anderton was seated in the Italian parlor with the two ancient hostesses when Halcyone at last came into their midst. They had evidently exhausted all possible topics of conversation and were extremely glad of an interruption.

Miss La Sarthe had been growing more and more annoyed at her great-niece's lengthy absence, while Miss Roberta felt so nervous she would like to have sniffed at her vinaigrette, but, alas! the stern eye of her sister was upon her and she dared not.

Mrs. James Anderton—good, worthy woman—had not passed an agreeable afternoon either. She felt herself hopelessly out of tune with the two old ladies, whose exquisitely reserved polished manners disconcerted her.

She had been made to feel—most delicately, it is true, but still unmistakably—that she had committed a breach of taste in thus descending upon La Sarthe Chase unannounced. And instead of the sensation of complacent importance which she usually enjoyed when among her own friends and acquaintances, she was experiencing a depressed sense of being a very small personage indeed.

Her highly colored comely face was very hot and flushed and she rather restlessly played with her parasol handle. Miss La Sarthe's voice grew a little acid as she said:

"This is our great-niece, Halcyone La Sarthe, Mrs. Anderton"—and then—"It is unfortunate that you should have been so long absent, child."

"I am very sorry," Halcyone returned gently, and she shook hands. She made no excuse or explanation.

Mrs. Anderton plunged into important matters at once.

"Your father, Mr. Anderton,"—how that word "father" jarred upon Halcyone's sensitive ears!—"wished me to come and see you, dear, and hopes you will return with me to-morrow to London, for a little visit to us, that you may make the acquaintance of your brother and sisters."

Halcyone had already made up her mind what to do, before she had left her room. She would agree to anything they suggested in order to have no obstacles put in her way

131

—not admitting for a moment that these people had any authority over her. Then, if in the morning, she received a letter from her Beloved, she would follow its instructions implicitly. Always having at hand her certain mode of disappearance, she could slip away, and if it seemed necessary, just leave them to think what they pleased. Priscilla would be warned to allay at once the anxiety of her aunts, and for the Andertons she was far too desperate to care what they might feel.

"Thank you; it is very good of you," she said as graciously as she could. "My old nurse has told me of your kind invitation, and is already beginning the preparations. I trust you left Mr. Anderton and my stepbrother and sisters well?"

"Hoity-toity!" thought Louisa Anderton. "Of the same sort as the old spinsters. This won't please James, I fear!" But aloud she answered that the family were all well, and that James Albert, who was thirteen now, would soon be going to Eton.

Over Halcyone, in spite of her numbness and the tension she was feeling, though controlled by her firm will, there came the memory of the red, crying baby, for whose life her own sweet mother had paid so dear a price. And Mabel and Ethel—noisy, merry little girls!—she had thought of them so seldom in these latter years—they seemed as far-off shadows now. But James Anderton and her mother stood out sharp and clear.

The strain and anguish of the day had left her very pale. Mrs. Anderton thought her plain and most uncomfortably aloof; she really regretted that she had put into her husband's head the idea of giving this invitation. He would gladly have left Halcyone alone, but for her kindly thought. Mabel was just seventeen, and such a handful that her father had decided she should stay in the schoolroom with her sister for another year, and Mrs. Anderton had felt it would be a good opportunity for Halcyone to rejoin the family circle at a time when her presence, if she proved good-looking, could not in any way interfere with her stepsister's début.

And here, instead of being overcome with gratitude and excitement, this cold, quiet girl was taking it all as quite an ordinary circumstance. No wonder she, Louisa Anderton, felt aggrieved.

They had hardly time for any more words, for Mrs. Anderton had already put off her departure by the seven-twenty train from Applewood to Upminster on purpose to wait for Halcyone, and now proposed to catch the one at nine o'clock—her fly still waited in the courtyard—and they made rapid arrangements. Halcyone, accompanied by Priscilla, was to meet her the next day at Upminster junction at eleven o'clock, and they would journey to London together.

And all the while Halcyone was agreeing to this she was thinking, if in the improbable circumstance that she should get no letter in the morning, it would be wiser to go to London. There was her Cheiron, who would help her to get news. But of course she would hear, and all would be well.

Thus she was enabled to unfreeze a little to her stepfather's wife, who, as they said good-by at the creaking fly's door, felt some of her soft charm.

"Perhaps she is shy," she said to herself as she rolled towards the station. "Anyway, it is restful, after Mabel's laying down the law."

That night Halcyone took her goddess to the little summer house upon the second terrace.

"If I start with John to-morrow, my sweet," she said, "you will come with me as I have promised you. But if I must go to that great, restless city, to find him, then you will wait for me here—safe in your secret home." And then she looked out over the misty clover-grown pleasance to the country beyond bathed in brilliant moonlight. And something in the beauty of it stilled the wild ache in her heart. She would not admit into her thoughts the least fear, but some unexplained, unconquerable apprehension stayed in her innermost soul. She knew, only she refused to face the fact, that all was not well.

Of doubt as to John Derringham's intentions towards her, or his love, she had none, but there were forces she knew which were strong and could injure people, and with all her fearlessness of them, they might have been capable of causing some trouble to her lover—her lover who was ignorant of such things.

She stayed some time looking at the beautiful moonlit country, and saying her prayers to that God Who was her eternal friend, and then she got up to steal noiselessly to bed.

But as she was opening the secret door, to have one more look at the sky, after she had replaced Aphrodite in the bag, it seemed as though her lover's voice called her in anguish through the night: "Halcyone!" and again, "Halcyone! My love!"

She stopped, petrified with emotion, and then rushed back

onto the terrace. But all was silence; and, wild with some mad fear, she set off hurriedly, never stopping until she came to their trysting tree. But here there was silence also only the nightingale throbbed from the copse, while the faint rustle of soft zephyrs disturbed the leaves.

And Jeb Hart and his comrade saw the tall white figure from their hiding-place in the low overgrown brushwood and Gubbs crossed himself again, for whether she were living or some wraith they were never really sure.

At the moment when Halcyone opened the secret door John Derringham was just recovering consciousness in a luxurious bed at Wendover Park, whither he had been carried when accidentally found by the keepers in their round about eight o'clock. It was several days since they had visited this part of the park, and they had hit upon him by a fortunate chance. He had lain there in the haw-haw, unconscious all that day, while his poor little lady-love waited for him at the oak gate, and was now in a sorry plight indeed, as Arabella Clinker bent over him, awaiting anxiously the verdict of the doctors who had been fetched by motor from Upminster. Would he live or die?

Her employer had had a bad attack of nerves upon hearing of the accident, and was now reclining upon her boudoir sofa, quite prostrated and in a high state of agitation until she should know the worst—or best.

Arabella listened intently. Surely the patient was whispering something? Yes, she caught the words.

"Halcyone!" he murmured, and again, "Halcyone—my love!" and then he closed his eyes once more.

He would live, the physicians said after some hours of doubt—with very careful nursing. But the long exposure in the wet, twenty-four hours at least, with that wound in the head and the broken ankle, was a very serious matter and absolute quiet and the most highly skilled attention would be necessary.

It was Arabella who made all the sensible, kind arrangements that night, and herself sat up with the poor suffering patient until the nurses could come. But it was Mrs. Cricklander, who, dignified and composed, received the doctors after the consultation with Sir Benjamin Grant next day before the celebrated surgeon left for London, and she made her usual good impression upon the great man.

That the local lights thought far more highly of Arabella did not matter. Mrs. Cricklander was wise enough to know it is upon the exalted that a good effect must be produced

"And, you are sure, Sir Benjamin, that he will get quite well?" she said tenderly, allowing her handsome eyes to melt upon the surgeon's face. "It matters enormously to me, you know." Then she looked down.

Thus appealed to, Sir Benjamin felt he must give her all the assurance he could.

"Perfectly, dear lady," he said, pressing her soft hand in sympathy. "He is young and strong, and fortunately it has not touched his brain. But it will take time and gentlest nursing, which you will see, of course, that he gets."

"Indeed, yes," the fair Cecilia said. And when they were all gone, she summoned Arabella.

"You will let me know, Arabella, every minute change in him," she commanded, "especially when he seems conscious. And you will tell him how I am watching over him and doing everything for him. I can't bear sick people—they upset my nerves, and I just can't stand them. But the moment he is all right enough to see me so that it won't bore me, I'll come. You understand? Now I must really have a trional and get some rest."

And when she was alone she went deliberately to the glass and smiled radiantly to herself as she whispered aloud:

"So he isn't going to die or be an idiot. In a few years he can still be Prime Minister. And I have got him now, as sure as fate!"

Then she closed her mouth with that firm snap Arabella knew so well, and, swallowing her sleeping draught, she composed herself for a peaceful siesta.

CHAPTER XXII

It required all Halcyone's fortitude to act the part of
unconcern which was necessary after the post had come in
and no letter for herself had arrived. The only possibility
of getting through the time until she should reach London,
and be able to communicate with Cheiron would be resolutely to forbid her thoughts from turning in any speculative
direction. *She knew* nothing but good could come to her—
was she not protected from all harm by every strong force
of the night winds, the beautiful stars and the God Who
owned them all? Therefore it followed that this seeming
disaster to her happiness must be only a temporary thing,
and if she bore it calmly it would soon pass. Or, even if it
delayed, there was the analogy of the winter which for
more than four months of the year numbed the earth, often
with weeping rain and frost, but, however severe it should
be, there was always the tender springtime following, and
glorious summer, and then the fulfillment of autumn and its
fruits. So she *must not* be cast down—she must have faith
and not tremble.

She made herself converse gently with her stepfather's
wife, and won her liking before they reached Paddington
station. If she had not been so highly strung and preoc-
cupied, she would have been thrilled in all her fine senses at
the idea of leaving Upminster, further than which she had
never been for the twelve long years of her residence at La
Sarthe Chase; but now, except that all appeared a wild rush
and a bewildering noise, the journey to London made no
impression upon her. It was swallowed up in the one longing to get there—to be able somehow to communicate with
Cheiron, and have her anxiety laid to rest.

The newsboys were selling the evening papers when they
arrived, but her eyes, so unaccustomed to all these new
sights, did not warn her to scan the headlines, though as they
were reaching Grosvenor Gardens where Mr. Anderton's
town-house was situated, she did see the words: "Under-
Secretary of State for Foreign Affairs." The sheet had
fallen forward and only this line was visible.

They did not strike her very forcibly. She was quite

unacquainted with the custom of advertising sensational news in London. It might be the usual political announcements—it surely was, since she saw another sheet as they got to the door with "Crisis in the Cabinet" upon it. And it comforted her greatly. John, of course, was concerned with this, and had been summoned back suddenly, having had no possible time to let her know. He who was so true an Englishman must think of his country first. It seemed like an answer to her prayers, and enabled her to go in and greet her stepfather with calm and quiet.

James Anderton had come from the city in the best of tempers. The day had been a good one. He had received his wife's telegram announcing that Halcyone would accompany her on her return, and awaited her arrival with a certain amount of uneasy curiosity and interest. Would the girl be still so terribly like Elaine and the rest of the La Sarthe—especially Timothy, that scapegrace, handsome Timothy, her father, on whose memory and his own bargain with Timothy's widow he never cared much to dwell?

Yes, she was, d—d like—after a while he decided; with just the same set of head and careless grace, and that hateful stamp of breeding that had so lamentably escaped his own children, half La Sarthe, too. It was just Timothy of the gray eyes come back again—not Elaine so much now, not at all, in fact, except in the line of the throat.

His solid, coarse voice was a little husky, and those who knew him well would have been aware that James Anderton was greatly moved as he bid his stepdaughter welcome.

And when she had gone off to her room, accompanied by the boisterous Mabel and Ethel, he said to his wife:

"Lu, you must get the girl some decent clothes. She looks confoundedly a lady, but that rubbish isn't fair to her. Rig her out as good as the rest—no expense spared. See to it to-morrow, my dear."

And Mrs. Anderton promised. She adored shopping, and this would be a labor of love. So she went off to dress for dinner, full of visions of bright pinks and blues and laces and ribbons that would have made Halcyone shrink if she had known.

Mabel was magnificently patronizing and talked a jargon of fashionable slang which Halcyone hardly understood.

Some transient gleam of her beloved mother kept suggesting itself to her when Mabel smiled. The memory was not distinct enough for her to know what it was, but it hurt her. The big, bouncing, overdeveloped girl had so little of the personality which she had treasured all these years as of her mother—treasured even more than remembered.

Ethel had no faintest look of La Sarthe, and was a nice, jolly, ordinary young person—dear to her father's heart.

At last they left Halcyone alone with Priscilla, and presently the two threw themselves into each other's arms—for the old nurse was crying bitterly now, rocking herself to and fro.

"Ah! how it all comes back to me, my lamb," she sobbed. "He's just the same, only older. Hard and kind and generous and never understanding a thing that mattered to your poor, beautiful mother. Oh! she was glad to go at the end, but for leaving you. Dear lady!—all borne to pay your father's debts, which Mr. Anderton had took up. I can't never forgive him quite—I can't never."

And Halcyone, overcome with her long strain of emotion, cried, too, for a few minutes before she could resume her stern self-control.

But at dinner she was calm again, and pale only for the shadows under her wide eyes.

She had written her letter to Cheiron—she knew not of such things as messenger-boys or cabs, and had got Priscilla to post it for her, and now with enforced quiet awaited his answer which she thought she could receive on the morrow.

"There has been a crisis in the Cabinet, has there not?" she said to her stepfather, hoping to hear something, and James Anderton replied that there had been some split—but for his part, the sooner this rotten lot of sleepers had gone out the better he would be pleased; a good sound Radical he was, like his friend Mr. Hanbury-Green.

Halcyone abruptly turned the conversation. She could not, she felt, discuss her beloved and his opinions, even casually, with this man of another class.

Oh! her poor mother—her poor, sweet mother! How terrible it must have been to her to be married to such a person! —though her common sense prompted her to add he was probably, under her influence, not nearly so coarse and bluff in those days as now he appeared to be.

Her little stepbrother, James Albert, had not returned from his private school for the summer holidays, so she perhaps would not see him during her visit.

As the dinner went on everything struck her as glaring, from the footmen's liveries to the bunches of red carnations; and the blazing electric lights confused her brain. She, the little country mouse, accustomed only to old William's gentle shufflings, and the two tall silver candlesticks with their one wax taper in each!

She could not eat the rich food, and if she had known it, she looked like a being from some shadowy world among the hearty crew.

Next morning Mr. Carlyon received her letter as he began his early breakfast; and he tugged at his silver beard, while his penthouse brows met.

The matter required the most careful consideration. He enormously disliked to have to play the rôle of arbiter of fate, but he loved Halcyone more than anything else in the world, and felt bound to use what force he possessed to secure her happiness—or, if that looked too difficult, which he admitted it did, he must try and save her from further unnecessary pain.

He had the day before received John Derringham's letter written from Wendover and which Mrs. Porrit had redirected, containing the news of the intended wedding, and it had angered him greatly.

Hs blazed with indignation! His peerless one to be made to take a mistress's place where any man should be proud to make her his honored wife! "The brutal selfishness of men," he said to himself, not blaming John Derringham in particular. "He ought to have gone off and left her alone when he felt he was beginning to care, if he had not pluck enough to stand the racket. But we are all the same—we must have what we want, and the women must pay—confound us!"

He had never doubted but that, when he read the letter, Halcyone was already his old pupil's wife—if indeed such a ceremony were legal, she being under age. And this thought added to his wrath, and he intended to look the matter up and see. But, before he could do so, he got an evening paper and read a brief notice that John Derringham had met with a severe accident—of what exact nature the press association had not yet learned—and was lying in a critical condition at Wendover Park, the country seat of the "beautiful American society leader, Mrs. Vincent Cricklander," with whose name rumor had already connected the Under-Secretary of State for Foreign Affairs in the most interesting manner, the paragraph added.

So Fate had stepped in and saved his pure night flower, after all! But at what sort of price? And Cheiron stared into space with troubled eyes.

He passed hours of anxious thought. He never did any
thing in a hurry, and felt that now he must especially con
sider what would be his wisest course.

And then, this next morning, Halcyone's letter had come.
It was very simple. It told of Mrs. Anderton's arrival a
La Sarthe Chase and of her own return to London with
her—and then the real pith of it had crept out. Had he
heard any news of Mr. Derringham? Because she had seer
his writing upon a letter Mrs. Porrit was readdressing at the
orchard house and, observing it was from London, she pre
sumed he was there, and she hoped she would see him.

The Professor stopped abruptly here.

"What a woman it is, after all!" he exclaimed. He him
self had never noticed the postmark on John Derringham's
envelope! Then he folded Halcyone's pitiful little com
munication absently, and thought deeply.

Two things were evident. Firstly, John Derringham had
been disabled before the hour when he should have met his
bride; and secondly, she was, when she wrote, unaware that
he had had any accident at all. She must thus be very un
happy and full of horrible anxiety—his dear little girl!

But what courage and fortitude she showed, he mused on
not to give the situation away and lament even to him, her
old friend. She plainly intended to stand by the man she
loved and never admit she had been going to marry him until
he himself gave her leave.

"The one woman with a soul," Cheiron muttered, and
rubbed the mist away which had gathered in his eyes.

He revolved the situation over and over. Halcyone must
be made aware of the accident, if she had not already read
of it in the morning papers; but she must not be allowed
to do anything rash—and as he got thus far in his meditations, a waiter knocked at the old-fashioned sitting-room
door, and Halcyone herself brushed past him into the room.

She was deadly pale, and for a moment did not speak.
Mrs. Anderton, it appeared, thinking she would be tired
from her unaccustomed journey, had suggested she should
breakfast in bed, which Halcyone, thankful to be alone, had
gratefully agreed to; and when on her breakfast tray which
came up at eight o'clock she saw a daily paper, she had
eagerly opened it, and after searching the unfamiliar sheets
for the political news, her eye had caught the paragraph
about John Derringham's accident. In this particular
journal the notice was merely the brief one of the evening
before, but it was enough to wring Halcyone's heart.

She bounded from bed and got Priscilla to dress her in the shortest possible time, and the faithful nurse, seeing that her beloved lamb was in some deep distress, forbore to question her.

Nothing would have stopped Halcyone from going out, but she hoped to do so unperceived.

"Look if the way is clear to the door," she implored Priscilla, "while I put on my hat. I must go to the Professor at once—something dreadful has happened."

So Priscilla went and contrived so that she got Halcyone out of the front door while the servants were busy in the dining-room about the breakfast. She hailed a passing hansom, and in this, to the poor child, novel conveyance, she was whirled safely to Cheiron's little hotel in Jermyn Street, and Priscilla returned to her room, to make believe that her nursling was still sleeping.

"Halcyone! My child!" the Professor exclaimed, to gain time, and then he decided to help her out, so he went on: "I am glad to see you, but am very distressed at the news in the paper this morning about John Derringham—you may have seen it—and I am sure will sympathize with me."

Halcyone's piteous eyes thanked him.

"Yes, indeed," she said. "What does it mean? Ought not—we—you to go to him?"

Mr. Carlyon avoided looking at her.

"I cannot very well do that in Mrs. Cricklander's house," he said, tugging at his beard, to hide the emotion he felt. "But I will telegraph this minute and ask for news, if you will give me the forms—they are over there," and he pointed to his writing-table.

She handed them immediately, and as he adjusted his spectacles she rang the bell; no time must be lost, and the waiter could be there before the words were completed.

"When can you get the answer?" she asked a little breathlessly.

"In two hours, I should think, or perhaps three," the Professor returned. "But there is a telephone downstairs—it has just been put in. We might telephone to his rooms, or to the Foreign Office, and find out if they have heard any further news there. That would relieve my mind a little."

"Yes—do," responded Halcyone eagerly.

The tone of repressed anguish in her soft voice stabbed Cheiron's heart, but they understood each other too well for any unnecessary words to pass between them. The kindest thing he could do for her was to show her he did not mean to perceive her trouble.

The result of the telephoning—a much longer process then than it is now—was slightly more satisfactory. Sir Benjamin Grant's report, the Foreign Office official informed them, was that Mr. Derringham's condition was much more hopeful, but that the most complete quiet for some time would be absolutely necessary.

"John is so strong," Mr. Carlyon said, as he put down the receiver which he had with difficulty manipulated—to Halcyone's trembling impatience. "He will pull through. And all I can do is to wait. He will probably be up at the end of my fortnight, when I get back home." And he looked relieved.

"They would not give him a letter from you, of course, I suppose?" said Halcyone. "If his head has been hurt it will be a long time before he is allowed to read."

Cheiron nodded.

"I am interested," she went on, looking down. "You will let me know, at Grosvenor Gardens, directly you hear anything, will you not, Master?—I—" and then her voice broke a little.

And Cheiron stirred in his chair. It was all paining him horribly, but until he could be sure what would be best for her he must not show his sympathy.

"I will send Demetrius with the answer when it comes, and I will telegraph to Wendover morning and night, dear child," he said. "I knew you would feel for me." And with this, the sad little comedy between them ended, for Halcyone got up to leave.

"Thank you, Cheiron," was all she said.

Mr. Carlyon took her down to the door and put her in the waiting hansom which she had forgotten to dismiss, and he paid the man and reluctantly let her go back alone.

She was too stunned and wretched to take in anything. The street seemed a howling pandemonium upon this June morning at the season's full height, and all the gayly dressed people just beginning to be on their way to the park for their morning stroll appeared a mockery as she passed down Piccadilly.

Whether she had been missed or no, she cared not, and getting out, rang the bell with numbed unconcern, never even noticing the surprised face of the footman as she passed him and ran up the long flight of stairs to her room, fortunately meeting no one on the way. Here Priscilla awaited her, having successfully hidden her absence. It was half past ten o'clock.

Halcyone went to the window and looked out upon the trees in the triangular piece of green. They were not her trees, but they were still Nature, of a stunted kind, and they would understand and comfort her or, at all events, enable her to regain some calm.

She took in deep breaths, and gradually a peace fell upon her. Her friend God would never desert her, she felt.

And Priscilla said to herself:

"She's prayin' to them Immortals, I expect. Well, whoever she prays to, she is a precious saint."

CHAPTER XXIII

MEANWHILE, John Derringham lay betwixt life and death and was watched over by the kind eye of Arabella Clinker. She had gathered quite a number of facts in the night, while she had listened to his feverish ravings—he was light-headed for several hours before the nurses came—then the fever had decreased and though extremely weak he was silent.

Arabella knew now that he loved Halcyone—that wood nymph they had seen during their Easter Sunday walk—and that he had been going to meet her when the accident had happened. The rest was a jumble of incoherent phrases all giving the impression of intense desire and anxiety for some special event. It was:

"Then we shall be happy, my sweet," or "Halcyone, you will not think me a brute, then, will you, my darling," and there were more just detached words about an oak tree, and a goddess and such like vaporings.

But Arabella felt that, no doubt the moment he would be fully conscious, he would wish to send some message—for during the two following days whenever she went in to see him there was a hungering demand in his haggard eyes.

So Miss Clinker took it upon herself to stop at the Professor's house on one of her walks, meaning to beard Cheiron in his den, and find out how—should it be necessary—she could communicate with Halcyone. And then she was informed by Mrs. Porrit that her master would be away for a fortnight, and that Miss Halcyone La Sarthe had been taken off by her stepmother—she did not know where—and that the two old ladies had actually gone that day, with Hester and old William, to some place on the Welsh coast they had known when they were children, for a change to the sea! La Sarthe Chase was shut up. Arabella Clinker was not sufficiently acquainted with the habits of its inmates to appreciate the unparalleled upheaval this dislodgment meant, but she saw that her informant was highly surprised and impressed.

"I expect the poor old gentry felt too lonely to stop, once that dear Miss Halcyone was gone," Mrs. Porrit said, "but

144

there, when I heard it you could have knocked me down with a feather!—them to go to the sea!"

All this looked hopeless as far as communicating with Halcyone went—unless through a letter to the Professor. Arabella returned to Wendover rather cast down.

She had been reasoning with herself severely over a point, and when her letter went to her mother on the next Sunday, she was still undecided as to what was her course of duty, and craved her parent's advice.

The case is this [she wrote]. Being quite aware of M. S.'s. intentions, am I being disloyal to her, in helping to frustrate them by aiding Mr. Derringham to establish communications with the person whom I have already vaguely hinted to you I believe he is interested in? I do not feel it is altogether honorable to take my salary from M. E. and to go against what I know to be the strong desire of her life at the present time. On the other hand, my feelings of humanity are appealed to by Mr. Derringham's weakness, and by the very poor chance he will have of escaping M. E. when she begins her attack during his convalescence. I have felt more easy in conscience hitherto because I have merely stood aside, not aided the adversary, but now there is a parting of the ways and I am greatly disturbed. I like Mr. Derringham very much, he has always treated me with courteous consideration not invariably shown to me by M. E.'s guests; and I cannot help being sorry for him, if—which I fear is almost a certainty—she will secure him in the end.

Then the letter ended.

Arabella was much worried. However, she felt she might remain neutral so far as this, that, when Mrs. Cricklander indulged in endless speculations as to why John Derringham should have been trying to cross that difficult and dangerous haw-haw, she gave no hint that his destination could have been other than the Professor's little house. She did swerve sufficiently to the other side to remark that to cross the haw-haw would save at least a mile by the road if one were in a hurry. And then her loyalty caused her to repeat, with extra care, to John Derringham in a whisper the fib which Mrs. Cricklander wished—namely, that she, the fair Cecilia, was there ready to come to him and sit up with him, and do anything in the world for him, and was only prevented by the doctor's strict orders, fearing the slightest excitement for the patient—and that these orders caused her great grief.

John Derringham's eyes looked grateful, but he did not speak.

His head ached so terribly and his body was wracked with pain, while his ankle, not having been set for twenty-four hours, had swollen so that it rendered its proper setting a very difficult matter, and caused him unspeakable suffering. Sir Benjamin Grant had come down to Wendover twice again before things looked in more hopeful state.

And what agonizing thoughts coursed through his poor feverish brain—until through sheer weakness there would be hours when he was numb.

What could Halcyone have thought waiting for him all that day! and now she, of course, must have heard of his accident and there was no sign or word.

Or was there—and were those cruel doctors not giving him the message? The day came—the Wednesday after Arabella had sent her letter to her mother—when he was strong enough to speak. He waited for the moment when Miss Clinker always arrived with Mrs. Cricklander's bunch of flowers and morning greeting—and then, while the nurse went from the room for a second, he whispered with dry lips:

"Will you do me a kindness?" And Arabella's brown eyes gleamed softly behind her glasses. "Let Miss Halcyone La Sarthe know how I am—she would come and meet you any day at Mr. Carlyon's—" then he stopped, dismayed by the blank look in Miss Clinker's face.

"What is it?" he gasped, and Arabella saw that pale as he had been, with his poor head all bandaged, he grew still more pale—and she realized how terribly weak he must be, and how carefully she must calculate what she could reply.

"I understand that Mr. Carlyon is in London upon a visit, and that the Misses La Sarthe have gone to the sea—" and then, as his eyes touched her with their pitiful questioning surprise, she blurted out the truth.

"Miss Halcyone La Sarthe was fetched away on last Thursday by her stepmother—I did not hear the name—and no one knows where she has gone. La Sarthe Chase is shut up."

John Derringham closed his eyes—his powers of reasoning were not strong enough yet to grasp the actual meaning of this—it seemed to him as though Halcyone were dead, taken away from him by some fate and that all things were at an end.

Arabella grew very frightened.

"Mr. Carlyon telegraphs from London every day," she ventured to announce.

But this appeared to bring no comfort, and the nurse returning, signed to her to leave the room, for John Derringham lay still as one dead.

And, when Arabella arrived at her own sanctum, she burst into tears. What a fool she had been to tell him that, she felt.

All these days, Halcyone passed in a repressed agony in spite of her prayers and unshaken beliefs. She knew it was her winter time and she must bear it until the spring should come, though it was none the less hard to support. But she got through the hours with perfect surface calm—and her stepsisters thought her stupid and dull, while Mrs. Anderton decided there was something unnatural about a girl who took not the slightest interest in shopping, and was perfectly indifferent about all the attractive garments which were put upon her back. She always expressed her thanks so gently, and was ever sweet and willing to be of use, but the look of pain remained deep in those star-like, mysterious eyes, and caused sensations of discomfort to grow in Mrs. Anderton's kindly breast.

Cheiron's laconic messages were delivered to Halcyone every day by Demetrius.

John Derringham was no worse.

He was having every care.

Sir Benjamin Grant had gone down again.

His ankle was satisfactorily set.

But never a word that he had asked for her, and yet she read in the morning papers each day, as well as knew from her Professor's information, that her lover was going on splendidly, and would soon be embarked upon a convalescence. The paper appeared to regard the accident as safely over, and the patient as returning to health.

For Mrs. Cricklander, well-skilled in the manipulating of reporters in her own country, knew exactly what impression she wished to give to the press. And she had no intention of the idea getting abroad that her injured visitor was in a very exhausted condition, because there were those she knew who would suggest that she had bagged him while he was at her mercy—when, later on, they heard the news of her engagement, which she felt was each day growing more certain of becoming a fact. And in Halcyone's brave heart not a doubt ever entered—she waited and believed and endured, in silent pain.

After Arabella's unfortunate announcement, for two or three days John Derringham was too ill to know or care what occurred, and then other and further tormenting thoughts began to trouble his weary brain.

If Halcyone had a stepmother who had come and taken her away, there were then more persons than her ancient aunts to reckon with. She could not now slip off into a secret marriage with himself with small chance of awkward questionings. That phase of the dream was over, he felt.

No letters of any sort were given him by the doctor's strict orders, and his private secretary had come down, an amiable and intelligent youth, and was dealing with the necessary official correspondence—as best he could—growing each day more infatuated with his fair hostess who felt that no pawn on the chessboard which contained John Derringham as king was worth neglecting. The Professor was not enjoying his fortnight in London, and almost tugged his silver beard out while he smoked innumerable pipes. He had come to some conclusions.

John Derringham having been unable to keep the tryst with Halcyone was plainly the working of the hand of Fate, which did not intend that his sweet girl should occupy the invidious and humiliating position of secret wife and apparent mistress to the ambitious young man. Therefore he —Arnold Carlyon—had no right to assist her again into John Derringham's arms. They must both suffer and work out their destinies however cruel that might seem.

"If John really feels she is a necessity, he will brave everything and marry her openly as soon as he is well. If he does not—then I will not assist her into a life of misery and disillusion."

He remembered a talk they had had long ago, when his old pupil had given his views about women and their place in the scheme of things. Not one must expect a man to be faithful to her, were she wife or mistress, he had said. So starting heavily handicapped in the rôle of his secret and unacknowledged wife, Halcyone would stand a very poor chance of happiness. Cheiron pictured things—John Derringham flattered and courted by the world and surrounded by adoring women, while Halcyone sat at home in some quiet corner and received the scraps of his attentions that were left.

No! decidedly he would have no hand in aiding the sorry affair.

So he used his influence and even a little cunning in preventing Halcyone from writing to her lover. He was too ill yet to be troubled, and she must wait until he should send some message to her.

"You do not want Mrs. Cricklander to read your letter, child," he said, when she timidly suggested one day that it would seem kinder if she wrote to say she was concerned at the accident to her old friend.—The sad comedy was still kept up between them.—And Halcyone had stiffened. No, indeed! not that! She was woman enough in spite of the ennobling and broadening effects of her knowledge of nature, to feel the stab of jealous pain, though she had resolutely crushed from her thoughts the insinuation she had read of in the first notice of the disaster—about Mrs. Cricklander's interest in her lover. Her pride took fire. Certainly until he could receive letters and read them himself, she must wait. Cheiron would, of course, inform her when that time came. A doubt of John Derringham's loyalty to her never even cast its shadow upon her soul, nor a suspicion that he could doubt her either.

All these things were the frosts and rains of their winter, but the springtime would come and the glorious sun and flowers.

She was growing accustomed to London and the life of continual bustle, and was almost grateful for it all as it kept her from thinking.

Her stepfather and his wife mixed in a rising half-set of society where many people who were not fools came, and a number who were, but to Halcyone they all seemed a weariness. No one appeared to see anything straightly, and they seemed to be taken up with pursuits that could not divert or interest a cat. She saw quite a number of young men at dinners and was taken to the theater and suppers at the fashionable restaurants, and these entertainments she loathed. She was too desperately unhappy underneath to get even youth's exhilaration out of them, and when she had been in London for nearly three weeks and Cheiron was preparing to return to his cottage, having delayed his departure much beyond his ordinary time, she felt she could endure the martyrdom no more.

She had stilled every voice which had whispered to her that it was indeed time that she heard some word from her lover. Because there were now only occasional notices in the papers about his health, he was supposed to be getting well.

"I will implore Cheiron to let me go back with him," she

decided firmly, as she went downstairs to breakfast. "I will ask if I may not go out and see him this morning," and, comforted with this thought, she entered the dining-room with a brisker step than usual. No one but her stepfather was down.

He had grown accustomed, if not quite attached, to the quiet, gentle girl, and he liked her noiseless, punctual way —they had often breakfasted alone.

He was reading his *Chronicle* propped up in front of him, and handed her the *Morning Post* from the pile by his side. He silently went on with his cutlet which an obsequious butler had placed for his consumption. Halcyone turned rapidly to the column where she was accustomed to look daily for news of her lover. And there she read that Mrs. Cricklander had been entertaining a Saturday to Monday party, and that Mr. John Derringham's recovery was now well advanced, even his broken ankle was mending rapidly and he hoped soon to be well.

A tight feeling grew round her heart, and her eyes dropped absently down the columns of the engagement announcements in which she took no interest, and then it seemed that her very soul was struck with agony as she read:

"A marriage has been arranged and will shortly take place between the Right Honorable John Derringham of Derringham in the County of Northampton, Under-Secretary of State for Foreign Affairs, and Mrs. Vincent Cricklander of New York, daughter of Orlando B. Muggs of Pittsburgh, U. S. A."

And it was here that the La Sarthe breeding stood Halcyone in good stead, for she neither fainted nor dropped the paper—but, after a few seconds of acute anguish, she rose and, making some little remark about having forgotten something, quietly left the room.

CHAPTER XXIV

It is possible that, if his revolver had been lying quite near, the morning John Derringham awoke to the remembrance that he was more or less an engaged man, he would have shot himself, so utterly wretched and debased did he feel. But no such weapon was there, and he lay in his splendid gilt bed and groaned aloud as he covered his eyes with his hand.

The light hurt him—he was giddy, and his head swam. Surely, among other things in the half-indistinct nightmare of the preceding evening, he must have had too much champagne.

From the moment, now over a week ago, that he had been allowed to sit up in bed, and more or less distinct thought had come back to him, he had been a prey to hideous anxiety and grief. Halcyone was gone from him—had been snatched away by Fate, who, with relentless vindictiveness, had filled his cup. For the first letters that he opened, marked from his lawyers so urgently that they had been given to him before the bandages were off his head, contained the gravest news of his financial position. The chief mortgagee intended to foreclose in the course of the next three months, unless an arrangement could be come to at once, which appeared impossible.

He was actually at bay. Thus, although in his first moments of consciousness, he had intended to go directly he was well and demand his love openly and chance the rest, this news made that course now quite out of the question. He could not condemn her to wretched poverty and tie a millstone round both their necks. The doctors had absolutely forbidden him to read or even know of any more letters—the official ones the secretary could deal with—but he became so restless with anxiety that Arabella Clinker was persuaded to bring them up and at least let him glance at the addresses.

There was one from Cheiron, which he insisted upon opening—a brief dry line of commiseration for his accident, with no mention of Halcyone in it. The complete ignoring of his letter to announce their marriage cut him deeply. He realized Mr. Carlyon guessed that the accident had happened before the event could take place, and his silence about it showed what he thought. John Derringham quivered with discomfort, he hated to feel the whip of his old master's contempt. And he could not explain matters or justify himself—there was nothing to be said. The Professor, of course, knew of Halcyone's whereabouts— but, after his broad hint of his want of sympathy about their relations, John Derringham felt he could not open the subject with him again. This channel for the assuagement of his anxieties was closed. The immense pile of the rest of his correspondence was at last sorted. He knew most of the writings, and the few he was doubtful about he opened but none were from his love. So he gave them all back to Arabella, and turned his face from the light physically exhausted and with a storm of pain in his heart.

Mrs. Cricklander had carefully gone through each post as it came, and longed to destroy one or two suspicious-looking communications she saw in the same female handwriting— from his old friend Lady Durend, if she had known!—but she dared not, and indeed was not really much disturbed. She had laid her own plans with too great a nicety and felt perfectly sure of the ultimate result of their action. Arabella was each day sent up with the subtlest messages to the poor invalid, which her honor made her unwillingly repeat truthfully.

Cecilia Cricklander was an angel of sweet, watchful care it seemed, and John Derringham really felt deeply grateful to her.

Then the moment came when she decided she would see him

"I will go this afternoon at tea-time, Arabella, if you can assure me there won't be any horrid smell of carbolic or nasty drugs about—I know there always are when people have cuts to be dresed, and I really could not stand it It would give me one of my bad attacks of nerves."

And Miss Clinker was reluctantly obliged to assure her employer that those days were passed, and that Mr. Derringham now only looked a pale, but very interesting invalid, as he lay there with a black silk handkerchief tied round his head.

"Then I'll go," said Mrs. Cricklander—and, instead of sending the message with her daily flowers, she wrote a tiny note.

I can't bear it any longer—I must come !

                                               CECILIA.

Arabella Clinker watched his face as he read this, and saw a flush grow in his ivory-pale skin.

"Oh! Poor Mr. Derringham!" she thought, "it isn't fair! How can he hold out against her when he is so weak—what ought I to do? If I only knew what is my loyal course!"

Arabella was perfectly aware how the reports of his rapid recovery had been circulated—and guessed the reason—and all her kind woman's heart was touched as she watched him lying there in splints, as pitiful and helpless as a baby. To pretend that he was making a quick return to health was so very far from the truth. She, herself, saw little change for the better from day to day; indeed, his large, proud eyes seemed to grow more anxious and haggard as the time went on.

Mrs. Cricklander donned her most suitably ravishing tea-gown, one of subdued simplicity—and, like a beautiful summer flower, she swept into the invalid's room when the lowered sun blinds made the light restful and the June roses filled the air with scent. It was the end of the month and glorious weather was over the land.

Nothing could have been more exquisite than Cecilia's sympathy. Indeed, she did feel a good deal moved, and was a superb actress at all times.

She only stayed a very short while, not to tire him, and John Derringham, left alone, was conscious that he had been soothed and pleased, and she departed leaving the impression that her love for him was only kept within bounds by fear for his health!

She had suffered *so* during all the days! she told him, she could hardly eat or sleep. And then to be debarred from nursing him!—the cruelty of it! Why the doctors should have thought her presence would be more disturbing than Arabella's, she could not think! And here she looked down, and her white hand, with its perfectly kept nails, lying upon the coverlet so near him, John Derringham lifted it in his feeble grasp and touched it with his lips. He was so grateful for her kindness—and affected by her beauty; he could not do less, he felt.

And after that, with a deliciously girlish and confused gasp. Mrs. Cricklander had hastily quitted the room.

It was not until the second day that she came again—and he had begun to wish for her.

This time she was bright and amusing, and assumed airs of authority over him, and was careful never to sit so that her hand might be in reach, while she used every one of her many arts of tantalization and enjoyed herself as only she knew how to do.

It was perfectly divine to have him there to play upon like a violin and to know it was only a question of time before she would secure him for her own!

After this, she had visitors in the house and did not come for three days, and John Derringham felt a little peevish and aggrieved. It rained, too, and his head ached still with the slightest exertion.

He now began to put all thoughts of Halcyone away from him, as far as he was able. It was too late to do anything —she must think him base, as she had never sent him one word. This caused him restless anguish. What was the meaning of it all? Could she have learned in the light of the world that it was not a very great position he had offered her, and so despised him in consequence? What aspect of it might they not have put into her head—these people she was with—this stepmother of whom he had never heard? In all cases Fate had parted them, and he must cut the pain of it from his life or it would destroy him. It never occurred to him to reflect upon the possible agony she might be suffering, his poor little wood-nymph, all alone. The fact of his own unhappiness filled his mind to the exclusion of any other thought for the time. In his dire physical weakness Cecilia Cricklander's gracious beauty seemed to augment, and Halcyone's sylph-like charm to grow of less potent force. For Love had not done all that he would yet do with John Derringham's soul.

That underneath, if he could have chosen between the two women, he would have hesitated for a second was not the case; only physical weakness, and circumstance and propinquity were working for the one and against the other —and so it would appear was Fate.

Thus, the day the visitors left, Mr. Hanbury-Green among them, the invalid was experiencing a sense of exasperating neglect. He felt extremely miserable. Life, and all he held good in it, seemed to be over for him, and his financial position was absolutely desperate—quite beyond any question of marriage it threatened to swamp his actual career. He felt impotent and beaten, lying there like a log unable to move.

Mrs. Cricklander sent him another little note in the afternoon. Arabella had reported that the patient was restless, and this might mean one of two things—either that he was becoming impatient to see her, or that he was growing restive and bored with bed. In either case it was the momeant to strike—and to strike quickly.

"The doctors have said you may have a taste of champagne to-night," she wrote, which was quite untrue, but a small fib like this could not count when such large issues were at stake. "And so I propose, if you will let me and will have me for your guest, to come and dine with you to celebrate the event. Say if I may. Cecilia."

And he had eagerly scribbled in pencil, "Yes."

So she came, and was all in white with just a red rose in her dress, and she was solicitous about his comfort—had he enough pillows?—and she spoke so graciously to the nurse who arranged things before she went to supper.

She, Cecilia, would be his nurse, she whispered—just for to-night! and then her own personal footman brought in an exquisite little dinner upon a table which he set near the bed, all noiselessly—it had been arranged outside—and she would select just the tenderest morsels for John Derringham, or some turtle soup?—He was not hungry!—Well, never mind, she would feed him!—and he must be good and let her pet him as she felt inclined.

She was looking quite extraordinarily beautiful, with all the light of triumph in her sparkling eyes, and she sat down upon the bed and actually pretended that if he were disobedient she would put pieces into his mouth!

John Derringham was a man—and, although he felt very ill and feeble, after she had made him drink some champagne, the seduction of her began to go to his head. Stimulant of any kind was the last thing he should have had, and would have caused the nurse a shock of horror if she had known. How it all came about he could not tell, what she said or he said he could never remember, only the one thing which stood out was that as the time for the nurse's return arrived, he knew that Cecilia Cricklander was kissing him with apparent passion, which he felt in some measure he was returning, and that she was murmuring: "And we shall be married, darling John, as soon as you are well."

He must have said something definite, he supposed.

But, at that moment, the nurse was heard in the next room and his *fiancée*—yes, his *fiancée*—got up and, when the woman came in in her stiff nurse's dress, slightly apologetic that she had been so long, she was greeted by this speech from the lady of the house:

"Ah, Nurse Brome, you have been so good to Mr. Derringham, you must be the first to wish us happiness and share our news. We are going to be married as soon as ever you get him well—so you must hasten that, like the clever woman you are !"

And she had laughed, a soft laugh of triumph, which even in his light-headed state had seemed to John Derringham as the mocking of some fiend.

Then she had left him quickly, while the footman carried the table from the room—and after that he remembered nothing more, he had fallen into a feverish sleep. But the next morning, when he awoke, he knew captivity had indeed tumbled upon him, and that he was chained hand and foot.

And all the day his temperature went up again, and he was not allowed to see even Arabella of the kind heart, who would have come and condoled with him, and even wept over him if she had dared, so moved did the good creature feel at his fate.

It was only upon the third day, when telegrams of congratulation began to pour in upon him by the dozen, that he knew anything about the announcement that had appeared in the *Morning Post*.

Yes, he was caught and chained at last, and for the next week had moods of gnashing his teeth, and feeling the most degraded of men, alternating with hours of trying to persuade himself that it was the best thing which could have happened to him.

Mrs. Cricklander, now that she had gained her end, wisely left him for a day or two in peace to the care of Arabella and the nurses, drawing the net closer each hour by her public parade of her position as his *fiancée*. She wrote the most exquisite and womanly letter to thank her many friends for their kind congratulations—and lamented, now that the truth being known would not matter, that John had had a slight relapse, and was not quite so well.

But, of course, she was taking every care of him, and so he soon would be his old exuberant self !

Thus the period of John Derringham's purgatory began.

CHAPTER XXV

GRIEVING is such a satisfactory and dramatic thing when you can fling yourself down upon the ground and cry aloud and tear your hair. But if some great blow must be borne without a sign, then indeed it wrings the heart and saps the forces of life.

When Halcyone got to her room, the housemaids were there beginning to make her bed—so it was no refuge for her—and she was obliged to go down again. The big drawing-rooms would be untenanted at this moment, so she turned the handle of the door and crept in there. The modern brightly gilt Louis XVI furniture glared at her, but she sank into a big chair thankful to find any support.

What was this which had fallen upon her?—The winter, indeed—or, more than that, not only the winter but the end of life, like the flash of lightning which had struck the tree in the park the night before that day which was to have seen her wedding?

And as she sat there in dumb, silent, hideous agony which crushed for the moment belief and hope, a canary from the aviary beyond set up a trilling song. She listened for a second; it seemed to hurt her more. The poor bird was in captivity, as was her soul. And then, while the little songster went on, undismayed by its cage, a reaction set in. If the soft-feathered creature could sing there beyond the bars, what right had she to doubt God for one second? No —there should never be any disbelief. It was only the winter, after all. She was too young to die like the tree which had been there for some hundreds of years. She would be as brave as the bird, and those forces of nature which she had loved and trusted so long, would comfort her.

She sat there for a quarter of an hour saying her prayers and stilling the pain in her heart—and then she got up and deliberately went back to the dining-room, where the family were all assembled now.

They chaffed about everything, and were boisterous and jovial as usual, and when she asked if she might go and see her old master, should Mrs. Anderton not wish especially for her company that morning, her stepfather offered to

157

drive her there in his phaeton on his way to the city.

"She grows upon one, Lu," he said to his wife, when Halcyone had gone up to put on her hat. "She is like some quiet, soothing book; she is a kind of comfort—but she looks confoundedly pale to-day. Take her to the play to-night, or ask some young fellows in to dinner, to cheer her up."

The drive did Halcyone good, and, to the astonishment of Cheiron who had also read the news, she walked into his sitting-room with perfect calm. He himself was raging with indignation and disgust.

But, when he looked into her deep eyes, his astonishment turned to pain, for the expression in them as they burned from her lifeless face was so pure, so pitiful and so tragic, that it left him without words for the moment.

At last he said—when she had greeted him:

"I have been thinking, Halcyone, that I have not had a trip abroad for a long time, but I am too old now to care about going alone. Do you think that your aunts and these step-relations of yours would spare you to accompany me, my dear?"

And Halcyone had to turn away to the window to hide the tears which suddenly welled up; he was so kind and understanding always—her dear old master.

"Yes, I am sure they would," she said in a very low voice. "How good of you. And if we could start at once—that would be nice, would it not? I suppose they would not let me go without Priscilla, though," she added; "would that matter?"

"Not at all," said the Professor.

They neither of them mentioned John Derringham's engagement. They talked long about the possibilities of their foreign journey, and Cheiron felt himself repaid when he began to observe a look of returning life creep into her white face.

"I will call and see your stepfather in the city directly after lunch," he said. "If you will write to your Aunts La Sarthe, I do not think there can be any objection."

"We could take Aphrodite, could we not?" Halcyone asked. "She is very heavy, I know, but I would carry her, and I do not think I would like to leave her there in the dark away from me for all that time."

"We would certainly take her," said Cheiron.

Halcyone knew enough about London now to know where Kensington Gardens were. Whenever she went to see Mr.

Carlyon, it was an understood thing he would bring her safely back, so no one would be sent to fetch her. Might they not go to Kensington Gardens this morning, she asked. She remembered to have noticed, when she had driven past with Mr. Anderton, that there seemed to be big trees there. She wanted to get into some open space, London was stifling her.

Mr. Carlyon put on his hat, and prepared to accompany her. They drove to the first gate and got out, neither having spoken a word, as was their habit when both were thinking.

They wandered in among the trees and found two chairs and sat down.

These were real trees, Halcyone felt. And, although she would have preferred to be alone to-day without even Cheiron, the great trunks and vast leafy canopy above them comforted her.

She would not permit herself to think, the beauty of the summer day must just saturate her, and soothe the cold, sick ache in her heart. And, presently, when she was strengthened, she would face it all and see what it could mean, and what would be best to do to bear the blow as a La Sarthe should, and show nothing of the anguish.

And, as she mused, her eyes absently wandered to a couple under a tree some twenty yards beyond them. There was something familiar in the girl's graceful back, and, as she turned her fresh face to look at her companion, Halcyone saw that it was Cora Lutworth.

Some magnetic spark seemed to connect them, for the pretty American girl turned completely round in her chair, and catching sight of the two jumped up and came towards them—with glad, laughing eyes and outstretched hands.

"To see you!" she exclaimed. "That is so good! There is no Styx here, and we must have some fun together!"

She sat down upon a chair which Lord Freynault dragged up for her, and he himself took another beyond the Professor—so the two girls could talk together.

"I am going to be married—you know!" Cora announced gayly. "Freynie and I settled it at a ball last night, but we haven't told anyone yet! Isn't it lovely? We just slipped out here for a little quiet talk."

"I am so glad. I hope you will be very happy," Halcyone said, and tried not to let the contrast of Cora's joyous prospect make her wince.

"I am always happy," Cora returned, "and it's dear of you to wish me nice things."

Halcyone attracted her immensely, her quite remarkable personal distinction was full of charm, and, now in fresh and pretty modern clothes, to Cora's eyes she looked almost beautiful; but why so very pale and quiet, she wondered; and then, with a flash, she remembered the news she too had read in the paper that morning. Perhaps Halcyone minded very much. She decided rapidly what to do. If she did not mention it at all, she reasoned, this finely strung girl would know that she guessed it would be painful to her—and that might hurt her pride. It was kinder to plunge in and get it over.

"Isn't it wonderful about Mr. Derringham and Cecilia Cricklander?" she said, pretending to be busy untangling her parasol tassel. "She always intended to marry him—and she is so rich I expect he felt that would be a good thing. Freynie says he is very much harder up than anyone knows."

Her kind, common sense told her that a man's doing even a low thing for expediency would hurt a woman who loved him, less than that the motive for his action should have been one of inclination.

Halcyone came up to the scratch, although a fierce pain tightened her heart afresh.

"Yes," she said, "I suppose no one was surprised to read of the engagement in the papers to-day. I can imagine that a man requires a great deal of money to support the position in the government which Mr. Derringham has, and no doubt Mrs. Cricklander is glad to give it to him—he is so clever and great." And not a muscle of her face quivered as she spoke.

"If it does hurt—my goodness! she is game!" Cora thought, and aloud she went on, "Cecilia isn't a bad sort— a shocking snob, as all of us are who not the real thing and want to be—like your own common pushers over here. We used to laugh at her awfully when she first came from Pittsburgh and tried to cut in before she married my cousin. Poor old Vin! He was crazy about her." Then she went on reflectively, as Halcyone did not answer. "We often think you English people are so odd—the way you can't distinguish between us! You receive, with open arms, the most impossible people if they are rich, that we at home would not touch with a barge pole, and you say: 'Oh, they are just American,' as if we were all the same! And then we are so awfully clever as a nation that in a year or two these dreadful vulgarians, as we would call them in New York, have picked up all *your* outside polish, and pass as *our* best! It makes lots of the really nice old gentle-folk at home perfectly mad—but I can't help admiring the spirit. That is why I have stuck to Cis, though the rest of the family have given her the cold shoulder. It is such magnificent audacity—don't you think so?"

"Yes, indeed," agreed Halcyone. "All people have a right to obtain what they aspire to if they fit themselves for it."

"That is one of Mr. Derringham's pet theories," Cora laughed. "He held forth one night, when I was staying at Wendover at Easter, about it—and it was such fun. Cis did not really understand a single thing of the classical allusions he was making—but she got through. I watch her with delight. Men are sweetly simple bats, though, aren't they? Any woman can take them in—" and Cora laughed again joyously. "I have sat sometimes in fits to hear Cis keeping a whole group of your best politicians enthralled, and not one seeing she is just repeating parrot sentences. You have only to be rich and beautiful and look into a man's eyes and flatter him, and you can make him believe you are what you please. Now Freynie thinks I am absolutely perfect when I am really being a horrid little capricious minx—don't you, Freynie, dear!" and she leaned over and looked at her betrothed with sweet and tender eyes —and Lord Freynault got up and moved his chair round, so that the four were in a circle.

"What preposterous thing is Cora telling you?" he laughed, with an adoring glance at her sparkling face. "But I am getting jealous, and shall take her away because I want to talk to her all to myself!"

And, when they had settled that the two girls should meet at tea the following day in Cora's sitting-room at Claridge's, where she was staying with a friend, the newly engaged pair went off together beaming with joy and affection.

And Halcyone gazed after them with a wistful look in her sad eyes, which stabbed the old Professor's heart.

She was remembering the morning under their tree, when she and her lover had sat and made their plans, and he had asked her if she had any fear at the thought of giving him her future.

It was only three weeks ago. Surely everything was a dream. How much he had seemed to love her. And then unconsciously she started to her feet, and strode away among the trees, forgetful of her companion—and Cheiron sat and watched her, knowing she would come back and it was better to let her overcome alone the agony which was convulsing her.

Yes, John Derringham had seemed to love her—not seemed—no—it was real—he *had* loved her. And she would never believe but that he loved her still. This was only a wicked turn of those bad forces which she knew were abroad in the world. Had she not seen evil once in a man's face crouching in the bracken, as he set a trap for some poor hare one dark and starry night? And she had passed on, and then, when she thought he would be gone, she had returned and loosened the spring before it could do any harm. That poacher had evil forces round him. They were there always for the unwary, and had fastened upon John. She would never doubt his love, and she herself could never change, and she would pour upon him all her tender thoughts, and call to the night winds to help her to do her duty.

So presently she remembered Cheiron, and turned round to see him far away still, sitting quietly beneath a giant elm stroking his long, silver beard.

"My dear, kind master!" she exclaimed to herself, and went rapidly back to him.

"That is a charming girl—your young friend," he said to her, as he got up to stroll to the gate; "full of life and common sense. There is something wonderful in the vitality of her nation. They jar dreadfully upon us old tired peoples in their worst aspects—but in their best we must recognize a new spring of life and youth for the world. Yonder young woman is not troubling about a soul, if she has one; she is a fountain of living water. She has not taken on the shadows of our crowded past. Halcyone, my dear, you and I are the inheritance of too much culture. When I see her I want to cry with Epicurus: 'Above all, steer clear of Culture!'" And then he branched from this subject and plunged into a learned dissertation upon the worship of Dionysus, and how it had cropped up again and again with wild fervor among the ancient worlds whose senses and brains were wearied with the state religions, and he concluded by analogy that this wild longing to return to youth's follies and mad ecstasies, to get free from restraints, to seek communion with the spiritual beyond in some exaltation of the emotions—in short, to get back to nature—was an instinct in all human beings and all nations, when their zeniths of art and cultivation had come.

And Halcyone, who had heard it all before and knew the subject to her finger tips, wandered dreaming into a shadowland where she felt she was of these people—those far back worshipers—and this was her winter when Dionysus was dead, but would live again when the spring came and the flowers.

CHAPTER XXVI

Mrs. Cricklander felt it would be discreet and in perfect taste if she announced her intention of going off to Carlsbad the week after her engagement was settled—she was always most careful of decorum. And, if the world of her friends thought John Derringham was well enough to be making love to her in the seclusion of her own house, it would be much wiser for her to show that she should always remain beyond the breath of any gossip.

In her heart she was bored to tears. For nearly the whole of June she had been cooped up at Wendover—for more than half the time without even parties of visitors to keep her company—and she loathed being alone. She had no personal resources and invariably at such times smoked too much and got agitated nerves in consequence.

John Derringham—strong and handsome, with his prestige and his brilliant faculties—was a conquest worth parading chained to her chariot wheels. But John Derringham, feeble, unable to walk, his ankle in splints and plaster of Paris, and still suffering from headaches whenever the light was strong, was simply a weariness to her—nothing more nor less.

So that, until he should be restored to his usual captivating vigor, it was much better for her pleasure to leave him to his complete recovery alone, now that she had got him securely in her keeping.

Arabella could ask her mother down and keep house and see that he had everything in the world that he wanted— and there were the devoted nurses. And, in short, her doctor had said she must have her usual cure, and that was the end of the matter!

She had only made him the most fleeting visits during the week. He had really been ill after the fever caused by the champagne. And she had been exquisitely gentle and not too demonstrative. She had calculated the possibility of his backing out under the plea of his health, so she determined not to give him a chance to have the slightest excuse by overtiring him.

No one could have better played the part of devoted,

understanding friend who by excess of love had been betrayed into one lapse of passionate outburst, and now
wished only to soothe and comfort.

"She is a good sort," John Derringham thought, after
her first visit. "She will let me down easy in any case," and
the ceasing of his anxiety about his financial position comforted him greatly.

The next time she came and sat by his bed, a vision of
fresh summer laces and chiffons, he determined to make the
position clear to her.

She always bent and kissed him with airy grace, then sat
down at a discreet distance. She felt he was not over-
anxious to caress her, and preferred that the rendering of
this impossible should come from her side. Indeed, unless
kisses were necessary to gain an end, she did not care for
them herself—stupid, contemptible things, she thought them!

John Derringham would have touched the hearts of most
women as he lay there, but Cecilia Cricklander had not this
tiresome appendage, only the business brain and unemotional
sensibilities of her grandfather the pork butcher. She did
realize that her *fiancé*, even there with the black silk handkerchief wound round his head and his face and hands
deadly pale and fragile-looking, was still a most arrogant
and distinguished-looking creature, and that his eyes, with
their pathetic shadows dimming the proud glance in them,
were wonderfully attractive. But she was not touched
especially by his weakness. She disliked suffering and never
wanted to be made aware of it.

John Derringham went straight into the subject which
was uppermost in his thoughts. He asked her to listen to
him patiently, and stated his exact financial situation. She
must then judge if she found it worth while to marry him;
he would not deceive her about one fraction of it.

She laughed lightly when he had ended—and there was
something which galled him in her mirth.

"It is all a ridiculous nothing," she said. "Why, I can
pay off the whole thing with only the surplus I invest every
year from my income! Your property is quite good security
—if I want any. We shall probably have to do it in a
business-like way; your house will be mine, of course, but
I will make you very comfortable as my guest!" and she
smiled with suitable playfulness. "Let the lawyers talk
over these things, not you and me—you may be sure mine
will look after me!"

John Derringham felt the blood tingling in his ears. There was nothing to take exception to in what she had said, but it hurt him awfully.

"Very well," he answered wearily, and closed his eyes for a moment. "If you are satisfied, that is all that need be said. As things go on, and I reach where I mean to get, I dare say to spend money to do the thing beautifully will please you as much as it will gratify me. I will give you what I can of the honors and glories—so shall we consider our bargain equal?"

This was not lover-like, and Mrs. Cricklander knew it, but it was better to have got it all over. She was well aware that the "honors and glories" would compensate her for the outlay of her dollars, but her red mouth shut with a snap as she registered a thought.

"When I come back it may amuse me to make him really in love with me." Then, watching carefully, she saw that some cloud of jar and disillusion had settled upon her *fiancé's* face. So with her masterly skill she tried to banish it, talking intelligently upon the political situation and his prospects. It looked certain that the Government would not last beyond the session—and then what would happen?

Mr. Hanbury-Green had given her a very clear forecast of what the other side meant to do, but this she did not impart to John Derringham.

She made one really stupid mistake as she got up to leave the room.

"If you want a few thousands now, John," she said, as she bent to lightly salute his cheek, "do let me know and I will send them to your bank. They may be useful for the wedding."

A dull flush mounted to the roots of his hair, and then left him very pale.

He took her hand and kissed it with icy homage.

"Thank you, no—" he said. "You are far too good. I will not take anything from you until the bargain is completed."

Then their eyes met and in his there was a flash of steel.

And when she had gone from the room he lay and quivered, a sense of hideous humiliation flooded his being.

The following day she came in the morning. She looked girlish in her short tennis frock and was rippling with smiles. She sat on the bed and kissed him—and then slipped her hand into his.

"John, darling," she said sweetly. "People will begin to

talk if I stay here at Wendover now that you are getting better—and you would hate that as much as I—so I have settled to go to Carlsbad with Lady Maulevrier—just for three weeks. By that time my splendid John will be himself again and we can settle about our wedding—" then she bent and kissed him once more before he could speak. "Arabella is going to get her mother to come down," she went on, "and you will be safe here with these devoted old ladies and your Brome who is plainly in love with you, poor thing!" and she laughed gayly. "Say you think it is best, too, John, dearest?"

"Whatever you wish," he answered with some sudden quick sense of relief. "I know I am an awful bore lying here, and I shall not be able to crawl to a sofa even for another week, these doctors say."

"You are not a bore—you are a darling," she murmured, patting his hand. "And if only I were allowed to stay with you—night and day—and nurse you like Brome, I should be perfectly happy. But these snatched scraps—John, darling, I can't bear it!"

He wondered if she were lying. He half thought so, but she looked so beautiful, it enabled him to return her caresses with some tepid warmth.

"It is too sweet of you, Cecilia," he said, as he kissed her. He had not yet used one word of intimate endearment—she had never been his darling, his sweet and his own, like Halcyone.

After she had gone again, all details having been settled for her departure upon the Monday, he almost felt that he hated her. For, when she was in this apparently loving mood, it seemed as if her bonds tightened round his throat and strangled him to death. "Octopus arms" he remembered Cheiron had called them.

When Mrs. Cricklander got back to her own favorite long seat out on the terrace, she sat down, and settling the pillows under her head, she had let her thoughts ticket her advantages gained, in her usual concrete fashion.

"He is absolutely mine, body and soul. He does not love me—we shall have the jolliest time seeing who will win presently—but I have got the dollars, so there is no doubt of the result—and what fun it will be! It does not matter what I do now, he cannot break away from me. He has let me see plainly that my money has influenced him—and, although Englishmen are fools, in his class they are ridiculously honorable. I've got him!" and she laughed aloud. "It is all safe, he will not break the bargain!"

So she wrote an interesting note to Mr. Hanbury-Green with a pencil on one of the blocks which she kept lying about for any sudden use—and then strolled into the house for an envelope.

And, as John Derringham lay in the darkened room upstairs, he presently heard her joyous voice as she played tennis with his secretary, and the reflection he made was:

"Good Lord, how thankful I should be that at least I do not love her!"

Then he clenched his hands, and his aching thoughts escaped the iron control under which since his engagement he had tried always to keep them, and they went back to Halcyone. He saw again with agonizing clearness her little tender face, when her soft, true eyes had melted into his as she whispered of love.

"This is what God means in everything." Well, God had very little to do with himself and Cecilia Cricklander!

And then he suddenly seemed to see the brutishness of men. Here was he—a refined, honorable gentleman—in a few weeks going to play false to his very instinct, and take this woman whom he was growing to despise—and perhaps dislike—into his arms and into his life, in that most intimate relationship which, he realized now, should only be undertaken when passionate calls of tenderest love imperatively forced it. She would have the right to be with him day—and night. She might be the mother of his children—and he would have to watch her instincts, which he surely would have daily grown to loathe, coming out in them. And all because money had failed him in his own resources and was necessary to his ambitions, and this necessity, working with an appeal to his senses when fired with wine, had brought about the situation.

God Almighty! How low he felt!

And he groaned aloud.

Then from a small dispatch box, which he had got his servant to put by his bed, he drew forth a little gold case, in which for all these years he had kept an oak leaf. He had had it made in the enthusiasm of his youth when he had returned to London after Halcyone, the wise-eyed child, had given it to him, and it had gone about everywhere with him since as a sort of fetish.

It burnt his sight when he looked at it now. For had he been "good and true"? Alas! No—nothing but a sensual, ambitious weakling.

CHAPTER XXVII

THE Professor and his protégée spent the whole of that July wandering in Brittany—going from one old-world spot to another. There had not been much opposition raised by Mr. and Mrs. Anderton to Halcyone's accompanying her old master. They themselves were going to Scotland, and there Mabel had decided she would no longer be kept in the schoolroom, and intended to come forward as a grown-up girl assisting in the hospitalities of her father's shooting lodge. And Mrs. Anderton, knowing her temper, thought a rival of any sort might make difficulties. So, as far as they were concerned, Halcyone might start at once. They always left for the north in the middle of the month, and if the Professor wanted to get away sooner, they did not wish to interfere with his arrangements. Halcyone must come and pay them another visit later on.

As for the Aunts La Sarthe—their heads appeared to be completely turned by their sojourn at the seaside! They proposed to remain there all the summer, and put forward no objection to their niece's excursion with Mr. Carlyon. The once quiet spot of their youth had developed into a fashionable Welsh watering place, and Miss Roberta was taking on a new lease of health and activity from the pleasure of seeing the crowded parade, while the Aunt Ginevra allowed that the exhilarating breezes and cerulean waters were certainly most refreshing!

Before the Professor could leave for a lengthy trip abroad, it was necessary that he should return to the orchard house for a day, and Halcyone accompanied him, leaving Priscilla in London. Her mission was to secure the goddess's head —but, as there was no one at La Sarthe Chase, she decided just to go there and get her treasure and sleep the night at Cheiron's.

It would be an excursion of much pain to her, to be so near to her still loved lover and to feel the cruel gulf between them, but she must face it if she desired Aphrodite to accompany them. The Professor suggested she might take him through the secret passage and try with his help to open the heavy box. No such opportunity had ever occurred be-

169

fore or was likely to occur again, her aunts being absent and even old William nowhere about. It made the chance one in a thousand. So she agreed, and determined to force herself to endure the pain which going back would cause her.

She was perfectly silent all the way from London to Upminster—and Mr. Carlyon watched her furtively. He knew very well what was passing in her mind, and admired the will which suppressed the expression of it. She grew very pale indeed in the station-fly when they passed the gates of Wendover. It was about half past three in the afternoon—and the Professor had promised to come to the archway opening of the secret passage at five.

So Halcyone left him and took her way down the garden and through the little gate into the park. It seemed like revisiting some scene in a former life, so deep was the chasm which separated the last time she walked that way from this day. She passed the oak tree without stopping. She would not give way to any weakness or the grief which threatened to overwhelm her. She kept her mind steadily fixed upon the object she had in view, with a power of concentration which only those who live in solitude can ever attain to.

Aphrodite was there still in the bag lying on top of the heavy iron-bound box in the secret passage, and she carried her out into the sunlight and once more took the wrappings from the perfect face.

"You are coming with us, sweet friend," she whispered, and gazed long into the goddess's eyes. What she saw there gave her comfort.

"Yes, I know," she went on gently. "I did say that, whatever came, I would understand that it was life—and I do—and I know this evil pain is only for the time—and so I will not admit its power. I will wait and some day joy will return to me, like the swallow from the south. Mother, I will grieve not."

And all the softest summer zephyrs seemed to caress her in answer, and there she sat silent and absorbed, looking out to the blue hills for more than an hour.

Then she saw Cheiron advancing up the beech avenue, and covering up Aphrodite she went to meet him.

They came back to the second terrace and started upon their quest.

Mr. Carlyon had the greatest difficulty in keeping his old head bent to get through the very low part of the dark arched place, and he held Halcyone's hand. But at last they emerged into the one light spot and there saw the breastplate and the box. But at first it seemed as if they could not lift it; it had fallen with the lock downward. Cheiron, although a most robust old man, had passed his seventieth year, and the thing was of extreme heaviness. But at last they pushed and pulled and got it upright, and finally, with tremendous exertions with a chisel Mr. Carlyon had brought, managed to break open the ancient lock.

It gave with a sudden snap, and in breathless excitement they raised the lid.

Inside was another case of wood. This also was locked, but at its side lay an old key. The Professor, as well as his chisel, had prudently brought a small bottle of oil, and eventually was able to make the key turn in the lock, and they found that the box was in two compartments, one entirely filled with gold pieces, and the other containing some smaller heavy object enwound with silk.

They lifted it out and carried it to the light, and then with great excitement they unrolled the coverings. It proved to be a gold-and-jeweled crucifix and beneath it lay a parchment with a seal.

Leaving the pieces of gold in the box, they carried the crucifix and the parchment out in to the terrace, and then the Professor adjusted his strongest spectacles and prepared to read what he could, while Halcyone examined the beautiful thing.

The writing was still fairly dark and the words were in Latin. It stated, so the Professor read, that the money and the crucifix were the property of Timothy La Sarthe, Gentleman to Queen Henrietta Maria, and that, should aught befall him in his flight to France upon secret business for Her Majesty, the gold and the crucifix belonged to whichever of his descendants should find it—or it should be handed to; that all others were cursed who should touch it, and that it would bring the owner fortune, as it was the work of one Benvenuto Cellini, an artist of great renown in Florence before his day, and therefore of great value. The quaintly phrased deed added that if it were taken to one Reuben Zana, a Jew in the Jewry at the sign of the Golden Horn, he would dispose of it for a large sum to the French king. The crucifix had been brought from Florence in the dower of his wife Donna Vittoria Tornabuoni, now dead. If his son Timothy should secure it, he was advised not to keep it, as its possession brought trouble to the family.

"Then it is legally ours and not treasure-trove," said Halcyone. "Oh, how good! It will make the Aunts La Sarthe quite rich perhaps, and look how beautiful it is, the jeweled thing."

They examined it minutely. It was a masterpiece of that great craftsman and artist and of untold value. Cheiron silently thrilled with the delight of it—but Halcyone spoke.

"I am glad Ancestor Timothy suggested selling it," she said. "I would never keep a crucifix, the emblem of sorrow and pain. For me, Christ is always glorified and happy in heaven. Now what must we do, Master? Must we at once tell the aunts? But I will not consent to anyone knowing of this staircase. That would destroy something which I could never recover. We must pretend we have found it in the long gallery; there is a recess in the paneling which no one knows of but I, and there we can put it and find it again. It will be quite safe. Shall we leave it there, Cheiron, until we come back from abroad? How much do you think it is worth?"

"Anything up to fifty thousand pounds perhaps to a collector," the Professor said, "since it is an original and unique. Look at the splendid rubies and emeralds and these two big diamonds at the top, and there is so little of Benvenuto's work left that is authentic."

"That is an unusual sum of money, is it not?" Halcyone asked. "That would surely give them anything they want for their lives; perhaps we ought not to keep them waiting."

And so after much talk it was arranged that Halcyone should make several journeys, taking the gold to the long gallery and then the crucifix; and then the box could be lifted and repacked again there. And, when she had it all stowed away carefully in the recess of the paneling, she and Cheiron should go openly to the back door and let the caretaker know that they had arrived, and go into the house—and there ostensibly find the treasure. Then they would write to the Misses La Sarthe about their discovery, and take the box to Applewood and deposit it in the bank until their return.

All this took a long time but was duly carried out, and about eight o'clock Halcyone and the Professor were able to go back, carrying the crucifix with them, to keep it safe for the night and then to put it back with the gold and the parchment, before they took the box to the bank on the morrow.

"It may be worth more still and there is a good deal of gold," the Professor said, "and their coins would be worth more now. You will be quite a little heiress some day, dear child."

"I do not care the least about money, Cheiron," she said, "but I shall be so glad for the aunts."

And when eventually the old ladies received the news of their fortune there was much rejoicing, and by following Cheiron's advice they were not defrauded and might look forward to a most comfortable end to their lives. Miss Roberta even dreamed of a villa at the seaside and a visit to London Town!

But meanwhile the Professor and Halcyone went back to London and on the Saturday left for Dieppe.

London, perhaps from her numbed state of misery, had said nothing to Halcyone. It remained in her memory as a nightmare, the scene of the confirmation of her winter of the soul. Its inhabitants were ghosts, the young men—jolly, hearty, young fellows from the Stock Exchange, and rising Radical politicians whom she had met—went from her record of things as so many shadows.

The vast buildings seemed as prisons, the rush and flurry as worrying storms, and even the parks as only feeble reminders of her dear La Sarthe Chase.

Nothing had made the least real impression upon her except Kensington Gardens, and they to the end of her life would probably be only a reminder of pain.

But her first view of the sea!

That was something revivifying!

Her memory of the one occasion when she had gone to Lowestoft with her mother was too dim to be anything of a reality, and, when they go to Newhaven, the Professor and Priscilla and she, with a brisk summer wind blowing the green-blue water into crested wavelets, the first cry of life and joy escaped her and gladdened Cheiron's heart.

How wonderful the voyage was! She took in every smallest change in the tones of the sky—she watched the waves from the forepart of the bridge, and some new essence of life and the certainty that her night forces would never desert her made themselves felt and cheered her.

Of John Derringham she thought constantly. He was not buried in that outer cycle of oblivion from which the thoughts unconsciously shy—as we bury our dead, their going so shrouded in pain that we long to blot out the memory of them. John Derringham was always with her. She prayed for his welfare with the fervor and purity of her sweet soul. He was her spirit lover still. He could

never really belong to any other woman, she knew. And
as the days went by a fresh beauty grew in her pale face.
The night sky itself seemed to be melted in her true eyes
with the essence of all its stars.

Cheiron often wondered at her. There was never a word
or allusion to the past. She was extremely quiet, and sometimes the droop of her graceful head and the sad curves
of her tender lips would make the kind old cynic's heart
ache. But she was always cheerful, taking unfeigned interest in the country and the people, delighting in the simple
faith of the peasants and the glory of some of the old
cathedrals.

And Aphrodite traveled everywhere with them. A special
case had been made for her—and Halcyone often took her
out to keep them company in the late evenings or when a
rare rain storm kept them indoors.

Mr. Carlyon had not written to John Derringham since
his engagement had been announced. He wished all connection with his former pupil to be broken off. He had no
mercy for his action, he could not even use his customary
lenient common sense towards the failings of mankind.

John Derringham had made his peerless one suffer—and
his name was anathema. As far as Cheiron was concerned
he was wiped off the list of beings who count.

Halcyone's delicate sense of obligation had been put at
ease by her stepfather. He had made over to her a few
hundreds a year which he said had belonged to her mother
—the simple creature was too ignorant of all business to be
aware whether this was or was not the case. She had grown
to have a certain liking for James Anderton. There was a
hard, level-headed, shrewd honesty about him, keen to drive
a bargain—even the one about her mother to which Priscilla had alluded and to which they had never made any
further reference—but, when once he had gained his point,
he was generous and kind-hearted.

He could not help it that he was not a gentleman, Halcyone thought, and he did his best for everybody according
to his lights.

Her few hundreds a year seemed untold wealth to her who
had never had even a few sixpences for pocket money.
But there was always some instinctive dislike for the thing
itself. It remained to her a rather unpleasant medium for
securing the necessities of life, though she was glad she
now possessed enough not to be a burden upon her aunts.

and could hand what was necessary for her trip over to the Professor.

They wanted to get into Italy as soon as it should be cool enough. August saw them in an out-of-the-way village in Switzerland.

And the mountains caused Halcyone a yet deeper emotion than the sea had done. Nature here talked to her in a voice of supreme grandeur, and bade her never to be cast down but to go on bearing her winter with heroic calm.

She often stayed out the entire night and watched the stars fade and the dawn come—Phœbus with his sun chariot! Somehow Switzerland, although it was not at all the actual background, seemed to bring to her the atmosphere of her "Heroes." The lower hill near their village could certainly be Pelion, and one day she felt she had discovered Cheiron's cave. This was a joy—and that night, when it rained and she and the Professor sat before their wood fire in the little inn parlor, with Aphrodite lying near them in her silken folds, she coaxed her old master into telling her those moving tales of old.

"You are indeed Cheiron, Master," she said—and then her eyes widened and she looked into the glowing ashes. "And you have one pupil, who, like Heracles in his fight with the Centaurs, has accidentally wounded you. But I want you not to let the poison of the arrow grow in your blood; the wound is not incurable as his was. Master, why do you never speak to me now of Mr. Derringham?"

Cheiron frowned. One of his eyesbrows had grown in later years at least an inch long and seemed to bristle ready for battle when he was angry.

"I think he has behaved as no gentleman should," he growled, "and I would rather not mention him."

"You know of things perhaps with which I am not acquainted," said Halcyone, "but from my point of view, there is nothing to judge him for. Whatever he may have done in becoming engaged to marry this lady—because she is rich—we do not know the forces that were compelling him. It hurts me, Cheiron, that you take so stern a view—it hurts me, Master."

Mr. Carlyon put out his hand and stroked her soft hair as she sat there on a low stool looking up at him.

"Oh, my dear," he said, and could articulate no more because a lump grew in his throat.

"Everything is so simple when we know of it," she went on, "but everyone has not had the fortune to learn nature and the forces which we must encourage or guard against. And Mr. Derringham, who had to mix with the world, ran many dangers which could not come to you and me at La Sarthe Chase. Ah, Cheiron! Even you do not know of the ugly things which creep away out of sight in the night —my night that I love! And they could sting one if one did not know where to put one's feet. And so it must be with him—he did not always see where just to put his feet, so we must not judge him, must we?" she pleaded.

"Not if you do not wish," Mr. Carlyon blurted out. And then he began to puff wreaths of smoke from his long old pipe.

"Indeed, I do not wish, Cheiron," she said. "Perhaps he is very unhappy now—we do not know—so we should only send him good thoughts to cheer him. I dream of him often," she went on in a far-off voice, as though she had almost forgotten the Professor's presence, "and he cries to me in pain. And I could not bear it that you should be thinking badly of him, and so I had to speak because thoughts can help or injure people—and now he wants all the gentle currents we can send him to take him through this time."

The Professor coughed violently; his spectacles had grown dim.

Then Halcyone rubbed her soft cheek against his old withered hand.

"You knew it, of course, Master," she said very softly. "I loved him always and I love him still—and, if I have forgiven any hurt which he brought me, surely it need not stand against him with you. To-night—oh, he is suffering so! I cannot bear that there should be one shadow going to him that I can take away. Cheiron, promise me you won't think hardly ever any more—promise, me, Cheiron, dear!"

The Professor's voice was almost the growl of a bear— but Halcyone knew he meant to acquiesce.

"Cheiron," she whispered, while she caressed his stiff fingers, "the winter of our souls is almost past. I feel and know the spring is near at hand."

"I hope to God it is," Mr. Carlyon said, very low.

Next day they moved on into Italy, crossing the frontier and stopping the night at Turin, where they proposed to hire a motor. From thence they intended to get down to Genoa to continue their pilgrimage. It was not such an easy matter, in those few years ago, as it is now to hire a motor, but one was promised to them at last—and off they started. Halcyone took the greatest interest in everything in that

quaint and grand old town. Her keen judgment and that
faculty she possessed of always seeing everything from the
simplest standpoint of truth made her an ideal companion
to wander with on this journey of cultured ease.

"How strong a place this seems, Cheiron," she said, after
two days of their sight-seeing. "All the spirits at the zenith
of Genoa's greatness were strong—nothing weak or ascetic.
They must have been filled with gratitude to God for giving
them this beautiful life, those old patrons of decoration.
There is nothing cheap or hurried; it is all an appreciation
of the magnificence due to their noble station and their pride
of race. For the *Guelphist* of them seems to have been an
aristocrat and an autocrat in his personal *ménage*. Is it not
so, Master?"

"I dare say," agreed Cheiron. He was watching with
deep interest for her verdict upon things.

"It gives me the impression of solid riches," she went on,
"the encouragement of looms of costly stuffs, the encouragement for workers in marble, in bronze, in frescoes, all the
material gorgeous, tangible pleasures of sight and touch.
It is not poetic; in inspires admiration for great deeds,
victorious navies, triumphs—banquets—I have no sense of
music here except the music of feasting. I have no sense of
poetry except of odes to famous admirals or party leaders,
and yet it is a joy in its way and a noble monu-
ment to the proud manhood of the past." And she
looked down from the balcony of the Palazzo Reale, where
they were standing, into the town below.

Her thoughts had gone as ever to the man she loved. He
had this haughty spirit—he could have lived in those days—
and she saw him a Doria, a Brignole-Sale or a Pallavicinis,
gorgeous, masterful and magnificent. England in the present day was surely a *supplice* for such an arrogant spirit as
that of John Derringham.

The prosperous mercantile part of Genoa said nothing to
her—she wanted always to wander where she could weave
romances into the things round. She had never seen any
fine pictures before. The Anderton family were not lovers
of art and, while in London, Halcyone had been too unhappy to care or even ask to be taken to galleries—and
Cheiron had not suggested doing so; he was a good deal
occupied himself. But now it was a great pleasure to him
to watch and see what impression they would make upon a
perfectly fresh eye. The immense cultivation of her mind

would guide her state probably—but it would be an interesting experiment.

She stopped instantly in front of a Van Dyck, but she did not speak. In fact she made no observations at all about the pictures until they were back in their hotel. It was still very hot, although September had come, and they had their dinner upon an open terrace.

And then her thoughts came out.

"I like the Guido Renis, Cheiron," she said; "his Magdalen in the Reale Palazzo is exquisite—she is pure and good. But I do not like the saints and martyrs in the throes of their agony, they say nothing to me, I have no sympathy for them. I adore the Madonna and the Child; they touch me—here," and she laid her hand upon her heart. "The Sassoferarto Virgin in the Reale Palazzo is like Miss Lutworth, she is full of kindness and youth. The early masters' works, which are badly drawn and beautifully colored, I have to take apart—and it is unsatisfying. Because, while I am trying not to see the wrong shape, I have only half my faculties to appreciate the exquisite colors, and so a third influence has to come in—the meaning of the artist who painted them and perhaps put into them his soul. But that is altruistic—I could as well admire something of very bad art for the same reason. For me a picture should satisfy each of these points of view to be perfect and lift me into heights. That is why perhaps I shall prefer sculpture on the whole, when I shall have seen it, to painting."

And Mr. Carlyon felt that, learned in art and old as he was, Halcyone might give him a new point of view.

Next day they left for Pisa.

CHAPTER XXVIII

WHEN Arabella Clinker and her mother were settled together at Wendover, a strange peace seemed to fall upon the place. John Derringham was conscious of it upstairs as he lay in his Louis XVI bed. By the time he was allowed to be carried to a sofa in the sitting-room which had been arranged for him, July had well set in.

He had parted from his Cecilia with suitable things said upon either side. Even in his misery and abasement, John Derringham was too assured a spirit and too much a man of the world to have any hesitation or awkwardness. Mrs. Cricklander had been all that was sympathetic. She looked superbly full of vigor and the joy of life as she came to say farewell.

"John, darling," she purred, "you will do everything you are told to by the doctors while I am away, won't you?" and she caressed his forehead with her soft hand. "So that I may not have to worry as dreadfully as I have been doing, when I come back. It has made me quite ill—that is why I must go to Carlsbad. You will be good now; so that I may find you as strong and handsome as ever on my return." Then she bent and kissed him.

He promised faithfully, and she never saw the whimsical gleam in his eyes, because for the moment having gained her end her faculties had resumed their normal condition, which was not one of superlative sensitiveness. Like everything else in her utilitarian equipment, fine perceptions were only assumed when the magnitude of the goal in view demanded their presence. And even then they merely went as far as sentinels to warn or encourage her in the progress of her aims, never wasting themselves upon irrelevant objects.

When her scented presence had left the room, John Derringham clasped his hands behind his head, and, before he was aware of it, his lips had murmured "Thank God!"

And then Nemesis fell upon him—his schoolboy sensation of recreation-time at hand left him, and a blank sense of failure and hopeless bondage took its place.

Surely he had bartered his soul for a very inadequate mess of pottage.

And where would he sink to under this scorpion whip? Where would go all his fine aspirations which, even in spite of all the juggling of political life, still lived in his aims. Halcyone would have understood.

"Oh! my love!" he cried. "My tender love!"

Then that part of him which was strong reasserted itself. He would not give way to this repining, the thing was done and he must make the best of it. He asked for some volumes from the library. He would read, and he sent the faithful and adoring Brome to request Miss Clinker to send him up the third and fourth volumes of "The Decline and Fall of the Roman Empire." He often turned to Gibbon when he was at war with things. The perfect balance of the English soothed him—and he felt he would read of Julian, for whom in his heart he felt a sympathy.

Arabella brought the volumes herself, and placed them on his table, and then went to settle some roses in a vase before she left the room.

A thin slip of paper fell out of one of the books as he opened it, and he read it absently while he turned the pages.

On the top was a date in pencil, and in a methodical fashion there was written in red ink:

"Notes for the instruction of M. E.," and then underneath, "Subjects to be talked of at dinner to-night—Was there cause for Julian's apostasy? What appealed most to Julian in the old religions—etc., etc."

For a second the words conveyed no meaning to his brain, and for something to say, he said aloud to Arabella: "This is your writing, I think, Miss Clinker. I see you have a taste for our friend Gibbon, too," and then observing the troubled confusion of Arabella's honest face, a sudden flash came over him of memory. He recollected distinctly that upon the Sunday before his accident, they had talked at lunch of Julian the Apostate, and Mrs. Cricklander had turned the conversation, and then had referred to the subject again at dinner with an astonishing array of facts, surprising him by her erudition.

He looked down at the slip again—yes, the date was right, and her red-ink heading was evidently a stereotyped one; probably Arabella kept a supply of these papers ready, being a methodical creature. And the questions!—were they for her own education? But no—Arabella was a cultivated person and would not require such things, and, on that particular Sunday, had never opened the door of her lips at either meal.

"She prompts Cecilia," in a flash he thought, with a wild sense of bitter mirth. "No wonder she can reel off statistics as she does. 'Subjects to be talked of at dinner'—forsooth!"

And Arabella stood there, her kind plain face crimson, and her brown eyes blinking pitifully behind her glasses.

She was too fine to say anything, it would make the situation impossibly difficult if she invented an explanation. So she just blinked—and finally, after placing the fresh flowers by Mr. Derringham's bed, she left the room by the door beyond.

When she had gone it was as if a curtain were raised upon John Derringham's understanding. Countless circumstances came back to him when his *fiancée's* apparent learning had aroused his admiration, and with a twinge he remembered Cheiron's maliciously amused eyes which had met his during her visit to the orchard house, when she had become a little at sea in some of her conversation. The whole thing then was a colossal bluff—Arabella was the brain! Arabella was the erudite, cultured person and his admirable Cecilia played the rôle of extremely clever parrot! He laughed with bitter cynical merriment until he shook in his bed.

And he, poor fool, had been taken in by it all—he and a number of others. He was in company at all events! Then he saw another aspect, and almost admired the woman for her audacity. What nerve to play such a game, and so successfully! The determination—the application it required—and the force of character!

But the gall of it when she should be his wife! He saw pictures of himself trembling with apprehension at some important function in case mistakes should occur. He would have to play the part of Arabella, and write out the notes for the subjects to be "talked of at dinner!"

He lay there, and groaned with rage and disgust.

He could not—he would not go through with it!

But next day the irony of fate fell upon him with heavy hand. He received the news that Joseph Scroope, his maternal uncle, was dead, not having produced an heir, so he knew that he would inherit a comfortable fortune from him.

The noose had, indeed, tightened round his neck,—he could not now release himself from his engagement to Cecilia Cricklander. Some instincts of a gentleman still remained with him in full measure. The hideous, hideous mockery of it all. If he had waited, he would now have been free to seek his darling, his pure star, Halcyone, in

all honor. He could have taken her dear, tender hand, and
led her proudly to the seat by his side—and crowned her
with whatever laurels her sweet spirit would have inspired
him to gain. And it was all too late! too late!

He reviewed the whole chain of events, and perceived how
it had been his own doing—what had happened in his each
step—and this knowledge added to the bitterness of his pain.
It was from now onward that his nights were often agony.
Every movement, every word of Halcyone came back to him,
from the old days of long ago when she had given him the
oak leaf, to the moment of her looking into his eyes, with
all her soul in hers, as she had answered his passionate
question. "Afraid? How should I be afraid—since you are
my lord and I am your love? Do not we belong to one
another?"

And in spite of the peace Mrs. Cricklander's absence
caused in the atmosphere, John Derringham grew more un-
utterably wretched as time went on.

His cup seemed to be filling from all sides. The Government was going out in disaster, and, instead of being able
to stand by his colleagues and fight, and perhaps avert catastrophe by his brilliant speeches and biting wit, he was
chained like a log to a sofa and was completely impotent

It was no wonder his convalescence was slow, and that
Arabella grew anxious about him. She felt that some of
Mrs. Cricklander's wrath and disgust because of this state
of things would fall upon her head.

His ankle was a great deal better now, it was five weeks
since the accident, and in a day or two he hoped to leave
for London. Mrs. Cricklander would be obliged to take an
after-cure at the highly situated castle of an Austrian
Prince, an old friend of hers—where the air was most
bracing, she wrote. For her strict instructions to Arabella
before she left, after telling her she might have her mother
to keep her company, and so earning the good creature's
deep gratitude, had been:

"You must keep me informed of every slightest turn in
Mr. Derringham—because, until he is perfectly well and
amusing again, I simply can't come back to England. His
tragic face bores me to death. Really, men are too tiresome when there is the slightest thing the matter with them.'

And Arabella had faithfully carried out her instructions
In common honesty she could not inform her employer
that John Derringham was perfectly well or amusing!

Poor Miss Clinker's happy summer with her mother was

being a good deal dimmed by her unassuaged sympathy and commiseration.

"Of course, he is grieving for that sweet and distinguished girl, Miss Halcyone La Sarthe," she told herself—and with the old maid's hungering for romance, which even the highest education cannot quite crush from the female breast, she longed to know what had parted them.

Mr. Carlyon had gone abroad, she had ascertained that, and La Sarthe Chase was still closed.

The night before John Derringham left for London, he hobbled down to dinner on crutches. He was not to try and use his foot for some weeks still, but the cut on his head was mended now. It was a glorious July evening, the roses were not over on the terrace, and every aspect of nature was gorgeously beautiful and peaceful.

They did not delay long over their repast, and there was still twilight when Mrs. and Miss Clinker left their invalid alone with his wine. A letter was in his pocket, arrived by the evening post from Mrs. Cricklander, which he had not yet opened. It would contain her reflections upon his changed conditions of fortune, of which he had, when he learned of its full magnitude, duly informed her.

He was alternately raging with misery now, or perfectly numb, and, as he sat there a shattered wreck of his former *insouciant* self, gaunt and haggard and pitifully thin, some of his friends would hardly have recognized him.

He felt it was his duty to read the missive presently, but he told himself the lights were too dim, and taking a cigar he hobbled out upon the terrace. His return to public life would now be too late to help to avert disaster, he must just stand aside in these last weeks of the session and see the shipwreck. An unspeakable bitterness invaded his spirit. The moon was rising when he got outside, one day beyond its full. It seemed like a golden ball in the twilight of opal tints, before it should rise in its silver majesty to supreme command of the night. Nature was in one of her most sensuously divine moods. The summer and fulfillment had come.

John Derringham sat down in a comfortable chair and gazed in front of him.

There had been moonlight, too, when he had spent those exquisite hours with his love, now six weeks ago—a young half moon. Could it be only six weeks? A lifetime of anguish appeared to have rolled between. And where was she? Then, for the first time, the crust of his self-absorption seemed to crumble, and he thought with new stabs of pain how she, too, must have suffered. He began to picture her waiting by the gate—she would be brave and quiet. And then, as the day passed—what had she done? He could not imagine, but she must have suffered intolerably. When could she have heard of the accident, since the next day she had been taken away? Why had she gone? That was unlike her, to have given in to any force which could separate them. And if he had known this step also was unconsciously caused by his own action in having his letter to Cheiron posted from London, it would have tortured him the more. Another thought came, and he started forward in his chair. Was it possible that she had written to him, and that the letter had got mislaid, among the prodigious quantity which accumulated in those first days of his unconsciousness.

Then he sank back again. Even if this were so, it was too late now. Everything was too late—from that awful night when he had become engaged to Cecilia Cricklander.

She had put the announcement into the paper not quite three weeks after the accident. What could Halcyone have thought of him and his unspeakable baseness? Now she could have nothing but loathing and contempt in her heart, wherever she was—and what right had he to have broken the beliefs and shattered the happiness of that pure, young soul?

He remembered his old master's words about a man's honor towards women. It was true then that it was regulated, not by the woman's feelings or anguish, but by the man's inclination and whether or no the world should hold him responsible. And he realized that this latter reason was the force which now prevented his breaking his engagement with Mrs. Cricklander. He had behaved with supreme selfishness in the beginning, and afterwards with a weakness which would always make him writhe when he thought of it.

His self-respect was receiving a crushing blow. He clasped his thin hands and his head sank forward upon his breast in utter dejection; he closed his eyes as if to shut out too painful pictures. And when he opened them again it was darker, and the moon made misty shadows through the trees, and out of them he seemed to see Halcyone's face quite close to him. It was tender and pitiful and full of love. The hallucination was so startlingly vivid that he almost fancied her lips moved, and she whispered: "Courage, beloved." Then he knew that he was dreaming, and that he was gazing into space—alone.

CHAPTER XXIX

MRS. CRICKLANDER, at Carlsbad, was not altogether pleased to receive the news of her *fiancé's* accession to fortune. She realized that John Derringham was not the sort of man to give up his will to any woman unless the woman had entirely the whip hand, as she would have had if he had been dependent upon her for the financial aid wherewith to obtain his ambitions. She would have practically no hold over him now, and, when he was well, he was so attractive that she might even grow to care too deeply for him for her own welfare. To allow herself to become in love with a husband who was answerable to her for his very food and lodging, and whom she could punish and keep in bondage when she pleased, was quite a different matter to experiencing that emotion towards an imperious, independent creature going his own way, and even, perhaps, compelling her to conform to his.

"How stupid of the old man, Mr. Scroope, to have married so late!" she said to herself, as usual finding everyone wrong who in any way interfered with her wishes.

John Derringham's letters—only two a week she received from him—were his usual masterpieces of style, and in them he employed his skill to say everything—and nothing.

She felt pleased as she read, and then resentful when she thought over them. He had never once used a word of personal endearment, although the letters were beautifully expressed. He seemed most happy and comfortable with Arabella. After all, perhaps she would not go and stay with Prince Brunemetz at Brudenstein. She might make John come out and join her and go on to St. Moritz—that would do him good. She could wire for Arabella. The *convenances* were so dear to her. The wedding should take place in October, she decided.

And two days after John Derringham had arrived in London at his old rooms in Duke Street, she wrote and suggested this plan to him—and then the first preliminary crossing of swords between them happened. He answered that he would come and join her later, but until the session was over he could not leave town, and he begged her to go

186

and stay with Prince Brunemetz, or do anything else which
would amuse her. He was still upon crutches, he said, and
not fitted to be a cavalier to any lady.

She shut her mouth with a snap, and, sitting down, wrote
a long letter to Mr. Hanbury-Green, with whom she kept
up a brisk correspondence. Very well, then! she would go
to Brudenstein; she would not martyrize herself by being
with a man on crutches! So half of her August passed in
a most agreeable manner, and towards the end of the month
she summoned her *fiancé* to Florence. He could walk with
a stick now—and to meet her there and go on to Venice
and out to Lido would be quite delightful, and could not
hurt him. She deserved some attention after this long
time.

The end of the session had come, and still the Government
hung on, but it was obvious that they had been so much dis-
credited that the end could not be long postponed, and that,
as soon as Parliament met again, a hostile vote would be
carried against them. But for the time there was nothing
to keep John Derringham in England, and with intense reluctance he started for Italy, the ever-nearing date for his
wedding looming in front of him like some heavy cloud.
He had plunged headlong into work when he had returned
from Wendover, for which he was still quite unfit. His
whole system had received a terrible shock, and it would be
months before he could hope to be his old robust self again;
and an unutterable depression was upon him. The total
silence of Halcyone, her disappearance from the face of the
earth as far as he was concerned, seemed like something
incredible.

There were no traces of her. Mrs. Porrit was out, and
the orchard house shut up, so he obtained no information.
He had stopped there to enquire on his way to the station
when he had left Wendover. La Sarthe Chase was entirely
closed, except for a woman and her husband from the
village who slept there. But what right had he to be interested now, in any case? He had better shut the whole
matter out of his mind, and keep his thoughts upon his coming marriage with Cecilia Cricklander.

And it was this frame of mind which caused him to
plunge recklessly into work as soon as he reached London,
though he found that nothing really assuaged his misery.

It was a glorious day towards the end of August when he
got onto the boat at Dover, and there ran across Miss Cora
Lutworth, bent upon *trousseau* business in Paris. She was

with her friend, the lady who chaperoned her, and greeted him with her usual breezy charm.

They sat down together in a comfortable corner on deck, while the lady went to have a sleep. They talked of many things and mutual friends. He was doing what was a comparatively rare thing in those days, taking over a motor to tour down to Venice in, and Cora was duly interested. Freynie adored motoring, too, she said, and that was how they intended to spend their honeymoon. She was going to be married in a few weeks, and was radiantly happy.

This was the first time she had seen John Derringham since his engagement and his accident, and the great change in him gave her an unpleasant shock. There were quite a number of silver threads in his dark hair above the temples, and he looked haggard and gaunt and lifeless. Cora's kind heart was touched.

"I am sure he does not care a rush for Cis," she thought to herself, "and I am sure he did for that sweet Halcyone. He and Cis are not married yet; there can be no harm in my mentioning her." So aloud she said:

"You remember our meeting that charming Miss Halcyone La Sarthe across the haw-haw on Easter Sunday? Well, fancy, I came across her in London at the end of June—in Kensington Gardens, sitting with the long-haired old Professor. I was surprised; somehow one could not picture her out of her own park." She watched John Derringham's face carefully, and saw that this information moved him.

"Did you?" he said, with an intense tone in his deep voice. "What was she doing there, I wonder?"

"She looked too sweet," Cora went on. "She was wearing becoming modern clothes, and seemed to me to have grown so pretty. But she was very pale and quiet. She came to tea with me the next day—I cannot say how she fascinates me. I just love her—and then, on the Saturday she was to go abroad with the Professor."

"Really?" said John Derringham, while he could feel his heart begin to beat very fast. "Where were they going, do you know? I would like to run across my old master."

"I think to Brittany for July, and then Switzerland; but they intended to get into Italy as soon as it was cool enough. They seemed to be going to have a lovely trip and take a long time about it."

"I had no idea Miss La Sarthe had any relations in

London," he said. "Who was she staying with there? Did she tell you?"

"Her stepfather, I think," Cora said. "Her mother married twice, it appears, and then died, and the man married again. This second wife, her sort of stepmother, came and fetched her from La Sarthe Chase quite suddenly one day."

"I cannot think of her in London," said John Derringham. Did she like it, do you think? And was she changed?"

"Yes, very changed," Cora answered, and made her voice casual. "She looked as if the joy of life had fled forever, and as if she were just getting through the time. Perhaps she hated being with her step-family—people often do."

Then she glanced at him stealthily as he stared out at the sea, while she thought: "I am sure some awful tragedy is here underneath; it is not only his broken ankle and his illness that has made him such a wreck. I wish I could help them. I would not care a snap for Cis, who is a rattlesnake if she wants something."

"When was it, exactly, you saw her?" John Derringham asked. "But perhaps you don't remember the date?"

"Yes, I do," Cora responded quickly. "It was the day your engagement was announced in the papers, because we spoke about it."

"Did you?" he said, and drew in his breath a little. "And what did you say?"

"Just the usual things—how fortunate you were. And Halcyone said you were clever and great."

John Derringham did not answer for a moment. This stunned him. Then he replied, very low, "That was good of her," and Cora noticed that even with the fresh wind blowing in his face he had grown very pale.

"Cis writes you are going to be married at the beginning of October," she said, to change the conversation. "I do hope you will be awfully happy. It is so exquisite to be in love, isn't it? I adore being engaged!"

But John Derringham could not bear this—the two things were so widely severed in his case. He did not answer, and Cora saw, although his face remained unmoved, that pain grew deep in his eyes.

"Mr. Derringham," she said, "I am going to say something indiscreet and perhaps in frightful taste—but I am so happy I can't bear to think that possibly others are not quite. I know Cis awfully well—her character, I mean. Is there anything I can do for you?"

John Derringham turned with a chillingly haughty glance intended to wither, but when he saw her sweet face full of frank sympathy and kindness, it touched him and his manner changed.

"We have each of us to fulfill our fates," he said. "I suppose we each deserve what we receive, and I am so glad yours seems to be such a very happy one."

Then he made some excuse to get up and leave her—he could bear no more.

And Cora, left alone, smiled sadly to herself while she reflected what a foolish thing pride was, and all the other shams which robbed life of the only thing really worth having.

"Well, I should not let any of that nonsense ever stand between Freynie and me, thank goodness!" she concluded.

But John Derringham limped off to the bows of the ship, quivering with pain. So Halcyone had spoken of his engagement and said he was "clever and great." What could it all mean? Did he no longer interest her then—even at that period? This stung him deeply. There was no light anywhere. When once he had grasped the full significance of his own conduct he was much too fine an intelligence to deceive himself, or persuade himself to see any other aspect but the hopeless one, that the entire chain of events was the result of his own action. But surely there must be some way out? If he wrote straight to Cecilia and told her the truth? And then he almost laughed bitterly as he realized the futility of this plan. What would the truth matter to Mrs. Cricklander? She could very well retort that he had known all this truth from the beginning, and had been willing to marry her while his financial position made it an advantage to himself, but was now *recalcitrant* only because fortune had otherwise poured gold into his lap.

No, there was no hope. He must go through with it.

So he crushed down his emotions and forced himself to return to Miss Lutworth and talk brightly to her until they landed.

And when they parted at the Gare du Nord, Cora was left with the impression that, whatever might be the undercurrent, John Derringham was strong enough to face his fate, and not give anyone the satisfaction of knowing whether in it he found pleasure or pain.

When he arrived about ten days later at the hotel in Florence, where Mrs. Cricklander was staying, waiting for him to accompany her on to Venice, he found her in a very bad temper. She felt that she had not been treated with that deference and respect which was her due, to say nothing of the ardor that a lover ought to have shown by hastening to her side. Why had he motored, spending ten days on a journey that he could have accomplished in two? And he made no excuses, and seemed quite unimpressed by her mood one way or another. He was so changed, too! Gaunt and haggard—he had certainly lost every one of his good looks, except his distinction—that seemed more marked than ever. His arrogant air that she had once admired so much now only caused her to feel a great irritation. He had made the excuse of the waiter not having quite closed the door, apparently, for only kissing her hand by way of greeting, and then he said just the right thing about her beauty and his pleasure in seeing her, and sat down by her side upon the sofa in far too collected a manner for a lover to have shown after these weeks of separation. Mrs. Cricklander grew very angry indeed. Cold and capricious behavior should only be shown upon a woman's side, she felt!

"Your Government made a colossal mess of things before the session was over, did they not?" she said by way of something to start upon. "Mr. Hanbury-Green tells me you will have to face a hostile vote when you reassemble, and that the whole thing is a played-out game. How long would the Radicals last if they do come in?—and it looks like a certainty that they will."

"Seven years, most likely," said John Derringham a little bitterly. "Or perhaps to the end of time. Your friend Mr. Green could tell you more accurately than I. Does the fact interest you very deeply?"

"Yes," she said, and narrowed her eyes. "I am wildly interested in everything that concerns you, of course—that is obvious."

"You will help me to fight, then, for the Opposition. Your social talents are so great, dear Cecilia, you will make a most brilliant Tory hostess," and he took her hand—he felt he must do something.

"I have always been on the winning side," she said, not more than half playfully. "I do not know how I should like seven years of fighting an uncertain fight. I might get extremely bored by it. I had no idea it would last so long." And she laughed a little uncomfortably. "However, we are perfectly modern, aren't we, John, and need not spend the entire year fighting together—fortunately?"

"No," he said. "I am sure we shall be an admirable pair

of citizens of the world. And now I suppose I must let you
go and dress for dinner. How is our estimable friend, Miss
Clinker? She is with you, I suppose?—or have you friends
staying in the hotel? You did not tell me in your letters."

"I never waste sweetness upon the desert air," she said,
smiling, with a glitter in her eyes. "You did not appear
over-anxious to hear of my doings. Our correspondence
made me laugh sometimes. You never wrote as though you
had received any of my letters—yours were just masterpieces of how little to say—and of how to say it beautifully!"

John Derringham shrugged his shoulders slightly; he did
not defend himself, and her anger rose. So that she was
leaving the room with her head in the air and two bright
spots of pink in her cheeks.

Then he felt constrained to vindicate his position, so he
put his arm round her and drew her to him, intending to kiss
her. But she looked up into his face with an expression in
her eyes which left him completely repulsed. It was mocking and bitter and cunning, and she put out her hand and
pushed him from her.

"I do not want any of your caresses to-night," she said.
"When I do, I'll pay for them." And she swept from the
room, leaving him quivering with debasement.

CHAPTER XXX

THERE was fortunately a company assembled for dinner when John Derringham descended to the restaurant and again joined his *fiancée*—who never dined alone if she could help it, and reveled in gay parties for every meal, with plenty of brilliant lights and the chatter of other groups near at hand. Wherever she went, from Carlsbad to Cairo, in the best restaurant you could always find her amidst her many friends, feasting every night. And now the party consisted of some of her compatriots, a Russian Prince, and an Italian Marchese. She looked superbly beautiful; anger had lent a sparkle to her eyes and a flush to her cheeks; no rouge was needed to-night, and she could scintillate to her heart's content. She flashed words occasionally at John Derringham, and he knew, and was horribly conscious all the time, that once he would have found her most brilliant, but that now it was exactly as when he had looked at the X-ray photograph of his own broken ankle, where the sole thing which made a reality was the skeleton substructure. He could only seem to see Cecilia Cricklander's vulgar soul— the pink and white perfection of her body had melted into nothingness.

He found himself listening for some of her parrot-utterances, as a detached spectator, and taking a sort of ugly pleasure in recognizing which were the phrases of Arabella. The man upon her left hand was intelligent, and was gazing at her with the rapt attention beauty always commands, and she was uttering her finest platitudes.

And once John Derringham leant back in his chair, when no one was observing him, and laughed aloud. The supreme mockery of it all! And in five weeks from this night this woman would be his wife!

His wife! Ye gods!

They had no *tête-à-tête* words before the party broke up, and had hardly exchanged a sentence when, as the last guest was saying farewell, Arabella, too, retired from the sitting-room.

So they were alone.

"Cecilia," he said, coming up quite close to her, "we

193

started rather badly to-night—at least let us be friends."
And he held out his hand. "Believe me, I wish to do all
that I can to please you, but I am afraid I make a very
indifferent sort of lover. Forgive me."

"Oh, you are well enough, I suppose," she said. "No
man values what he has won—it is only the winning of it
that is any fun. I understand the feeling myself. Don't let
us talk heroics."

John Derringham smiled.

"Certainly not," he said.

And then she put up her face and let him kiss her, which
he did with some sickening revolt in his heart. Even her
physical beauty had no more any effect upon him—he would
as soon have kissed Arabella.

So she sailed from the room again, with her mouth shut
like a vise, and her handsome eyes glancing at him over her
shoulder.

Next day, after having kept him waiting for an hour to
take her out, she decided they should spend what remained
of the morning at the Bargello. And, when they got there,
she did her best to be a charming companion, and pressed
him to lean upon her instead of his stick. But to his awak-
ened understanding what was even probably true in their
talk and comprehension of the gems of art, seemed false
and affected, and he was only conscious of one continual jar
as she spoke.

A thousand little trifles, never remarked before, now appeared to loom large in his vision. At last they came to
the galleries above, to the collection of the Della Robbias,
and Mrs. Cricklander rhapsodized over them, mixing them
up with delightful unconcern. They were all just bits of
cheap-looking crockery to her eye, and it was impossibly
difficult to distinguish which was Luca's, Andrea's, or
Giovanni's; and, security having made her careless, she committed several blunders.

John Derringham laid no pitfalls for her—indeed, he
helped her out when he could. To-day each new discovery
no longer made him smile with bitter cynicism, he was only
filled with a sense of discomfort and regret.

He stopped in front of Andrea's masterpiece, the tender
young Madonna. Something in the expression of the face
made him think of Halcyone, although the types of the two
were entirely different; and Cecilia Cricklander, watching,
saw a look of deep pain grow in his eyes.

"I wish to goodness he would get well and be human and

masterful and brilliant, as he used to be," she thought. "I am thoroughly tired out, trying to cope with him. He is no more use now than a bump on a log. I am sorry I made him come here!"

"It is about time for lunch," said John Derringham, who could no longer bear her prattle; and they returned to the hotel.

Arabella and an American man made the *partie carrée*, and Miss Clinker did her best to help to get through the repast, and afterwards wrote in a letter to her mother:

"Mr. Derringham has arrived. He still looks dreadfully ill and careworn, and I can see is feeling his position acutely. Since that dreadful day when he found my notes in Gibbon, ►I have never dared to look at him when in the company of M. E. I feel that distressing sensation of hot and cold during the whole time. M. E., now that no further great efforts are needed, chatters on with most disquieting inconsequence. I can see she is very much upset at Mr. Derringham's attitude. The impression that the Conservative Government cannot last has had also a great effect upon her, and she has set me to find out exactly the position and amount of prestige the wife of a rising member of the Opposition would have. This morning she sent for me, when she was dressing to know if it were true, as Mr. Derringham had told her, that, if the Radicals got in, they might last seven years—because, if so, she would then be almost thirty-eight, and the best days of her youth would be over. I do not dare to think what remarks may mean, but in connection with the fact that she receives daily letters from Mr. Hanbury-Green—that unpleasant Socialist person who is coming so much to the front—I almost fear, and yet hope, that there is some chance for Mr. Derringham's escape. He is bearing his trouble as only an English gentleman could do, and at lunch paid her every attention."

And old Mrs. Clinker smiled when she got this letter.

But by the end of the afternoon John Derringham's face wore no smiles; a blank despair had settled upon him.

They drove along the Arno and into the Gardens.

It was warm and beautiful, but, so forceful is a hostile atmosphere created between two people, they both found it impossible to make conversation.

Mrs. Cricklander was burning with rage and a sense of impotency. She felt her words and all her arts of pleasing were being nullified, and that she was up against an odious situation in which her strongest weapons were powerless. It made her nervous and very cross. She particularly resented not being able to ascertain the cause of the change in him, and felt personally aggrieved at his still being a wretched wreck hobbling with a stick. He ought to have got quite well by now—it was perfectly ridiculous. What if, after all, he would not be worth while? But the indomitable part of her character made her tenacious. She felt it was a different matter, throwing away what she had won, to having to relinquish something that she knew she had never really gained. She would make one more determined effort, and then, if he would not give her love, he should be made to feel his bondage, she would extort from him to the last ounce, her pound of flesh.

"John, darling," she said, slipping her hand into his, under the rug as they rode, "this beautiful place makes me feel so romantic. I wish you would make love to me. You sit there looking like Dante with a beard, as cold as ice."

"I am very sorry," he answered, startled from a reverie. "I know I am a failure in such sort of ways. What do you want me to say?"

This was not promising, and her annoyance increased.

"I want you to tell me you love me—over and over again," she whispered, controlling her voice.

"Women always ask these questions," he said to gain time. "They never take anything for granted as men do."

"No!" she flashed. "Not when a man's actions point to the possibility of several other interpretations of his sentiments—then they want words to console them. But you give me neither."

"I am not a demonstrative person," he responded. "I will do all I can to make you happy, but do not ask me for impossibilities. You will have to put up with me as I am."

"I shall decide that!" And she snatched away her hand angrily, and then controlled herself—the moment had not yet come. He should not have freedom, which now she felt he craved; he should remain tied until he had at all events paid the last price of humiliation. So for the rest of that day and those that followed she behaved with maddening capriciousness, keeping him waiting for every meal and every appointment—changing her mind as to what she would do—lavishing caresses upon him which made him wince, and then treating him with mocking coldness; but all with such extreme cleverness that she never once gave him the chance to bring things to an open rupture. She was beginning really to enjoy herself in this new game—it required even more skill to torture and hold than to attract and keep at arm's length. But at last John Derringham could bear no more.

They had continuous lunches and dinners with the gay party of Americans who had been of the company on the first evening, and there was never a moment's peace. A life in public was as the breath of Cecilia Cricklander's nostrils, and she did not consider the wishes of her betrothed. In fact, but for spoken sympathy over his shattered condition and inability to walk much, she did not consider him at all, and exacted his attendance on all occasions, whether too fatiguing for him or not.

The very last shred of glamour about her had long fallen from John Derringham's eyes, and indeed things seemed to him more bald than they really were. His proud spirit chafed from morning to night—chafed hopelessly against the knowledge that his own action had bound him as no ordinary bond of an engagement could. His whole personality appeared to be changing; he was taciturn or cynically caustic, casting jibes at all manner of things he had once held sacred. But after a week of abject misery, he refused to bear any more, and when Mrs. Cricklander grew tired of Florence, and decided to move on to Venice, he announced his intention of taking a few days' turn by himself. He wished to see the country round, he said, and especially make an excursion to San Gimignano—that gem of all Italy for its atmosphere of the past.

"Oh! I am thoroughly tired of these moldy places," Mrs. Cricklander announced. "The Maulevriers are in Venice, and we can have a delightful time at the Lido; the new hotel is quite good—you had better come on with me now. Moping alone cannot benefit anyone. You really ought to cheer up and get quite well, John."

But he was firm, and after some bickerings she was obliged to decide to go to Venice alone with Arabella, and let her *fiancé* depart in his motor early the next morning.

Their parting was characteristic.

"Good night, Cecilia," John Derringham said. No matter how capricious she could be, he always treated her with ceremonious politeness. "I am leaving so very early tomorrow, we had better say good-by now. I hope my going does not really inconvenience you at all. I want a little rest from your friends, and, when I join you at Venice again, I hope you will let me see more of yourself."

She put up her face, and kissed him with all the girlish rippling smiles she had used for his seduction in the beginning.

"Why, certainly," she said. "We will be regular old Darbys-and-Joans; so don't you forget while you are away that you belong to me, and I am not going to give you up to anything or anybody—so long as I want you myself!"

And John Derringham had gone to his room feeling more chained than ever, and more bitterly resentful against fate.

As soon as he left her, she sat down at her writing-table and wrote out a telegram to be sent off the first thing the next day. It contained only three words, and was not signed.

But the recipient of it, Mr. Hanbury-Green, read it with wild emotion when he received it in his rooms in London— and immediately made arrangements to set off to Florence at once.

"I'll beat him yet!" he said to himself, and he romantically kissed the pink paper. For, "You may come" was what he had read.

CHAPTER XXXI

An hour or so before sunset the next day John Derringham in his motor was climbing the steep roads which lead to San Gimignano, the city of beautiful towers, which still stands, a record of things mediæval, untouched by the modernizing hand of men.

A helpless sense of bitterness mastered him, and destroyed the loveliness and peace of the view. Everything fine and great in his thoughts and aims seemed tarnished. To what stage of degradation would his utter disillusion finally bring him! Of course, when Cecilia Cricklander should once be his wife, he would not permit her to lead this life of continuous racket—or, if she insisted upon it, she should indulge in it only when she went abroad alone. He would not endure it in his home. And what sort of home would it be? He was even doubtful about that now. Since she had so often carelessly thrown off her mask, he no longer felt sure that she would even come up to the mark of what had hitherto seemed her chief charm, her power of being a clever and accomplished hostess. He could picture the scenes which would take place between them when their wishes clashed! The contemplation of the future was perfectly ghastly. He remembered, with a cynical laugh, how in the beginning, before that fateful Good Friday when the Professor first planted ruffling thoughts in his mind, and before the spell of Halcyone had fallen upon him, he had thought that one of the compensations for having to take a rich wife he had found in Cecilia. She would be his intellectual companion during the rather rare moments he would be able to spare her from his work. He would be able to live with a woman cultured in all branches which interested him, capable of discussing with him any book or any thought, polished in brain and in methods. He had imagined them, when alone together, spending their time in a delightful and intellectual communion of ideas, which would make the tie of marriage seem as almost a pleasure. And what was the reality?— An absolute emptiness, and the knowledge that, unless Arabella Clinker continued her ministrations, he himself would have to play her part! He actually regretted his accession

199

to fortune. But for it he could have broken off the engagement with decency, but now his hands were tied. Only Cecilia could release him, and she did not seem to have the slightest intention of doing so.

He savagely clenched his white teeth when he remembered the ridiculous waiting lackey he had been made to turn into in the last week. Then he looked up and tried to take interest in the quaint gateway through which he was passing and on up to the unique town and the square where is the ancient Podesta's palace, now the hotel. But he was in a mood of rasping cynicism—even the exquisite evening sunlight seemed to mock at him.

His highly trained eye took in the wonderful old-world beauty around him with some sense of unconscious satisfaction, but the saintly calm of the place made no impression upon him. Santa Fina and her flowers could not soften or bring peace to his galled soul. The knowledge that the whole situation was the result of his own doings kept his bitterness always at white heat. The expression of his thin, haggard face was sardonic, and the groups of simple children, accustomed to ask any stranger for stamps for their collections—a queer habit of the place—turned away from him when once they had looked into his eyes.

He left his motor at the hotel and wandered into the square where the remains of the palazzos of the two great Guelph and Ghibelline families, the Ardinghelli and the Salvucci, frown at one another not fifty yards apart—shorn of their splendors, but the Salvucci still with two towers from which to hurl destruction at their enemies.

John Derringham looked up at the balcony whence Dante had spoken, and round to the Cathedral and the picturesque square. The few people who passed seemed not in tune with his thoughts, so calm and saintly was the type of their faces—all in keeping with a place where a house of the sixteenth century is considered so aggressively modern as not to be of any interest. It was too late for him now to go into the Cathedral; nothing but the fortress battlements were possible, and he hobbled there, desiring to see the sunset from its superb elevation.

The gate-keeper, homely and simple, opened to him courteously, and he went in to the first little courtyard, with its fig tree in the middle and old grass-grown well surrounded by olives and lilac bushes; and then he climbed the open stairs to the bastion, from whose battlements there is to be obtained the most perfect view imaginable of the country, the like of which Benozzo Gozzoli loved to paint.

It has not changed in the least since those days, except that the tiles of the roofs, which are now dark gray with age, were then red and brilliant. But the cypress trees still surround the monasteries, and the high hills are still crowned with castellos, while the fields make a patchwork of different crops of olives and vines and grain.

John Derringham mounted the stairs with his head down, musing bitterly, so that, until he reached the top, he was not aware that a slender girl's figure was seated upon the old stone bench which runs round the wall. Her hat lay upon the seat beside her, while she gazed out over the beautiful world. He paused with a wildly beating heart in which joy and agony fought for mastery, but, as she turned to see who this stranger could be, thus breaking in upon her solitude, his voice, hoarse with emotion, said aloud her name:

"Halcyone!"

She started to her feet, and then sank back upon the bench again unsteadily, and he came forward to her side. They both realized that they were alone here in the sunset—alone upon this summit of the world.

He sat down beside her and then he buried his face in his hands, letting his cap fall; and all the pent-up misery and anguish of the past week seemed to vibrate in his voice as he murmured:

"Ah, God!—my love!"

Her soft eyes melted upon him in deepest tenderness and sorrow. To see him so pale and shattered, so changed from the splendid lover she had known!

But he was there—beside her—and what mattered anything else? She longed to comfort him and tend him with fond care. Had he been the veriest outcast he would ever have found boundless welcome and solace waiting for him in her loving heart.

"John!" she whispered, and put out gentle fingers and caressed his hair.

He shivered and let his hands fall from his haggard face.

"Darling," he said, "I am not worthy to touch the hem of your garment. Why do you not turn from such a weakling and brute?"

"Hush! Hush!" she exclaimed, aghast. "You must not speak so of yourself. I love you always, as you know, and I cannot hear him whom I love abused."

And now he looked into her eyes while he took her slender hand, and there he saw the same wells of purity and devotion brimming with divine faith and tenderness that he had last seen glistening with happy love.

He folded her to his heart; the passionate emotion each was feeling was too deep, too sacred for words; and then their eyes streamed with scorching tears.

They sat thus close for some seconds. The thirst and hunger of all these days of rack and anguish must be assuaged before either could talk. But at last she drew a little back and looked up into his face.

"John," she said softly, "I read in an English paper a week ago that your wedding was fixed for the seventh of October—my birthday. Is it the truth?"

He clasped his hands in agony.

"It can never now be so," he said. "I cannot, I will not go through with it. Oh, Halcyone, my darling one, you would pity me, although you would despise me, if you knew—"

"I could never despise you," she answered, nestling once more in his arms. "John, for me nothing you could do would make any difference—you would still be my love; and if you were weak I would make you strong, and if cold and hungry, I would feed and comfort you, and if wicked, I would only see you good."

"Oh, my dear, my dear," he said, "you were always as an angel of sweetness. Listen to the whole degrading story, and tell me then of that which I must do."

She took one of his hands and held it in both of hers; and it was as if some stream of comfort flowed to him through their soft warm touch and enabled him to begin his ugly task.

He told her the whole thing from the beginning. Of his ambitions, and how they held chief place in his life, and how he had meant to marry Cecilia Cricklander as an aid to their advancement. He glossed over nothing of his own baseness, but went on to show how, from the moment he had seen her upon that Good Friday at the orchard house, his determination about Cecilia Cricklander had begun to waver, until the night under the tree when passion overcame every barrier and he knew he must possess her—Halcyone—for his wife.

He made no excuse for himself; he continued the plain tale of how, his ambitions still holding him, he had selfishly tried to keep both joy and them, by asking her—she who was so infinitely above him—to descend to the invidious position of a secret wife.

She knew the rest until it came to the cause of his accident, and, when she heard it occurred because of his haste to get to her before she should reach home, she gave a little moan of anguish and leaned her head against his breast.

So the story went on—of his agonized thoughts and fever and fears—of his comprehension that she had been taken from him, and of the utter hopelessness of his financial position, and the whole outlook, until he came to the night of his engagement; and here he paused.

"Do not try to tell me any of this part, John, my dear lover," she said. "I know the standard of honor in a man is that he must never give away the absent woman, and I understand—you need not put anything into words. I knew you were unhappy and coerced. I never for a moment have doubted your love. You were surrounded with strong and cruel forces, and all my tenderness could not reach you quite, to protect you as it should have done, because I was so full of foolish anguish myself. Dearest, now only tell me the end and the facts that I must know."

He held her close to him in thankfulness, and then went on to speak of the shame and degradation he had suffered for his weakness; the drawn-out days of aching wonder at her silence, and finally the news of his Uncle Joseph Scroope's death and the fortune that would come to him, and how this fact had tied and bound his hands.

"But it has grown to such a pass," he said, "that I had come to breaking-point, and now I can never go back to her again. I have found you, my one dear love, and I will never leave you more."

Halcyone shook her head sadly, and asked him to listen to her side. And when he knew about her leaving La Sarthe Chase had been brought about because of his letter to Cheiron having been posted from London, so that she hoped to find him there, it added to his pain to feel that, even in this small turn of events, his action had been the motive force.

But, as she went on, her pure and exquisite love and perfect faith shining through it all seemed to draw his soul out of the mire in which it had lain. And at last they knew each other's stories and were face to face with the fateful moment of to-day, and he exclaimed gladly:

"My darling, now nothing else matters—we will never, never part again."

Then, as he looked into her eyes, he saw that not gladness but a solemn depth of shadow grew there, and he clasped both her hands. A cold agony chilled his whole being. What, O God, was she going to say?

"John," she whispered, all the tenderness of the angels in her gentle voice as she leaned and kissed the silver threads in his dark hair. "John, do you remember, long ago when we spoke of Jason and Medea, and you asked me the question then, Must he keep his word to her even if she were a witch?—and I told you that was not the point at all: it was not because she was or was not a witch, but because it was *his word?*"—Here her voice broke, and he could hear the tears in it, and he wildly kissed her hands. Then she went on:

"Oh, my dear lover, it is the same question now. *You cannot break your word.* Nothing but misfortune could follow. It is a hard law, but I know it is true, and it is fate. We put in action the force which brings all that we receive, and we who have courage pay the price without flinching, and, above and beyond all momentary pleasure or pain, we must be true to ourselves."

"I cannot, I cannot!" he groaned in agony. "How can you condemn me to such a fate?—tied to this woman whose every influence is degrading to me; parted from you whom I adore—I would rather be dead. It is not fair—not just, if you only knew!"

Then he continued wildly. "Ah, God—and it is all because I forgot the meaning of your dear and sacred pledge with me that I must always be good and true! If I could suffer alone—my darling, my soul!—then I would go without a word back to hell, if you sent me. But you, too—think, Halcyone! Can you bear your life? You who are so young, separated for evermore from love and me. Oh! my own, my own—"

Here he stopped his mad rush of words—her face was so white and grave—and he let her draw herself from him, and put her hands upon his shoulders, while her eyes, with tender stars of purity melting in their depths, gazed into his.

"John," she said, "do not try to weaken me. All Nature, who is my friend, and the night-winds and their voices, and that dear God Who never deserts me, tell me that for no present good must we lower ourselves now. Nothing can ever hurt me. Go back and do that which being a gentleman entails upon you to do—and leave the rest to God. This is the winter of our souls, but it will not last forever. The spring is at hand. if you will only trust, and believe with me that first we on our side must be ready to pay the price."

Then she bent forward and kissed him as an angel might have done, and, without speaking more, rose and prepared to walk toward the stairway which descended to the lower court.

He followed her, and she turned before she began to descend the steps, while she pointed to the beautiful country.

"Look at the vines, all heavy with grapes," she said, "and the fields shorn of their corn, and the olives shimmering in the sunset; and then, dear lover, you will know that all things have their sequence, and our time of joy will come. Ah! sweetheart, it is not farewell for ever; it is only that we must wait for our spring."

"Halcyone," he said, while his proud eyes again filled with tears, "you have the absolute worship of my being. You have taught me, as ever, the truth. Go, my darling, and I will do as you wish, and will try to make myself more worthy of your noble soul. God keep you until we meet again."

She did not speak; she only looked at him with a divine look of love and faith, and he watched her as she went down, it seemed, out of the very heart of the setting sun and into the shadows beneath, and so disappeared from his adoring eyes in a peaceful purple twilight.

Then he returned to the old stone seat and leaning forward gazed out over the exquisite scene.

A great hush had fallen upon his torn heart. And thus he stayed motionless until the night fell.

CHAPTER XXXII

Mrs. Cricklander awaited Mr. Hanbury-Green's coming quite impatiently. She felt she wanted a little warmth and humanity after the chilling week she had passed with her betrothed. What she meant to do with this latter she had not yet made up her mind—the justice of an affair never bothered her, and her complete unconsciousness of having committed any wrong often averted her action's immediate consequence. That Mr. Hanbury-Green should suffer, or that John Derringham should suffer, mattered to her not one jot. She was really and truly under the impression that only her personal comfort, pleasure and feelings were of any importance in the world. Her brain always guarded these things, and when they were not in any jeopardy or fear of being inconvenienced, then she was capable of numbers of kind and generous actions. And, if she had even been reproached about her colossal selfishness, she would have looked up astonished, and replied:

"Well, who is nearer to oneself than oneself?"

Common sense like this is not to be controverted.

It would only be when she was growing old that she would feel the loneliness of knowing that, apart from the passion which she had inspired because of her sex and her beauty, not a single human being had ever loved her. For the present she was Venus Victrix, a glorious creature, the desired of men—and that was enough.

Mr. Hanbury-Green was a forceful person, unhampered be any of the instincts of a gentleman, and therefore armed with a number of weapons for winning his battles. He had determined to rise to the top upon the wave of class hatred which he had been clever enough to create, and he neither knew nor cared what state of devastation he might bring the country. He was a fitting mate in every way for Cecilia Cricklander, and completely equipped to play with her at her own game.

So, when they met in her sitting-room in the Florentine hotel, each experienced a pleasurable emotion.

His was tempered—or augmented—by a blunt and sufficiently brutal passion, which only the ideal of circumspect outward conduct which dominates the non-conformist lower middle classes, from which he had sprung, kept him from demonstrating, by seizing his desired prize in his arms.

He was frankly in love, and meant to leave no stone unturned to oust John Derringham from his position as *fiancé* of the lady—John Derringham, whom he hated from the innermost core of his heart!

Mrs. Cricklander fenced with him admirably. She did not need Arabella's coachings in her dealings with him; he was quite uncultured, and infinitely more appreciated what her old father had been used call her "horse sense" than he would have done her finest rhapsody upon Nietzsche. Mrs. Cricklander had indeed with him that delightful sense of rest and ceasing from toil that being herself gave. She felt she could launch forth into as free a naturalness as if she had been selling little pigs' feet in her grandfather's original shop. And all to a man who was rising—rising in that great country of England, where some day he might play a *rôle* no less than Tallien's, and she could be "Notre dame de Thermidor."

Arabella had once told her of this lady's story, and she felt that the time in Bordeaux when the beautiful Thérèse wore the red cap of Liberty and hung upon the arm of one who had swum in the blood of the aristocrats, must have been an experience worth having in life. Her study of Madame Tallien went no further; it was the lurid revolutionary part in her career that she liked.

Mr. Hanbury-Green was very careful at first. He was quite aware that he was only received with *empressement* because he was successful; he knew and appreciated the fact that Cecilia Cricklander only cared for members of a winning side. He felt like that about people himself, and he respected her for the way she fought to secure a footing among the hated upper classes, and then trampled upon their necks. There were no shades of her character which would have disgusted or dismayed him; even the knowledge that her erudition was merely parrot-talk would only have appealed to his admiration as a further proof of her sagacity.

They went on to Venice the day after he arrived, with Arabella to make a chaperoning third, and for the first two days afterwards Cecilia kept him at arm's length, but not waiting for his dinner! Some instinct told her that in his home circle he would probably have been accustomed to worthy, punctual women, and, while she enjoyed tantalizing him, she knew that he had a nasty temper and could not be provoked too far. No bonds of honor or chivalry would control his actions as they would those of John Derringham. She was dealing with as lawless a being as herself, and it was very refreshing. Mr. Hanbury-Green knew her one weak point—she was intensely sensitive of the world's opinion, as are all people who inwardly know they are shams. She would have hated to be the center of a scandal, from the point of view that it would irreparably close doors to her; and her resentment of barriers and barrier-makers was always present.

This he would remember as his strong card—the last to be played.—If she continued being capricious until the moment of her *fiancé's* expected return, he would use all his cunning—and it was no inconsiderable quantity—and compromise her irrevocably, and so get her to surrender upon his terms. For he had made up his mind, as he sped to Florence, that Cecilia Cricklander should return to England as his wife.

They had four days of the usual gay parties for every meal—there happened to be a number of people passing through and staying in Venice—and the early September weather was glorious and very hot.

Mrs. Cricklander delighted in a gondola. There was something about it which set off her stately beauty, she felt, and she reveled in the admiration she provoked; and so did Mr. Hanbury-Green—he prized that which the crowd applauded. But time was passing, and nothing the least definite was settled yet, although he knew he had obtained a certain mastery over her.

On the Friday evening a telegram was received from John Derringham saying he would return on the Saturday night, and Mr. Hanbury-Green felt this was the moment to act. He had no intention of having any quarrel with his rival, or of putting himself in the position of being called upon to give an account of himself. The news of his dismissal must be conveyed to John Derringham by the lady as that lady's free and determined choice.

So Mr. Green was very cautious all the Friday evening, and made himself as irresistible as he could, using all his clever wits to flatter and cajole Cecilia, and leaving not a trifle unconsidered which could interfere with his plans.

They were simple enough.

He claimed to have discovered a quite new and quite charming spot on the Lido, which he was most anxious to take Mrs. Cricklander to see alone—he put a stress upon the word *alone,* and looked into her eyes. They would go quite early and be back before tea, as John Derringham had timed himself to arrive upon the mainland about seven o'clock, and would be at the Daniellis, where they were all staying, for dinner.

Mrs. Cricklander felt she must have one more delightful afternoon, and, as this excursion might contain a spice of adventure, it thrilled her blood. She had been exquisitely discreet—in public—forcing Arabella always to talk to Mr. Hanbury-Green, and devoting herself to Lady Maulevrier, or any other lady or old gentleman who happened to be present. And then she felt free to spend long hours alone with Mr. Hanbury-Green in her sitting-room, whose balcony hung over the beautiful canal. No one could say a word—Arabella's discretion could always be counted upon; and pleasure was secured.

She looked, perhaps, more beautiful than she had ever done in her life as they started. Mr. Hanbury-Green had hired a special gondola, not the one they were accustomed to float about in,—and off they went. Where was the harm, in broad daylight! and with Arabella to accompany them—as far as the last steps, and then to be dropped? Cecilia felt like a school-girl on a forbidden treat.

When they were well out of sight of all observation, Mr. Hanbury-Green began. He told her that he loved her, in all the most impressive language he was master of; he felt that with her he might with safety and success use the same flamboyant metaphors and exaggerations with which he was accustomed to move his constituents. No restraint or attention to accuracy was necessary here. And if his voice in his honest excitement would have sounded a little cockney in Arabella's cultured ears, Cecilia Cricklander did not notice it. On the contrary, she thought the whole thing was the finest-sounding harangue she had ever heard in her life.

He went on to say that he could not live without her, and implored her to throw over John Derringham and promise to be his wife.

"He thinks you are madly in love with him, darling," he said, knowing this would sting, "and will stand any of his airs. Let him see you are not. Give him the snub he deserves for deserting you, and fling his dismissal in his face."

Cecilia Cricklander reddened and thrilled, too. Here, at all events, was warmth. But she was not won yet. So she looked down, as if too full of emotion to speak. She must

gain time to consider what this would mean, and, if worth
while, how to lay her plans.

Should the scheme contain certain elevation for herself
and certain humiliation for John Derringham, then there
was something worthy of consideration in it, for undoubtedly Percy Hanbury-Green suited her the better of the
two, as far as just the men themselves were concerned.
She knew she would get desperately tired of having to live
up to John Derringham's standard, and a divorce in England
would not be so easily obtained, or so free from scandal, as
her original one in America had been. But she must think
well, and weigh the matter before plunging in.

Mr. Hanbury-Green saw her hesitation and instantly applied another forceful note. He dwelt upon the political
situation and grew eloquent and magnetic, as when he was
on the platform—for was he not playing for stakes which,
for the moment, he valued even more than some thousands
of votes?

It was no wonder Cecilia Cricklander's imagination grew
inflamed. He let her see that as his wife she would, for
seven years or more, ride on the crest of the wave of an
ever-rising tide to undreamed-of heights of excitement and
intrigue. "With you at my side, darling," Mr. Green said
passionately, "I could be stimulated into being Dictator myself. The days of kings and constitutions are over. The
people want a strong despotic leader who has first brought
about their downfall. And they will get him—in ME!"

This clinched the matter, and Cecilia, seeing visions of herself as Madame Tallien, allowed herself to be drawn into his
arms!

.   .   .   .   .   .

"Do you know, my beauty," the triumphant lover said, as
they floated back to pick up Arabella upon the last steps,
rather late in the afternoon, "I had meant to get you somehow to-day. If you had refused to listen, I intended to
take you to the Lido and keep you there all night—the gon-
dolier and the people there are bribed—then you would have
had no choice but to marry me. Oh, you cannot balk me!"

And all Cecilia Cricklander replied was, with a girlish
giggle of pleasure:

"Oh, Percy, dear!"

In the innermost recesses of their hearts there are a number of cold women who adore a bold buccaneer!

She had made one stipulation with him before they landed,
and this was one which in the future—little as she knew it

then—would rob her of all her triumph over John Derringham, and plant an everlasting and bitter sting in her breast.

She insisted that, as she did not wish to create a nine days' wonder, no mention of his engagement to herself should be made public by Mr. Hanbury-Green for at least a month after people were aware that she had closed hers with John Derringham. All should be done with decency and in order, so as not to militate in any way against her future position as queen of the winning side.

And, knowing that he had already telegraphed the announcement that the marriage arranged between the Right Honorable John Derringham and Mrs. Vincent Cricklander would not take place, so that it should appear in the Monday morning papers—Mr. Hanbury-Green felt he could safely comply with her caprice and bide his time. He had not the slightest intention of ever permitting a whim of hers to interfere with his real wishes in any way, and having a full command of her own weapons and methods, he looked forward to a time of uninterrupted bliss when once she should be his wife. To dissemble for a month or so would not hurt him, and might even amuse him as a new game.

So they entered Daniellis in subdued triumph, and said good-night before Arabella, with prim decorum, and then Cecilia mounted to make herself look beautiful for the flinging of his *congé* in John Derringham's face.

CHAPTER XXXIII

When Halcyone left the Fortezza she was conscious of no feeling of depression or grief. Rather a gladness and security filled her heart. She had seen him with her mortal eyes—her dear lover—and he was in truth greatly in need of all her care and tender thoughts. Her beliefs were so intense in those forces of protection with which that God Whom she worshiped so truly surrounded her, that she never for a moment doubted but these invisible currents would be directed to the disentangling of destiny's threads.

She made no speculations as to how this would be—God would find the way. Her attitude was never one of pious resignation to a divine chastisement. She did not believe God ever meant to chastise anyone. For good or ill each circumstance was brought about by the individual's own action in setting the sequence of events in motion, as the planting of seed in the early spring produced fair flowers in the summer—or the bruising of a limb produced pain. And the motion must go on until the price had been paid or the pleasure obtained. And, when long ago she had heard Cheiron and John Derringham having abstruse arguments upon Chance, she used silently to wonder how they could be so dull as not to understand there was no such thing really as Chance—if people were only enabled to see clearly enough. If they could only trace events in their lives to their sources, they would find that they themselves had long ago—even perhaps in some former existence—put in motion the currents to draw the events to themselves. What could be called "chance" in the matter was only another name for ignorance.

And, if people knew about these wonderful forces of nature, they could connect themselves with only the good ones, and protect themselves from the bad. Misfortune came through—figuratively—not knowing just where to put the feet, and through not looking ahead to see what would be the result of actions.

Only, above and beyond all these forces of nature and these currents of cause and effect, there was still the great eternal Source of all things, who was able to dispel ignorance and to endow one individual with the power to help another by his prayers and thoughts. This God could hasten and bring Happiness, if only He were believed in with absolute faith. But that He would ever stoop to punish was an unheard-of blasphemy. He was only and entirely concerned with good. Punishments came as the results of actions. It followed then that John Derringham, having paid the price of much sorrow for all his mistakes, would now come into peace—and her prayers, and exceptional advantages in having been allowed for years to learn the forces of nature, would be permitted to help him. That he would be obliged to marry Mrs. Cricklander would seem to be an over-exaction, and not just. But they were not the judges, and must in all cases fulfill their part of honesty and truth, no matter what might betide.

These were her convictions, and so they caused her to feel only a God-like calm—as she went away into the purple shadows of the old streets.

Cheiron and she had been at San Gimignano for half a week, and almost every child in the place knew and loved her. She had always a gracious word or a merry smile when they clustered round her, as is their friendly way with all travelers, when she came from the Cathedral or the strange old solitary chapel of St. Jacopo.

The Professor was waiting for her on the hotel steps, and he saw by some extra radiance in her face that something unusual had happened.

"What is it, my child?" he asked, as they went in and up to their dinner in the big *salle à manger* upon the first floor, which was then nearly always empty of guests.

"John Derringham is here, Master," she said—"and we have talked, and now all shadows are gone—and we must only wait."

"I am glad to hear it," replied Cheiron, and bristled his brows.

This is all that was said between them on the subject, and, immediately the meal was over, they retired to their rooms. But when alone in hers, Halcyone took from the silken wrappings the Goddess Aphrodite, and in the divine eyes read a glad blessing, and, as soon as her head touched her pillow, she fell into a soft sweet sleep, while the warm night winds flew in at the wide-opened windows and caressed her hair.

And John Derringham, when the dark had fallen, came down from his high watch tower, and walked slowly back to the hotel, leaning upon his stick. He was still filled with the hush of his loved one's serene calm. Surely, after all, there must be some truth in her beliefs, and he would trust to them, too, and wait and hope—and above all keep his word, as she had said, with that honor which is entailed upon a gentleman.

He ordered his motor for dawn the next morning, so as to be away before the chance of disturbing the two should occur.

The rare and wonderful sight of a motor in those days caused a crowd to collect whenever one should arrive or depart. It was an unheard-of thing that two should visit the city at the same time—there had only been three in the whole year—so Halcyone, when she heard the whizz next morning, bounded from her bed and rushed to peep between the green shutters. Some instinct told her that the noise indicated it was he—her dear lover—about to start, and she had the happiness of gazing down upon his upturned face unperceived, as his eyes searched the windows, perhaps in some vague hope of being able to discern which was hers. And she showered upon him blessings of love and tenderness, and called all the currents of good from the sky and the air, to comfort and protect him and give him strength to go back and keep his word. And, just as he was starting, a white pigeon flew down and circled round John Derringham's head—and he was conscious that at the same moment the sun must have risen above the horizon, for it suddenly gilded the highest towers. And he passed out of the dark gate in its glory, and took the Siena road, a mighty purpose of strength in his heart.

After a few days of wandering, during which he strove not to let grief or depression master him again, he sent a telegram to Venice to Cecilia Cricklander. And on that Saturday evening, he walked into her sitting-room with a pale and composed face.

She was seated upon the sofa and arranged with every care, and was looking triumphantly beautiful as she smoked a cigarette. Her fine eyes had in them all the mocking of the fiend as she greeted him lazily.

"How are you, John?" she said casually—and puffed rings of smoke, curling up her red lips to do so in a manner that, John Derringham was unpleasantly aware, he would once have found attractive, but that now only filled him with disgust.

"I am well," he said, "thank you,—better for the change and the sight of some most interesting things."

"And I, also," she responded with provoking glances from under her lids, "am better—for the change! I have seen—a man, since which I seem to be able the better to value your love!"

And she leaned back and laughed with rasping mockery, which galled his ears—although for some strange reason she could no longer gall his soul. He felt calm and blandly indifferent to her, like someone acting in a dream.

"I am glad you were, and are, amused," he said. He had not made the slightest attempt to kiss her in greeting—and she had not even held out her hand.

"You are quite rich now, John, aren't you?" after a short silence she presently asked nonchalantly—"this is, as you English count riches—ten or twelve thousand a year. I suppose it will keep you in comfort."

He leaned back and smiled one of his old cynical smiles.

"Yes," he said, "it is extremely rich for me; my personal wants are not great."

"That is splendid, then," she went on, "because I shall not feel I am really depriving you of anything by doing what I intend to do in throwing you over—otherwise I should have been glad to settle something upon you for life!"

As he listened, John Derringham's eyes flashed forth steel, but the pith of her speech had in it such divine portent, as it fell upon his ears, that the insult of its wording left him less roused than she hoped he would have been.

She saw that it was joy, not rage, which lay deep in his eyes, and the fury of her whole nature blazed up, so that she forgot the years of polish that she had acquired—forgot her elaborately prepared plan that for an hour she would torture and play with him, as a cat plays with a mouse, and, crimsoning with wrath, she hurled forth her displeasure, cutting things short.

"You are only a paltry fortune-hunter, John Derringham, for all your fine talk," she said loudly, raising her voice, and allowing it to regain its original broad accent, "and I have kept you on just to punish you. But, if you thought I was ever going to marry you now that you are no better than a cripple, and don't amount to thirty cents in the opinion of the world—you or your Government either!—you made a great mistake. I have something much more delightful on hand—so you can take back your ring and your freedom—

and go and find some meeker woman who will put up with your airs."

And she picked up from a table beside her his diamond gage, which she had taken from her hand before his entrance, and threw it over to him—and then leaned back as if exhausted with anger among the cushions.

John Derringham had grown very pale as the insulting words fell from her lips—and now he rose to his feet, and standing there looked at her with pitying contempt.

"Then I will say good-by, Cecilia," he said. "The manner of your release of me cancels the pain it might otherwise have caused me. I can only wish you all success with any new venture you may make—and assure you always of my deep respect."

And, calmly putting the ring in his pocket, he turned round and slowly left the room—when, meeting Arabella upon the stairs, she was startled to see him shaking with sardonic laughter.

"Good-night, and good-by, dear Miss Clinker," he said; "I am glad to have had this opportunity of thanking you again and again for your sweet goodness to me when I was ill; it was something which I shall never forget."

"Oh, Mr. Derringham!" said Arabella, "you haven't parted from Mrs. Cricklander, have you?" But she saw from his laughing eyes that he had, and, before she was aware of it, good, honest soul, she had blurted out: "Oh, I'm so glad!"

Then they shook hands heartily, to hide her dreadful confusion, and John Derringham went on to his rooms at the Britannia, where he was staying, with nothing but a mad, wild joy in his heart.

What did Cecilia Cricklander's insults matter? What did anything on earth matter? He was free to go and seek his beloved one—and have every sorrow healed as he held her to his heart. The only necessary thing now was to find her immediately, which would require some thinking out. It was too late to get an answer to any telegrams to England— he must wait until the morning. Mrs. Porrit would know where Cheiron's next address would be. Yes, he could hope to come up with the wanderers perhaps not later than the day after to-morrow.

But when Arabella entered her employer's sitting-room after wishing him good-by, she found Mrs. Cricklander in violent hysterics, and she had to have the doctor and a sleeping draught before she could be calmed.

The hatefulness, the impossible arrogance and insolence

of the man, she thought! and the humiliation to herself of knowing full well that, instead of making this dismissal a scene of subtle superlative cleverness, so that through all his torture he would be obliged to admire and respect her skill—she had let her temper get the better of her, and had shown him a side of herself that, she was well aware, was most unrefined, so that he had been able to leave her, not as a humbled, beaten cur, as she had intended, but feeling what she knew to be unfeigned contempt.

No wonder she had hysterics! It was galling beyond compare, and not all Mr. Hanbury-Green's devotion or flattery next day could heal the bitter hurt.

"Oh, how I will help you, Percy!" she said, "to pull them all down from their pedestals, and drag them to the guillotine!"

And Mr. Hanbury-Green had laughed, and said it gratified him greatly to feel her sympathy and coöperation would be with him, but he feared they would never have the humorous pleasure of getting as far as that!

And, it being a Sunday, Arabella Clinker wrote to her mother to apprise her of these events.

"The engagement is over [Mrs. Clinker was told]—the advent of Mr. Hanbury-Green (a very unpleasant personality, afraid of being polite to me in case I should fancy myself his equal) seemed to clinch matters in M. E.'s mind. I suppose he was able to give her some definite assurance of the future of the Government. In any case, I could see, when they returned from their excursion in the gondola yesterday, that things were upon a very familiar footing between them. Mr. H. G. has none of Mr. Derringham's restraint or refinement, and, after M. E. had seen Mr. Derringham and, I presume, returned him his freedom, she had a terrible fit of hysterics, only calmed when Mr. Hanbury-Green entered the room and suggested emptying the water jug over her. It appears he has a sister who is subject to these attacks, and this is the only method which has any effect upon her. I suppose in his circle they would have a number of crude remedies which we are unaccustomed to, but it seemed to be the right one for M. E., who pulled herself together at once.

They told me privately that they are engaged, but do not intend to announce it yet, and I believe they are really suited to each other. I had thought at one time that Mr. Derringham might be equally a mate for her, because of his

selfishness, but, after I grew to know him when he was ill, I
saw that he was infinitely above her, and not really more
selfish than other men—and, as you know, I have extended
to him my pity and commiseration ever since. Your liking
of him confirmd my good opinion. I am to stay on with
M. E. as long as I will, because Mr. Hanbury-Green, she
says, is not cultivated either, and I may be of use to them
both, she thinks, in the future, although she has not imparted
this to him. I do not believe I shall like having to render his
speeches erudite, because my political convictions are all
upon the other side. But something else may turn up, and
it is a comfort to know things are settled for the present.
Mr. Derringham looked so joyous as he came from her
sitting-room, after his dismissal, that I am sure he will
go off at once to that person I have often given you a hint
about,—and his restoration to health may consequently be
looked upon as a certainty. I fear the influences we shall
have to live under now will not encourage that high tone
which endeavoring to keep up with Mr. Derringham and his
party entailed, and it may grow more than I can bear. The
inference to be drawn from M. E.'s defection to the other
side is not felicitous, and gives me cause for the most
gloomy foreboding as to the future of the country, because
she would never have done it if she had not received from Mr
Hanbury-Green absolute guarantees that with him she will
occupy the highest position. Everything Conservative is
vieux jeu now, she says, and she must go with the tide.

And from this the letter wandered on to personal matters.
Meanwhile John Derringham had received Mrs. Porrit's
answer and had ascertained the Professor's probable address, and was joyously speeding his way on to Rome.

CHAPTER XXXIV

THE Palace of the Cæsars was lying in blazing heat when Halcyone and the Professor decided to spend the afternoon there. People had warned them not to get to Rome until October, but they were both lovers of the sun, and paid no heed. It would be particularly delightful to have the eternal city to themselves, and they had come straight down from San Gimignano, meaning to pick up their motor again at Perugia on their way back, as the roads to the south were so bad.

They had only arrived the evening before, and felt the Palatine hill should be their first pilgrimage. It was completely deserted in the heat and they wandered in peace. They had gone all through the dark rooms which overlook the Forum, and had reached the garden upon the top, with its cypress and cool shade. Here Halcyone sat down on a bench, looking over the wonderful scene. She wanted to re-read a letter from her Aunt Roberta which had arrived as they were starting out.

The old ladies were delighted with their accession to a modest fortune, the matter was turning out well, and they hoped to have their ancient brougham repainted and a quiet horse to draw it, before very long, so that, even when it rained, they could have the pleasure of going to church.

William, the Aunt Roberta added, was really growing a little old for so many duties, and would, under the new and more prosperous *régime,* confine himself to being only butler. Halcyone would find several changes on her return; among them the four gates had been mended!

As she read this part of the letter, Halcyone almost sighed! The gates, especially the one of the beech avenue, had always been such friends of hers, she knew and loved each crack. And then her thoughts wandered, as ever, to her lover. Where was he and how had it fared with him? Her serene calm was not disturbed—she felt certainty in every breath of the soft warm air—the certainty that the springtime of their souls had come.

Now, that same morning, John Derringham had arrived at the Grand Hotel, and, after breakfasting, had made his

219

way to the hotel to which Mrs. Porrit had informed him the Professor's letters were to be addressed. And Demetrius, whom he asked for, hearing Mr. Carlyon was out, was able to give him information as to where his master had gone; so that he set off at once.

The Palace of the Cæsars was rather a labyrinth to expect to find anybody in, but he would do his best. And so it happened, after about an hour's search, that he came upon Cheiron alone, just as he reached Livia's house.

Mr. Carlyon held out his hand.

"Well, John," he said, "and so we meet again."

His old pupil shook it heartily, and Cheiron, seeing that joyous light in his eyes, raised his left penthouse with a whimsical smile.

"Got clear of the Octopus, I should imagine," he said laconically. "Well, better late than never—Halycone is over on the bench under the cypress, gazing upon the Tarpeian rock; perhaps you may like to go to her—" and he pointed in that direction.

"It is what I have come at post-haste from Venice to do, Master," John Derringham said. "Mrs. Cricklander was kind enough to release me on Saturday evening—she has other views, it seems!"—and he laughed with his old boyish gayety.

"Well, I won't keep you," Cheiron answered. "Bring my little girl back to the hotel when these gates shut. No doubt you will have enough to talk about till then," and he smiled benignly.

"You will give us your blessing, Master?" John Derringham asked. But the Professor growled as he turned to go on.

"She has my blessing always," he said, "and you will have it, too, if you make her happy, but you don't deserve her, you know, John."

John Derringham drew himself up and looked straight out in front of him—his face was moved.

"I know I do not," he said, "but I hope you believe me, Cheiron, when I tell you that I mean to devote the rest of my life to attain that object—and at least no man could worship her more."

"Get on with your courting then, lad!" said the Professor, pointing with his stick in Halycone's direction, while his wise eyes smiled. "I suppose she will think you perfect in any case—it is her incredible conviction!" And with this he shook his old pupil's hand again, and the two men went their separate ways; John Derringham forgetful of even his lame ankle as he rapidly approached his beloved.

She saw him coming—she had been thinking of him deeply in an exquisite day-dream, and this seemed just the sequence of it, and quite natural and yet divine.

She rose and held out both hands to him, the radiance of heaven in her tender eyes. For she knew that all was well and joy had come.

And they spoke not a word as he folded her in his arms.

. . . .

A week later they were married very quietly at the Embassy, and went south to spend their honeymoon, leaving Mr. Carlyon to go back to England alone. He was tired of wandering, he said, and sighed for the comforts of the orchard house and his pipe and his Aristotle.

And Aphrodite went with the bridal pair, no doubt content.

The manner of Mrs. Cricklander's dismissal of John Derringham had left him unimpaired by any consideration for her feelings.

And when she read the announcement in the *New York Herald* the day after the wedding, she burned with furious rage.

So this was the meaning of everything all along! It had not been Cora Lutworth or his political preoccupations, or anything but simply the odious fact that he had been in love with somebody else! This wretched English girl had taken him from her—a creature of whose existence she had never even heard!

And the world would know of his marriage before her own news had been made public! The gall of the whole thing was hardly to be borne!

She felt that, had she been aware that John Derringham's affections were really given elsewhere, nothing would have induced her to break off the engagement! Mr. Hanbury-Green was all very well, and was being a most exceptional lover, only this hateful humiliation and blow to her self-love mattered more than any mere man!

But of such things the married two recked not at all. Their springtime of bliss had come.

And, as they sat absolutely alone upon the inner steps of the Temple of Poseidon at Paestum, looking out upon the sapphire sea and azure sky, the noble columns in front of them all bathed in golden light, and a solemn crow perched above as priest to bless them, Halcyone drew the wrappings from the goddess's head.

"See, John," she said. "Aphrodite is perfectly happy; she is smiling as never before. She knows that we have found all her message." And she laid her head against his shoulder as he encircled her with his arm.

"Dear," she went on, with that misty look in her serene eyes as though she could see into the beyond, "for me, however much beautiful things exalt me and take me to God, I can never go there alone. It always seems as if I must put out my hand and take your hand."

"Sweetheart," he answered, holding her close, "and long ago I called love a draught of the poison cup—what a poor blind fool was I!"

"Yes," she said tenderly. "John, we are much wiser now —and, when we return to the world out of this divine dream-country, you will teach me of that life which you must live in the fierce arena where you will fight for a principle against such odds; and I shall be always there to comfort you and give you of my sympathy and tenderness. And, as you instruct me in the day and its strenuous toils, I will teach you of the soothing, peaceful currents of the night. And we shall know only joy, because we have seen how it always comes if we go straight on and leave the tangled threads to God."

John Derringham bent and kissed her lips and he murmured:

"My darling—my one woman with a soul."

THE END